"We'd be finish
project if t
scattere

Meg sighed. "Yeah."

"Does that happen often?"

"You mean border patrol roundup? They swarmed all over us until a few months ago. They've kind of left us alone lately. At least, until today." Meg shrugged.

Now *that* was worthwhile information. "Must be frustrating to get a job half-done and have your crew disappear." His new "boss" clearly had only a vague understanding of the way the system worked.

Jack could have explained it to her in four words: *Illegals in, illegals out.* Employers going for cheap labor and willing to take the consequences when they got caught. Sometimes even greedy enough and power-hungry enough for murder.

For the hundredth time Jack reminded himself it hadn't been *his* greed or *his* grab for power that had killed his partner. He and Rico had simply been in the wrong place at the wrong time.

THE TEXAS GATEKEEPERS: Protecting the
borders...and the women they love.

ELIZABETH WHITE

As a teenager growing up in north Mississippi, Elizabeth White often relieved the tedium of history and science classes by losing herself in a romance novel hidden behind a textbook. Inevitably she began to write stories of her own. Torn between her two loves—music and literature—she chose to pursue a career as a piano and voice teacher.

Along the way Beth married her own Prince Charming and followed him through seminary into church ministry. During a season of staying home with two babies, she rediscovered her love for writing romantic stories with a Christian worldview. A previously unmined streak of God-given determination carried her through the process of learning how to turn funny mushy stuff into a publishable novel. Her first novella saw print in the banner year 2000.

Beth now lives on the Alabama Gulf Coast with her husband, two high-maintenance teenagers and a Boston terrier named Angel. She plays flute and pennywhistle in church orchestra, teaches second-grade Sunday school, paints portraits in chalk pastel and—of course—reads everything she can get her hands on. Creating stories of faith, where two people fall in love with each other and Jesus, is her passion and source of personal spiritual growth. She is always thrilled to hear from readers c/o Steeple Hill Books, 233 Broadway, Suite 1001, New York, NY 10279, or visit her on the Web at www.elizabethwhite.net.

Under Cover
of Darkness

ELIZABETH WHITE

Steeple
Hill®

Published by Steeple Hill Books™

STEEPLE HILL BOOKS

**Steeple
Hill®**

ISBN 0-373-44218-1

UNDER COVER OF DARKNESS

Copyright © 2005 by Elizabeth White

www.SteepleHill.com

Printed in U.S.A.

I am the gate; whoever enters through Me
will be saved. He will come in and go out,
and find pasture. The thief comes only to steal
and kill and destroy; I have come that they
may have life, and have it to the full.

—*John* 10:9–10

This book is dedicated to my husband, Scott. I love you more than I can say.

Abundant thanks to my critique partners, Tammy and Sheri. I feel sorry for other writers who don't have you two, but I'm not sharing!

I would also like to express my gratitude to several people who let me pick their brains for this project. First I'm overwhelmed by the bravery and dedication of our U.S. Border Patrol Service, now under the Department of Homeland Security. These men and women tirelessly guard our far-flung national boundaries. For the sake of the story, I had to make up a bad guy, but I never ran across one "in real life." These guys are true heroes! In particular, I'd like to thank Border Patrol Chaplain Brian Henderson and retired Agent Bill Harrington for helping with story details. All mistakes are mine.

Credit also goes to Robin Burgin and Carolyn Whittington, who both allowed me to trot along behind them learning a little about landscaping design and gas-powered augers. Thank you for sharing your time and creativity.

Muchas gracias to Señor Garry Morrison and Señora Jane Myers Perrine, who helped with Spanish translation. I hope I understood you correctly!

One more note. Thanks to my brother in Christ, Pastor Gabriel Cortes, who ministers to the Spanish-speaking community of south Fort Worth. Your loving, joyful congregation richly blessed me when I visited. May the Lord continue to multiply the Kingdom through you.

Prologue

The black iron skeleton of the old railroad bridge known as *el puente negro* arched across the Rio Grande in bold relief against a clear, starlit sky. The odors of jasmine, fish and mud drifted on a damp summer breeze down to the two uniformed men searching the riverbank.

U.S. Border Patrol Agent Jack Torres struggled through tall banks of carrizo cane as he followed behind his partner, their powerful flashlights cutting a path through the heavy vegetation. They were looking for broken stalks that would indicate human movement, listening for the sounds of fearful panting and rustling, the telltale ripple of water.

Jack stopped Rico by touching his elbow. "Too quiet around here, man," he whispered. "Something's wrong."

"I know," Rico agreed. "Not even a bullfrog singin' us a lullaby."

Shoulders tight, Jack moved closer to the water. The illegals often chose to come across under the bridge, where the darkness hid them until they crawled right up into the cane along the bank. Jack wondered how they could stand it. He had recurring nightmares about going under, sucking river water into his lungs. Submersion had always scared him; he'd had to make himself learn to swim just before going into the Academy.

Rico had been after him to get baptized since his conversion a month ago, but Jack continued to resist. "I'm thinking about it, man," he would say, and Rico would laugh and call him a sissy, giving him a hard time until Jack found something to razz back with.

They stood listening until Rico, always hyper, started to move. Jack motioned for him to wait. "Turn off your light."

Rico complied. "We should've been off thirty minutes ago," he grumbled under his breath. "Isabel worries when I don't call."

"I'll tell her you were unavoidably detained."

Jack lifted his night-vision glasses to scan the blackness downriver. Not so long ago the only thing ground agents worried about was controlling the swimmers. They came across without benefit of steel or pavement—some on rafts or inner tubes, many floating on planks or doors, most simply dog-paddling across. Lately, however, as dope peddlers moved into Piedras Negras over in Mexico, the action had gotten a little more interesting.

"Did you hear about Zuniga and Berg?" Rico said.

Jack loved Rico like a brother, but he wished he'd shut up. Had that been a footfall on the bridge? He couldn't be sure. He trained the glasses on the apex, but didn't see anything.

Rico kept whispering. "Last week they caught three MAK-90's. Sixty-one hundred rounds of ammo, too. Then the very next night they picked up 450 pounds of marijuana. Can you believe that, man?"

Rico talked too much when he was nervous. Jack knew his partner was tired, had been up 'til all hours last night with a sick kid. Maybe they should call it quits after all—

The noise on the bridge again. Louder, footsteps running, a body slamming against the side rail, somebody yelling Spanish curses. Where were the border patrol guys at the checkpoint?

The lights on the bridge went out.

Jack stood up, heart pounding, hand on his gun. *"¡Párese y identifíquese!"* he shouted. "Rico, cover me." The running continued. Why didn't they listen to him and stop? *"¡Dije, 'Párese!'"* Jack stumbled toward the bridge, finally clear of the cane, but briars and other weeds caught at his clothes.

A gun fired, the bullet whizzing past his shoulder. Jack dove into the cane for cover. More gunfire blasted—deafening, confusing, bursting in obscene pops, making it impossible to identify the direction of the sound.

"Oh, God, protect us!" Jack groaned. "Rico, where are you?" He didn't know if his partner could hear him or not through the noise.

Where was Rico? He looked around, afraid to shoot because he couldn't find him. *Oh, God let him be all right.*

Shots blasted overhead again, and this time Jack placed the sound at the base of the bridge, only a hundred yards away. He raised up, saw three dark shapes running toward him; he fired and saw one of the figures fall. The other two split, one plunging into the river, the other disappearing.

As suddenly as the fusillade had begun, it was over. Numb dark silence dropped into place. Where was his backup? The agents from the bridge should have come running at the first sound of gunfire.

"Lord my God, please don't let any of those guys be down."

Jack got up on his hands and knees. He looked around and heard nothing, then half stood, chest heaving. The gun shook in his hand as if it were alive. He staggered to his feet.

"Rico?" he whispered into the unnatural stillness. Cold hard stars blinked in the sky. Rico was worse than a kid, playing tricks. "Rico, I'm telling you this isn't funny. I nearly got my shoulder blown off."

He stepped backward, turned around.

"Rico!" he shouted. Then he moved to the edge of the water, where the cane was crushed in a zigzag path.

The lights on the bridge flickered back on, and the wail of a siren blared from the direction of the city.

Jack remembered his flashlight. He turned it on and, slipping, nearly falling, shone it into the broken cane.

Broken cane. Broken cane. Water. Red water. Blood.

Rico.

Chapter One

⌒

Fort Worth, Texas

"Oh no, not again!" groaned Meg St. John. She dropped her forehead onto the steering wheel of her company truck. "Please tell me this is a heat mirage."

She was alone in the truck, but as a little girl she'd developed the habit of talking out loud to Jesus. She'd never seen any reason to abandon it. Meg lifted her head and looked again, letting the air-conditioning blast her in the face. It might be ninety degrees in the shade today, but she definitely wasn't seeing things. Or *not* seeing things, as the case may be.

"Lord, this is not funny," she muttered, rubbing her temple. Then she sighed. "Well, maybe it is."

Just over an hour ago she had left an eight-man crew preparing the new Fort Worth Savings and Loan site for planting. All but three of them had disappeared, leaving rakes abandoned midswipe and shovels stuck here and there like old grave markers.

Appropriate, she thought, *for the direction my career just took.*

Crew leader Manny Herrera stood on the front sidewalk, shoulders hunched and hands deep in his olive-drab uniform pants. His younger brother Tomás and their uncle Diego hunkered down in the meager shade of the little Bobcat dirt-mover that was parked, engine still running, near the drive-through. The Herrera family, loyal to the end.

With a deep breath for fortitude, Meg hopped out of the truck. As a licensed landscape architect, she was the official crew chief responsible for interpreting the design blueprints. Manny, however, was vital, because he oversaw most of the practical aspects of the job and served as translator for the Spanish-speaking crew.

"Manny!" She got his attention by waving her cap. "How many got caught?"

She didn't have to ask what had happened. The last time border patrol came by, five members of her crew had been bused back to Mexico. The job had been pushed several days behind while a new crew was hired and trained.

"Two." Manny gave one of the shrugs that accompanied almost every sentence out of his mouth. "Cruz and Rivera ran away when they saw the truck coming. Vega had good papers, but he left anyway. Said he'd be back Monday." Manny removed his black plastic sunglasses, revealing the anxiety on his thin, scarred face. "I'm sorry, ma'am. I tried to stop them."

"Good grief, it's not your fault." Though it wasn't *her* fault, either, she still felt responsible. Meg looked in despair at the six-foot trailer still loaded with crape myrtles, dwarf nandinas and begonias. Somehow she had to pull things together and finish the task. "The main problem is," she said, "the savings and loan is supposed to *open* on Monday."

Manny's expression tightened even more. "You better call the office and ask for help."

Meg gulped. If Kenneth Warner got wind of this, he'd find some way to blame it on her. "No, let's just install what we can by five o'clock. Maybe I can come back tomorrow and finish it myself." Her day off would be blown to pieces, and salaried employees weren't paid for overtime. But less than her best was out of the question.

According to some cultural custom she didn't understand, the Mexican men rarely met her eyes. But now, Manny's dark gaze lifted and held hers for a long moment. Meg saw that he understood exactly what she was afraid of. She felt an odd kinship with this quiet, sad-eyed man.

"Okay, ma'am," he said, "we'll do what we can." He turned and beckoned the other two men. "Tomás. *Tío. ¡Ven!*"

The four of them settled into a frantic teamwork that Meg would have enjoyed if she hadn't been aware of the sun moving over relentlessly, notch by notch, in the hard-baked blue sky.

Shortly after noon, she and Tomás were crouched in the center of a curved bed on the north side of the brick building. Meg's stomach had been rumbling for quite some time. Her bowl of Lucky Charms had been scarfed down at dawn while she stood on the porch waiting for Gilligan the Wonder Dog to sniff around the yard. She'd brought an apple with her, but had given it to Tomás. Yesterday he'd fainted, claiming it was the heat, but Meg suspected he couldn't afford more than one meal a day. She was going to have to call a break soon, before they all passed out from dehydration.

For nearly an hour she had been marking shrub spacing, Tomás following with the plants. They worked in quiet companionship, making steady progress, with little need for conversation. A bluegrass CD blasted from a boom box on the porch rail. Tomás had initially wrinkled his nose at Meg's choice of music, but during the last few minutes his bony shoulders had been rhythmically moving.

"Tomás, do you play an instrument?" She glanced at him and saw his dark eyes widen. Looking over her shoulder, she saw a red BMW sedan gliding up beside her truck.

"Okay, I see absolutely *no* humor here." She sat right down in the dirt, looking up.

"*¿Señorita?*" inquired Tomás. "*¿Está usted bien?*"

Was she all right? No. In that car was the one person who consistently made her life miserable.

Realizing the boy felt her anxiety, Meg took a stab at a smile and touched his shoulder. "Sure I am. *Sí.*" Stomach flipping, she got to her feet.

After her junior year of college, Meg had spent the summer in her hometown. Sunset Landscaping, owned by cattle baron, artist and entrepreneur Theodore "Ted" Crowley, had offered her a much-coveted internship. Discovering that she actually enjoyed the practice of what she'd been studying, Meg pushed herself hard and graduated at the top of her class with a master's degree in landscape architecture. To nobody's surprise, her old employer recruited her to come back, and Meg accepted the job with delight.

Then reality hit. The company's new financial officer took one look at Meg and decreed that she was too inexperienced—and too female, Meg secretly suspected—for a management position. He'd convinced Mr. Crowley that she needed another year of in-the-field "seasoning" before moving into the design office.

Hurt and confused, Meg had considered looking elsewhere for a job. But after a week of prayer and fasting, she regrouped, took her career delay in stride, and began to learn the landscaping business, quite literally, from the ground up.

The year would be up next Friday.

Unfortunately, Kenneth Warner could extend her probation for as long as he chose.

Meg yanked off her gloves and wiped her sweaty hands on the seat of her pants. She knew she had to show at least outward respect for this wretched man.

Scowling, Warner stepped out of the BMW and picked his way up the sidewalk, which was still littered with flats of monkey grass. In spite of the heat, he wore a red silk tie Windsorknotted at the throat of a crisp blue-striped Oxford. His dark-blond hair was carefully combed back to disguise its thinness. He was a smart, handsome man, and had a knack for dropping into conversations the fact that he'd put himself through college by modeling for Neiman's.

Warner approached, sharp blue eyes scouring Meg. He stopped, hands thrust into the pockets of immaculate Armani trousers. "May I have a moment of your time, Ms. St. John?" He ignored Tomás, who stole surreptitious glances at that brilliant tie.

Meg hated the way Warner looked at her. A couple of months ago he'd offered to take her to lunch—alone. Knowing he was married, she'd refused. Since then he'd treated her with roving eyes and patronizing sarcasm. Aware that her perfectly modest uniform shirt was drenched with sweat, she shifted her shoulders to loosen it.

"Sure." She hit the boom box to turn off Ricky Skaggs. Since Warner apparently hadn't noticed the absence of half her crew, Meg couldn't imagine what the man wanted. He rarely visited job sites, preferring to spend his days in the office dishing out orders by phone. "Have you met Tomás?"

Warner looked as startled as if she'd offered to introduce him to a boxwood. "Uh, no. Does he even speak English?"

Like most of her crew, Tomás understood more English than he actually spoke. But since he'd moved to the trailer for more shrubs, Meg shook her head. "What can I do for you, Mr. Warner?"

"The first thing you can do is check your cell phone and make sure it's charged up and turned on. I've been trying to reach you all day."

Meg gulped. No wonder he'd risked soiling his Italian shoes. "Oops. Sorry. I always forget about it."

"Well, welcome to the twenty-first century. I have a lunch appointment in ten minutes, so I'll get right to the point. Crowley has come up with a new project for you, starting Monday."

"Really?" Meg's emotions skidded in all directions. Since her original interview, she'd seen the owner of the company half a dozen times. She'd been afraid he had forgotten about her.

"Yes. But I warn you, this won't exactly be a cushy job."

Meg thought she detected a vindictive gleam in Warner's expression. So much for career advancement.

"Okay," she said cautiously, "so what sort of project is it?"

Warner rocked back on his heels. "I suppose you're aware that Crowley's sister, Mary Frances Grover-Niles, sits on the board of the Hysterical Society."

Meg nodded, refusing to be amused by his snide reference to the Fort Worth Historical Commission. In her opinion they served a valuable community service, and she enjoyed reading their articles in the Sunday paper. "I think I read that somewhere."

"Well, it seems they've decided to invest in the biggest money pit this side of the Mississippi River. And you, Ms. St. John, have been elected to excavate it."

"Me?" Meg's heart yo-yoed. "So I'm promoted to design?"

Warner snorted. "Wait until you see the budget before you get all starry-eyed. Over my objections—*strenuous* objections, I might add—Crowley insisted on bidding on this white elephant and won the contract. Since our other two architects are busy with *moneymaking* projects, the only way to do this one without putting ourselves out of business is to give it to you. If you bring it in on time and under budget—and if the Commission is completely satisfied, of course—I'll consider taking you off probation."

"A budget," Meg breathed. She wondered what Warner would say if she broke into a Snoopy dance across the parking lot. "Do I have a deadline?"

"In my opinion, it would take the next decade to bring the place out of the wilderness, but Mrs. Grover-Niles wants her daughter to be married there the second weekend of August."

Meg did the math. Today being May twenty-fourth, that left about ten weeks to research, plan, locate plant materials and install a—

"How big is this place anyway?"

"It's a five-acre turn-of-the-century estate called Silver Hill."

"That sounds beautiful!"

"It's a goat farm," he said flatly, "so you'd better get right on it. Sam Thornton's going to meet you out there in an hour to give you the specs." Warner looked around as if the lack of activity had suddenly penetrated his fog of self-absorption. "This isn't your whole crew, is it?"

"Border patrol came by while I was off-site," Meg blurted, caught off guard. "Apparently somebody hasn't been real careful about checking documentation." Then she remembered that Warner was in charge of paperwork. Her eyes widened. "No criticism intended—"

"Documentation is not your concern," Warner snapped.

Red stripes flagged his sculpted cheekbones. "What were you doing off-site?"

She might have known this would turn into a power play. "I had to go back to the nursery for—"

Warner slashed a hand through the air, cutting her off. "Never mind, I'm late for my meeting. Here's the address." He handed Meg a computer printout. "It's in the old Gloriana district."

He headed for his car and paused inside the open door. "One more thing. You have to finish this S and L job today. Crowley wants to see Silver Hill sketches next Thursday so he can present them to the board on Friday." A smirk curved his full lips. "Have a nice day."

As Warner's car slid around a corner, Meg evaluated the crew's progress. The three of them were working hard, but they'd hardly made a dent in the job. And she was going to have to leave them while she met with Sam.

Meg pressed her hands to her churning stomach. *Oh, Lord, what am I going to do? This isn't humanly possible.*

The implications of that simple truth struck her.

For the last year she'd been traveling in a wilderness of suppressed dreams and desires, wondering when deliverance would come. Now she faced equal amounts of opportunity and failure. This was no time to get self-sufficient…or to retreat in fear.

Heavenly Father, she prayed, *help me see Your hand. Help me hold on to You—*

"Ma'am, you okay?"

Meg's eyes flew open. Tomás was looking at her over his shoulder, his thin young face creased with concern.

She whipped the rolled-up blueprint out of her back pocket. "Everything's peachy, Tomás." At his confused look, she scoured her meager Spanish vocabulary. All she could come up with was *"bueno"* and a thumbs-up.

Tomás's face cleared, and he went back to work.

"Gotta spend a little more time with *Spanish for Gringos*," she muttered with a sigh.

When Sam Thornton's big Ford F-250 truck pulled up along the curb behind her, Meg was sitting in her truck, staring at the front elevation of Silver Hill and repeating, "It's not so bad. It's really not." But she had a sinking feeling even the Munsters would have hesitated to move into this place.

Sections of green tile roof were visible above a tangle of overgrown trees, briars, vines and crabgrass that had been chopped away to leave a narrow passage down the middle of a broken sidewalk. Through that opening, Meg could see a tiny section of the front porch and brick entryway. A service road leading up from the street had been hacked through the jungle; she assumed the remodeling of the house itself had been completed, but it was impossible to tell from here.

Why had she agreed to this project sight unseen? Kenneth Warner must be laughing up his sleeve. For the second time that day she laid her forehead on the steering wheel. "Ay-yi-yi."

"This ain't no time for takin' a nap, little girl." Her supervisor's dark Alabama drawl rolled through her open window, and she turned her head to find Sam opening her door. "Come on out and face the music."

Only Sam could call a grown woman "little girl" and get away with it. A fiftyish African-American built like a big black bear—and just about as grouchy—Sam had become more like a favorite uncle than a boss over the past year. In the words of her older brother Cole, Sam Thornton was "the real deal."

Meg got out and elbowed the door shut. "Did you know about this?"

He shook his gray-flecked head. "Um-mm. Mr. Ted kept it quiet until he was sure it was gonna happen. And I can see why," he added under his breath. "Hoo-boy, that is one whoppin' mess."

"Well," she sighed, "at least it's *my* mess, and I can do what I want to with it. Have you got a plot plan and stuff for me?"

Sam grunted. "Yeah, in a minute, but first I want you to meet somebody." He lifted a beefy hand and gestured with two fingers. For the first time Meg realized there was a passenger in his truck.

The man lifted his chin in acknowledgement, then got out and approached with a loose, athletic stride. He stopped next to Sam, thumbs hooked in the back pockets of faded-to-white jeans.

Meg compared every man she met to her father, and her first thought was, *He's even taller than Daddy.* He was probably in his early thirties, with dark hair pulled smoothly into a short ponytail at the back of his neck. A pair of mirrored sunglasses covered his eyes.

Who was he? Hispanic, obviously, but he didn't have the wiry, hungry look of the men who worked on her crew. Too rough-edged to be a crony of Warner or Mr. Crowley; a couple days' growth of black beard shadowed his angular jaw, and a tattoo of some sort stuck out from under the sleeve of his black T-shirt. A thin silver hoop pierced one ear.

Meg looked at Sam for explanation. Her boss was leaning, arms folded, against the hood of the truck, watching her with a twinkle in his mud-brown eyes. "Torres, this is St. John."

Meg felt the stranger's hidden gaze home in on her face. She thought with an amused inward shudder that if he took off the glasses, his eyes would surely glow red. All he needed was a black leather jacket and a laser gun.

Killer of plants and planters. Oh, baby.

"*You're* St. John?" he said, a slight Spanish inflection to the way he said her name, half Latino, half Texas cowboy.

"Last time I checked." She looked down at her shirt pocket, where her name was embroidered, and gave the Terminator a friendly smile.

His extraordinary mouth suddenly curled, and she forgot all about cyborgs. He had a very sweet smile for a guy who looked like a dope peddler. The incongruity of those white teeth and the dark hardness of his face got her attention and weakened her knees.

All Meg's defenses went up—*boom*—because Torres, whoever he was, took her back to her painful junior year of high school. The only skipped stitch in the fabric of Meg's spiritual development had occurred during what her mother liked to call her bad-boys-whatcha-gonna-do stage. A brief flirtation with life on the edge which, fortunately, her parents had put a stop to before she fell off.

A period which she had no desire to revisit. She jerked her gaze from Torres's mouth. "Sam thinks having a lady crew chief is funny," she said, to humor her boss. "I'm Meg." She waited a moment in vain for Torres to offer her his first name, then gave Sam a confused look. "So what's up? I have to get back to the savings and loan. Border patrol busted my crew again—"

"When?" Torres's posture remained relaxed, though the tone of the question had been abrupt.

Meg frowned. "Mid-morning. Left me with two days work and only three guys to help me."

Sam was shaking his head. "I keep tellin' Kenny Warner

he's got to be more careful about checking these guys' papers. We're gonna get stiffed with a fine one of these days."

"Yeah, well, he basically told me to mind my own business."

"Not a bad idea," Sam said dryly. "I'm killin' two birds with one stone here. Here's the specs for your job." He handed her a large yellow clasp envelope. "Plot plan and a few historic pictures to get you started. You'll want to come back Monday morning with your camera and graph paper. Make some drawings of what's already here. You know the drill."

She did. Her masters thesis project, a design for a Mississippi horse farm, had won several awards.

Meg hefted the thickly stuffed envelope, resisting the temptation to open it then and there. She wanted to savor the task when she didn't have another unfinished job hanging over her head. She felt like she'd just been given a birthday present. "Okay. What's the other bird?"

Sam nodded at Torres, who had followed their conversation intently. "You're training him to take over when you move into the office. Besides, you'll need more help with the heavy stuff on this—" Evidently searching for an apt description, Sam jerked a thumb at the house.

"Goat farm," Meg supplied, borrowing Warner's phrase. She glanced doubtfully at Torres. "Have you ever done landscaping work before?" *Maybe in prison?*

She mentally slapped herself. *Don't judge people on appearances, Meg.*

"I've done a little bit of everything," Torres replied.

Which didn't really answer her question. But if Sam recommended Torres, then he would no doubt work out fine.

Meg nodded. "Okay. Well, I'd better get back to the S and L." She took a step and paused, glancing at Torres. "Does he have to leave with you now, Sam, or can I borrow him this afternoon?"

Sam seemed to think that was a funny question. His eyes lit again. "He's all yours, baby girl. Just return him in the same condition you got him."

With that Parthian shot, he lumbered toward his truck, hitching up his pants. He got in and backed into the street, leaving Meg and Torres staring at one another. At least she assumed he was staring. The mirrored shades made it hard to tell.

"What's the matter?" asked Torres, folding his arms. The tattoo, Meg saw, was a Celtic cross. Interesting.

She shook her head. "I think you're an answer to a prayer, but don't quote me on that."

Chapter Two

For a long, focused year, Jack had thought of nothing but bringing down the smuggling ring responsible for Rico's murder. The kingpins had so far escaped identification, and Jack was one of three border patrol special agents chosen to infiltrate companies known for employing large gangs of illegal laborers. He knew he had the training, the experience and the motivation required to follow through with this investigation.

Or did he?

Here he was, caught off guard by Sam Thornton's little joke and thinking he wouldn't mind belonging to Meg St. John. True, her work boots and muddy uniform were hardly siren material, but that wide, lush mouth was made for kissing. Big, innocent eyes of a dark leaf-green had surveyed him with curiosity and interest. And there was something even more dangerous there, which he might have labeled innocence, if he'd still believed such a thing existed.

As Meg maneuvered onto the interstate, Jack watched her hands on the wheel. Strong, well-shaped hands with short unpolished nails and not a ring in sight. But there were concessions to femininity in two silver crosses dangling from her right earlobe, neither of which matched a third one in her left ear. No makeup, which was smart, because in her job it would've been sweated off in five minutes. Jack didn't see that she needed it anyway; straight dark brows and lashes marked those intensely colored eyes, and her skin was a perfect, clear olive.

She glanced over and caught him looking at her. "Where are you from, Torres?"

"Nowhere in particular."

She made a face. "Everybody's from somewhere."

"Well, let's see. Most recently, I guess, El Paso."

"Doing what?"

He'd thought she would take his laconic response as a hint to mind her own business. Wrong. "Why?" he asked, aware that she had been examining him. "You think I been in prison or something?"

"Of course not," she said, sounding exasperated. He watched doubt twitch her eyebrows together. "Were you?"

Jack tried not to smile. "I'd rather not talk about it," he said ominously, Jean-Claude Van Damme, Bruce Willis and Clint Eastwood all rolled into one. She was too easy to lead.

Her mouth fell open. "What did you do?"

Jack would have given twenty dollars to know what was going on in her head. Women sensed things they weren't supposed to see, and they were never satisfied with simple explanations. On the other hand, Meg could be a valuable source of information if he didn't scare her off.

"I'm yanking your chain, kiddo," he drawled. "I'm just a boring guy trying to make a living. You wouldn't be interested in my background."

Meg blew out a breath. "Boy, you had me going there for a minute." She glanced at him, pursing that sweet mouth.

"Listen, Torres, I'm sorry for jumping to conclusions. I'm not usually so suspicious. It's just that this has been a very... strange day."

"You mean the business with your crew?"

"Yeah. That and Mr. Warner—I guess you've met him?"

Jack had met Kenneth Warner all right. "Why?"

Meg frowned. "You always answer a question with a question, did you know that?"

Jack smiled. He did it out of habit, as an investigative technique, but most people didn't notice. "I do?"

"Yes. Anyway, about Mr. Warner. He dumped this job on me with no warning, gave me an impossible deadline, and now I've got just a skeleton crew to complete it. I'm glad to have your help, but I hope you don't mind taking orders from a woman. Otherwise this is going to be a very long summer, you know what I mean?"

"I suppose I do." Her tone hadn't been hostile, just honest. Having met Kenneth Warner, Jack could appreciate her concern.

"And for the record, I don't appreciate you calling me 'kiddo.' I'm twenty-five years old."

At that he laughed out loud. "Okay, Grandma, point taken. Why don't you tell me about the job we're taking on."

Wrinkling her nose at him, she did so with an enthusiasm that grabbed his interest and made him realize how the past year's events had aged him beyond his years. He had to force himself not to look at her in fascination.

Keep your mind on business, Torres.

Meg St. John was off-limits for anything except information.

Bareheaded in the broiling late-afternoon sun, Jack straddled a four-foot-deep hole in the ground while steadying a red maple tree in its center. Every stitch of clothes he had on was soaked with sweat. He'd known this assignment would be physical, but he hadn't put in this many hours of backbreaking labor since he'd worked on a roofing crew in college.

He covertly assessed the two undersized Mexicans shoveling dirt around the tree. Mustachioed Diego could have been anywhere between thirty and fifty; Tomás looked to be about sixteen but was probably younger. Though six-foot-four Jack towered over both of them like Gulliver in Lilliput, he had to make an effort to keep up. Blending into this crew wasn't going to be easy.

And it wasn't just his height. St. John kept glancing over her shoulder at him. He couldn't help wondering what she saw.

She was crouched in one of the front beds, setting out pots of pink-and-white flowers that would be dead within six months. Jack considered trees useful: shade, fruit, lumber. Flowers were a big waste of time.

When the maple was steady, Jack let go of it and pulled a bandanna out of his pocket to wipe his face. He tied it around his head to keep the sweat from running into his eyes, then picked up a shovel. The sooner they got this tree planted, the sooner they could all take a break.

He spoke in Spanish to the older man, Diego. "So who's the real boss around here—your nephew or the lady?"

Diego didn't look up. "They work together."

"She know what she's doing?"

Tomás paused with his shovel braced in both hands. "You treat her with respect." His angular chin jutted, and Jack noted a few hairs sprouting there. Maybe the kid was sixteen after all.

Jack glanced at Diego. "What's the big deal?"

Diego shrugged.

"She's a nice lady," Tomás muttered, his shovel biting deep. Stringy muscles bunched in his upper arms.

Jack filed away the fact that the men liked their pretty boss and would protect her. They seemed to regard her in the light of minor royalty.

As he worked, Jack kept an eye on Meg. She moved around, emptying pots and filling holes with practiced efficiency, occasionally flipping her thick red-brown braid over her shoulder when it got in her way. She had on a baseball cap embroidered with the Sunset logo, and she wore the same olive-green uniform pants as the men. But the crew all wore green shirts, while her white one was a stark contrast to the brick wall and dark earth beneath her. Her forearms were warmly tanned, slender but sturdy, with neat wrists and those deft, strong hands. Yeah, she knew what she was doing.

She caught his eye.

Rising in one lithe motion, she took off her gloves and approached as Diego tied the tree to its last stake.

"Good job, guys. I think we'll get through today after all." St. John stood relaxed, hands on hips, looking more like a twelve-year-old boy than a crew chief.

Jack knew that he would be better off to keep his distance, but her utter lack of self-consciousness made him want to shake her up.

"Then how about a break? Ma'am," he added teasingly. He'd seen her wince every time one of the Mexicans addressed her that way.

"Don't call me ma'am," she muttered, grabbing the radio clipped to her belt. "Hey, Manny, take a break for a minute, will ya?"

The radio crackled. "*Sí*, coming, ma'am."

Herrera appeared around the corner of the building. The five of them headed for the orange cooler in the back of the equipment trailer parked on the street. Jack followed St. John, watching her braid sway against her slender back. Nothing boyish about that walk.

She was the first to reach the stack of plastic Texas Rangers cups, but to Jack's surprise she filled one and handed it to Tomás with a smile. The boy grinned, said *"Gracias,"* and moved to sit in the shade of the newly planted maple tree. Jack hung back, watching as Diego and then Manny each received a cup and joined Tomás.

Meg filled the last cup and looked around, cheeks glowing and sweat beading in the deep bow of her upper lip. Suddenly he realized that she was holding the cup out to him, and that he was staring.

"I'm not taking the last of the water," he said gruffly, embarrassed. Good thing his glasses covered his expression. "Drink it yourself."

"Oh, come on, Arnold, lighten up." Her grin revealed pretty teeth, white and crooked enough to be charming. "You gotta be thirsty. I don't mind drinking out of the hose."

He frowned. "Arnold?"

"You know—'*Hasta la vista, baby,*'" she intoned with a deep Austrian accent.

He looked away because her eyes sparkled so brightly and it had been so long since he'd felt anything remotely like humor. "You drink it," he repeated. Ignoring the cup in Meg's outstretched hand, he walked off toward the hose attached to an outside spigot. He could feel her puzzled gaze on his back. After a deep drink he wiped his mouth with the back of his hand and turned off the water. When he looked around, Meg had her back to him, studying a blueprint. There was something defensive about the set of her shoulders.

Jack sat on his haunches, feeling guilty and resenting the guilt. Maybe he wasn't even capable of normal conversation with a beautiful woman. If only he could somehow manage a real time warp—go back a year, to humor and friendship and satisfaction in his job. All of that lost in one disastrous decision that had cost him his best friend.

In spite of the bright sun, black depression all but overwhelmed him. He pushed it away, knowing he'd better take advantage of every opportunity to get answers. *Come on, Torres, you can ask questions without getting personal.*

He walked over to Meg and reached across her shoulder to flick a finger across the blueprint. He was careful not to touch her. "How much left to do?" he asked.

She avoided his gaze. "The front is done. Manny's been marking the back, so we'll all move around there and finish up."

"We'd be done by now if the crew hadn't been scattered, wouldn't we?"

She sighed. "Yeah."

"Does that happen often?"

"You mean the border patrol roundup?" She looked thoughtful. "They swarmed all over us until a few months ago. They've kind of left us alone lately." She shrugged. "At least until today."

Now that was worthwhile information. "Must be frustrating to get a job half done and have your crew disappear." She clearly had only a vague understanding of the way the system worked.

Jack could have explained it to her in four words. Illegals in, illegals out. Employers going for cheap labor and willing to take the consequences when they got caught. Sometimes even greedy enough and power-hungry enough for murder.

For the hundredth time, Jack reminded himself it hadn't been *his* greed or *his* grab for power that had killed his partner. His only fault had been staying on duty longer than necessary. He and Rico had simply been in the wrong place at the wrong time.

The Border Patrol Department of Investigations had turned up leads indicating that somebody with nationwide contacts in the construction industry had hooked up with a network of "coyotes," or guides, and transportation facilitators. Evidence suggested the hub of the ring was in the Dallas/Fort Worth Metroplex.

Jack was pretty sure Ted Crowley—or somebody in his employ—was involved. And he was going to prove it.

"What about these guys?" He gestured toward the three men lounging in the shade.

Meg frowned. "What do you mean?"

"How come they didn't run?"

The question seemed to upset her. "Manny and his family have worked for Sunset for five summers. Nobody's ever sent them back."

Jack lifted his hands. "Just curious. Why do you think border patrol suddenly showed up again today?"

"I don't know. But I'm glad you came along." She looked at him as if she were trying to decipher him. "I didn't know what to expect, but you've been working like three men."

Silence ticked between them as Jack absorbed the unexpected sensation of sincere praise. "*De nada*," he finally said, taking a step backward. "You've got a good team here."

Meg smiled. "I do. But we'd better get back to it if we're gonna wrap it up by dark."

"Okay, guys, that looks great," said Meg, surveying their handiwork with satisfaction.

While Manny supervised the last-minute adjustment of the sprinklers, Meg picked up an armload of rakes and staggered to the equipment trailer. One more bag of mulch would have put her flat on the ground. They'd all worked straight through the long afternoon with only a slug of water every hour or so and a fifteen-minute supper break. The sun was a faint pink strip on the horizon, but they'd managed to finish on time.

"Thank You, thank You this is over," she breathed, barely aware of Torres, who followed her with the heavy gas-powered auger slung across his shoulder.

She could feel his gaze as he strapped the auger to the trailer with a bungee cord. "I assume that wasn't addressed to me." A faint smile curved his lips.

She shook her head, surprised to hear his deep voice. His questions at the water cooler had gotten her thinking, and she'd watched him all afternoon. He always seemed to be where he was needed, doing more listening than talking. "Just giving credit where credit is due."

Torres reached to help Meg with the hand tools.

"Thanks," she said, yawning and leaning against the side of the trailer, draping her forearms across the top rail. She'd never met a man with such a contradictory personality. Rough masculinity housing a deep, innate courtesy; hard, self-protective reticence that would occasionally lift to reveal unexpected humor. He conversed as fluently in Spanish as he did English, and she'd heard no swearing—which, unfortunately, she'd gotten used to in her years of working with men.

She wondered what her roommate would think about Torres. Bernadette had an uncanny knack for character discernment.

Meg felt an attack of nosiness coming on and went down without a fight. "I think you could do without the moon-glasses now," she suggested, resting her chin on her folded arms.

Torres vaulted down from the trailer and gave her an

amused look. "St. John, you are something else." He yanked off the glasses. "No bionic eyes, I promise."

No, they were dark, almond-shaped, exotic. "Are you part Asian?" she asked, fascinated. Why would he look so self-conscious?

"I'm American," he said firmly. "My mother was Mexican, and who knows what my father was. Frankly, I don't care."

Meg felt her smile falter. "I just wondered...I think family trees are fascinating."

"With a name like St. John, yours probably helped build the *Mayflower.*"

Meg straightened. Her curiosity had hurt him somehow. "I'm sorry—"

"For what?" Torres slammed the tailgate of the trailer, hailing the other three men. "Let's head to the house, *muchachos.* I got things to do tonight."

Kenneth Warner loved his office, particularly the massive cherry desk that backed up to a plateglass picture window looking out on Sunset's immaculately landscaped front lawn. Tonight, however, at eight o'clock in the evening, the view was completely dark. This perfectly suited his mood.

Enthroned in his leather executive chair, he tapped a Montblanc pen against the blotter and stared at his reflection in the black window. His phone—the land line, not his cellular toy— was clamped to his ear.

"I thought we had agreed," he snarled into the receiver, "that there would be no more interference with our crews."

The voice on the other end of the line was countrified, but the words precisely chosen in the way of law enforcement officers. "Our agreement was that funds would be released punctually on the first of every month. Punctually, Mr. Warner, means on time."

"I know what it means," Warner said, cursing. He wheeled the chair around to glare at a matted and framed photo of himself and Tiger Woods, standing on the first tee at last year's Colonial golf Pro-Am. "You'll get your money when I get mine. The last shipment hasn't paid off yet."

There was a deep chuckle in Warner's ear. "Cry me a river, Warner-boy. The first rule of business is, the job don't get done if you don't pay up."

"Look, after that royal botch-up down at Eagle Pass last year it's been nearly impossible to get the system rolling again." Warner hated working with this man, but the relationship ran too deep to throw it away. This was worse than a bad marriage— another institution with which he was intimately acquainted. "By the way, has the investigation calmed down in the last few months? What about the partner of the agent who was shot?"

"He left the agency." Tension thickened the slow voice. "Losing a partner is more than some guys can handle." Then more quickly, "But the situation's back under control on my end. You take care of your part—the money."

"I'll see what I can do," Warner choked out, then ground the phone into its cradle.

Headlights suddenly poured into the driveway leading to the equipment sheds, drawing his attention back to the window. Undoubtedly Meg St. John returning from her day's adventure. He wished he could catch her alone, just once. But the Mexicans protected her like she was the queen bee. He wished he knew what she found so fascinating about a bunch of ignorant Mexicans who couldn't even speak English.

Disgusted, he turned once again to the computer and pulled up a report of accounts due.

"Let's see what we can do," he repeated, scrolling down the list.

Ted Crowley was a creative genius when it came to making money, but he wasn't so good at managing what he made. During the last two years Crowley had been slowly turning over the financial reins of the business to Warner until, as chief financial officer, he pretty much had control.

Okay, Wolf, I'll get you your money.

Chapter Three

"'**I** got things to do tonight,'" Meg muttered to herself as she stepped out of the shower. Her little dachshund, nesting in a pile of Meg's discarded clothes, looked up with a question in his big brown eyes. "That's what he said, Gilligan. He's probably knocking back a few longnecks down at the Stockyards, huh?"

She'd been pondering the enigma of Torres since they'd parted ways in the parking lot, where he'd gotten on a wicked-looking Harley and roared off in the direction of the interstate with nothing more than a wave and "See you Monday."

"I guess this is one more thing that's not my concern," she said, toweling her hair.

When she'd finished high school as a babyish seventeen-year-old, choosing a career had been a simple matter of skimming a college catalog for ideas. Landscape architecture had seemed a perfect blend of her two "best talents," growing flowers and drawing, so she went for it. Her parents had taught her to believe that she could accomplish anything.

But nothing in college had prepared her for the reality of

dealing with the problems she was now facing. An ego-driven executive with the management skills of Fidel Castro. Trying to breach the language barrier between herself and her crew. And now encountering a man who frightened her and piqued her curiosity at the same time.

As she pulled on an oversize red nightshirt featuring Woodstock the bird, Torres's words ricocheted around in her brain.

You think I been in prison?

She'd apologized for jumping to conclusions, but she still thought it was a strong possibility. She grimaced at her sunburned face in the bathroom mirror. "'Yanking your chain, kiddo.'" Well, that was nothing new. Her family constantly teased her about her gullible streak. "'Constitutionally incapable of leaving people alone, too.'" That was her brother's favorite line.

"Are you talking to me, Meggins?" her roommate called from the adjoining room.

"No," Meg said, combing out tangles as she walked into the den, "but somebody needed to give me a lecture, and you were busy."

Bernadette Malone, seated cross-legged in the wicker Papasan chair with her computer on her lap, looked up and smiled. In a white eyelet nightgown, with her black hair spiraling around a dark, flowerlike face, she looked more like a Hawaiian princess than a seminary student hailing from Vancleave, Mississippi.

"I'm never too busy for a lecture," said Benny, closing the lid of the computer. "Want me to start with working by yourself after dark with all those men?"

Benny had a deeply cynical side, particularly toward men.

"Manny was there," Meg said. "You know I'd trust him with my life." She curled up on the sofa, and Gilligan hopped into her lap.

"Yeah, but you could've called *me* so I wouldn't worry." Benny's soft voice was gently reproving.

"I thought you'd be at the library." Meg combed her hair over her face to avoid her roommate's sharp gaze, then started working on a snarl at the back of her head. "You're the only person I know who can be as practical as a toaster one minute and discussing Hebrew declensions the next."

Benny was not to be distracted. "We both have cell phones."

"All right, Professor, I confess." Meg parted her hair and made a face at her best friend. "I let the battery run down again."

Benny rolled her eyes. "I might have known. One day that's going to get you in serious trouble."

"And one day you're going to make a great mother."

"Since having children presupposes the existence of a husband, I seriously doubt it."

Meg never made any headway on this particular argument, so she abandoned it. Besides, even if her roommate were actively looking for a husband, men were generally either blinded by her beauty or intimidated by an IQ in the 160s. It was hopeless.

"So anyway," Benny persisted, dogged as a terrier after a rat, "what kept you so late?"

"A visit from INS. I had to leave the site for a couple of hours, and when I came back half my crew was gone."

Benny frowned. "Oh, Meg, not again. I don't like to think of you working for a company that hires illegal aliens."

"They all do it. People complain about foreigners taking jobs, but Americans don't want to work for the peanuts these guys earn." Meg sighed, flopping onto her back, resting her head against the arm of the sofa. "It gives me a headache to think about it. *You've* got a good brain. Why don't you go to work for the State Department and figure it out?"

Benny shuddered. "I'd rather be eaten by cannibals."

"Which could happen," Meg said darkly.

"Oh, please." Benny laughed. "The people in Central America are poor, but they're not interested in snacking on skinny Americans."

"I guess you would be a pretty tough chew," Meg teased.

"You bet. So you wound up with just Manny to finish that job?"

"No, Diego and Tomás were left—plus the Terminator."

"The *Terminator?*"

"The new man, Jack Torres. Big tough-looking guy with an earring, a ponytail and Schwarzenegger glasses. Sam gave him to me to—" She sat up. She'd forgotten all about the new job.

"Sam *gave* him to you?"

"No, no, I meant Sam *hired* him for my new project. It's a run-down historical estate called Silver Hill, and Benny, I get to design it!"

"Boy, you *have* had an eventful day."

"You can say *that* again," Meg sighed, curling her legs beneath her.

Benny tipped her head. "What's the matter? I thought you were dying to get into the design office."

"You should see this place…" Meg didn't know where to begin to describe what she'd seen that afternoon. "I keep thinking about how God likes to send people into the wilderness."

Benny smiled. "Don't you think there's a reason for that?"

Meg stared at her roommate. "I never thought about it. Maybe to teach them to trust Him."

"Hah. Yes, and you'll notice that He only does that with choice servants."

Meg had to laugh. "Oh, Benny, I'm not any choice servant. I'm a spoiled rotten kid who's pretty much had everything I ever asked for, and now I'm pouting because I've had to wait for a whole year to get the job I want. *You're* the servant." She pressed a sofa pillow to her face. This was the first time she'd admitted the humiliating truth aloud.

There was a long silence.

"Meg, put that pillow down and look at me." Benny's voice was firm and gentle. Meg reluctantly obeyed and found tears standing in her roommate's eyes. "Listen. God's brought me through some things that you can thank Him you'll never have to see. But *He's* got a reason for keeping you pure and sheltered, even though you may not see it for a long time. He wants you innocent in what's evil and wise in what's good. So listen to what the Lord's telling you now. The challenge will make you stronger."

Meg had no idea what to say, so she simply nodded.

"Good." Benny rubbed her eyes, then looked at her damp fingers as though surprised. "I need to study some more before I go to bed, but let's pray together first. Okay?"

"Okay," Meg whispered and bowed her head.

Just after midnight, Jack pushed through the heavy outer door that had long ago replaced the traditional saloon doors of a dive known as the Electric Q. Located on Mule Alley in the Fort Worth Stockyards, it was not as cowboy-chic as the famous Billy Bob's. It was, however, perfectly suited for Jack's purpose.

He slipped into the smoke-filled room and paused inside the door, back to the wall. Steel guitars and the melancholy voice of Merle Haggard pulsed from an old jukebox in one corner, throwing out images that Jack used to find impossible to erase.

Once upon a time he'd relished any excuse to carry around a shot glass, a cigarette clipped between his fingers and a 9 mm Glock tucked under his armpit. Always on the job, inside the job, consumed with the job. Fresh out of the military and buzzed on freedom, he'd been eager to earn a reputation as the baddest border cop since Wyatt Earp.

Then Rico Valenzuela had shown him there was more to life than the job and its associated temptations. Jesus Christ had given value to his life. Once Jack grabbed on to that truth, the reputation didn't matter.

Now the music pounded against his chest, but got no further.

Jack tapped a cigarette from the pack rolled into the tight sleeve of his T-shirt and lit it with a cheap lighter. About three years ago he'd ditched the habit, but the prop was important cover. He'd learned to pretend to smoke.

Just don't inhale, Torres, he told himself with inward amusement.

Where was Carmichael? Jack hadn't yet met his OIC—Officer in Charge—in person, but had been told to look for a white straw Stetson with a black silk band…and an amputated arm. Word was, thirty years or so ago, when border patrol agents were even more underfunded and underequipped than now, Carmichael had had an unfortunate run-in with a rusty knife. Nobody knew the particulars, but it must have been a nasty scene.

Jack bought a beer—another prop—and continued to survey the room, noting the mixture of cultures represented here. Carmichael, though stationed in the Dallas regional office, was familiar with the area and had chosen the Electric Q, a haven for working men of all races, as a place where they could both blend in.

Sliding around to the back of the bar, Jack sat alone at a

table facing the crowded room. Idly he flicked ash off the end of the cigarette and occasionally lifted the bottle to his lips, pretending to drink.

Presently he intercepted the curious glance of a young woman seated on a stool at the bar. Dressed in tight clothes, she kept pushing a long fall of black hair over her shoulder. He looked away.

He couldn't help comparing the woman's overblown and underdressed figure to his little boss-lady. An image of Meg St. John's dark-green eyes and elusive dimple had stayed with him despite his best efforts to ignore it. He could picture her supple movements and unflagging encouragement of the pitiful crew left to her today. She was as wholesome as your best friend's little sister. Not at all his type.

To his relief, these disturbing thoughts were interrupted by a white hat appearing in the smoke by the door. Carmichael.

Jack stood as the tall, middle-aged man approached. He was over six feet, tightly packed with muscle, the empty left sleeve of his plaid western shirt pinned. His craggy face was etched by lines of responsibility and remembered pain, the mouth pulled down on one side as if by paralysis. The eyes hadn't lost the far-seeing squint common in longtime border patrol officers.

Jack felt weighed by those eyes as he shook hands and sat down.

Carmichael leaned in immediately, speaking softly in a rolling West Texas drawl. "You're in okay?"

Jack nodded. "The references were good."

"First impressions?"

"Haven't met Crowley or Warner yet. Thornton's a good man. I'm on a crew that got busted today, run by some little girl with a degree and no common sense." Well, that wasn't true or fair, but it would do for Carmichael's purposes. "The Mexicans I worked with today apparently have good documents."

Carmichael caught a waitress's eye and asked for a drink, then turned back to Jack. "We brought you in from out-of-sector on purpose. You haven't seen anybody you know, have you?"

"No, sir, and I'm not likely to. Besides, I've changed my looks significantly. I don't think I'd be recognized."

Carmichael studied him for a moment, a smile tugging the good side of those ruined lips. "I wouldn't want to run into you in a dark alley myself." He paid for his drink and set it on the table untouched. "Remember, though, this guy we're tracking is a killer. Watch your back."

Jack nodded. "Yes, sir."

Carmichael hesitated, frowning. "You're not carrying any ID. If you get in a jam—"

"I'll improvise," Jack assured him. "But I won't get caught."

On Monday morning, Meg braced herself for her first thorough inspection of Silver Hill. Maybe it wouldn't be as bad as she remembered it.

She'd spent most of Saturday going through the packet Sam had given her and marveling at the potential beauty of the estate. Besides the base map of the house, there were copies of faded black-and-white photos from the '20s and '30s; even a couple of interior shots of a beautiful woman in a bizarre hat and flowing dress, posed in front of the grand staircase in the foyer. Full color exteriors from the '60s revealed a lush green lawn, pruned hedges and a breathtaking garden with a view of blooming trees in the distance.

Meg couldn't wait to take those photos on-site and compare them to what was still in existence.

Dressed in a clean uniform, her hair in a neat French braid, she grabbed the packet and the digital camera her parents had given her the previous Christmas. Excitement in equal proportions to dread buzzed along her nerves as she drove to work.

She found Sam, standing in the shade of one of the nursery buildings. He was watching Manny, Torres and several other men load a flatbed truck with pallets of sod.

"Sam, I'm heading out to Silver Hill."

"Just hold your horses, missy," he said, arching his back as though it ached. "I'm going with you. That way I'll have a better idea what you're dealing with out there. You won't need your crew yet—I'm sending them to work on a job in midtown—but Torres is coming with us."

"Okay," she said reluctantly. She'd been looking forward to exploring Silver Hill alone. She glanced at Torres, who was sliding a hundred-pound stack of grass squares onto the trailer as easily as if it were a basket full of plastic Easter eggs. He didn't look any more civilized than the last time she'd seen him. In a faded red T-shirt that said "Take No Prisoners" and the same decrepit jeans he'd worn on Friday, he looked like a refugee from a Salvation Army yard sale. A blue bandanna was tied pirate-style around his head. "Torres, when are your uniforms supposed to come in?"

"Next week." He shrugged. "They tried to find me something temporary, but everything in the uniform closet was too small."

Meg's gaze skimmed Torres's long legs and the densely muscled shoulders. Flustered, she said, "You could have at least worn something with a few less holes."

"So call the fashion police."

"Ha-ha." Conceding she might have sounded a tad critical, she sighed. "Never mind. What can I do to help?"

* * *

Silver Hill *was* as bad as she remembered it but, undaunted, Meg bounced out of the back seat of Sam's truck armed with her camera, clipboard and Barol-Mirado #2 pencil, ready to go to war against weeds, faulty drainage and anachronistic plantings.

"If I had thirteen million dollars, I sure wouldn't spend it on a dump like this," growled Torres, shoving aside a bridal wreath spirea that had grown over the sidewalk. He held it for Meg to pass by. "After you, ma'am."

She stopped and bowed. "No, please. After you."

"Oh, no, I insist. You first."

Meg loved Chip and Dale. She loved anything old and funny. What a kick to discover that Torres would indulge in an absurd moment. She laughed and passed under his arm, glancing up at his hard face. He looked tired.

"Hard weekend at the honky-tonk?" she asked lightly as they struggled through the bushes behind Sam.

He gave her an inscrutable smile. "Guess so."

Disappointed, Meg stopped and thrust the plot plan into Torres's hands. "Here, can you read a blueprint? Take charge of this while I draw and make notes." Pulling her pencil from behind her ear, she held the clipboard like a shield.

He stared at her from behind those mirrored sunglasses. "I can read anything you want me to read."

Sam hollered, "Hey, what's goin' on back there?"

"Coming, Sam." Meg dragged her attention back to the business at hand.

Consulting the plot plan, the three of them tramped around the house, dodging briars and spider-infested hedges. Meg made rough sketches, marking the placement of the major trees left on the property.

The roof repair and interior remodeling had left a mélange of glass, broken green tiles and rotten shutters—among the more identifiable items—littering the ground. The crew would have at least a day's job clearing away the trash.

But none of the mess could take away from the classic beauty of rounded double porches on either end of the house, the grand front entryway flanked by tall ionic columns and steeply pitched gables soaring above the second story. The old brick was a warm pink-brown, its deep gray mortar still in good shape. The windows, newly replaced, were dusty and streaked with paint, but Meg could imagine standing inside one of the front rooms, looking out on a lovely sweep of lawn.

If she could just find it.

She sighed and followed Sam's limping gait around to the west side of the house, where a covered carriageway arched over the drive, ending in an ornamental brick wall. According to her notes, it had been constructed along with the free-standing carriage house sometime in the '30s. Whole sections of the tile roof had tumbled inward, leaving dangerous protrusions of fallen beam and joist waiting to whack the unsuspecting soul on the head.

She stopped at a safe distance with her hands on her hips. "Can that be repaired?"

Sam shook his head. "I think there's been a dogfight over it. The general contractor says it would be a waste of time, but Miz Grover-Niles keeps insisting the bride's gotta have a place to make her grand entrance."

"I think I'd like Mrs. Grover-Niles," Meg declared.

"She's an aggravating old biddy with too much time on her hands," Sam muttered, stumping through the safest visible opening in the rubble.

Meg laughed and followed him.

* * *

The three of them returned to the office at five o'clock, covered from head to toe with pollen and dusty sweat. Mid-afternoon they'd run into a quarter-acre field of sunflowers that Meg insisted on inspecting just because she'd never seen so many in one place at one time. Sam's dark brown skin had taken on a grayish cast, and Meg had sneezed until she nearly turned herself wrong side out. Still, Jack never heard her complain. Long days of heat and discomfort seemed to be right up her alley.

He had never seen such boundless energy and enthusiasm in one person. Rico had been hyper, for sure, but his had been the masculine, egocentric kind. Meg was sincerely interested in everything and everyone she came in contact with.

He knew she was curious about him, too, which left him feeling flattered and uneasy. He had no objection to flirtation, but in an undercover situation it could be dangerous.

He watched Meg teasing Sam, who tolerated her with the surly affection of an old German shepherd putting up with the antics of a puppy. She'd wrestled a sunflower stalk out of the ground and brought it back to the office, marching in with it as if it were a battle flag.

She poked her head in the door of the closet where the hourly workers were clocking out for the day. "Manny, remind me to bring filter masks tomorrow so we won't all suffocate on pollen."

"*Sí*, I will." Looking at Meg, Manny cracked a smile.

Jack had to laugh, too. The top of Meg's head was dark brown where her hat had been, but the rest of her hair and face was a nasty yellowish-taupe color. The sunflower waved above her head like a saffron-colored kite.

"What?" Her eyes sparkled in the dust.

"You are some sight to behold," Jack said. He rubbed his finger down her nose and held it up for her to see.

"Hah. You should see yourself." She sneezed again.

He looked down at his own filthy clothes. "Yeah, and ain't it a shame I didn't have on a new uniform so I could've ruined it instead?"

Meg grinned. "*Touché.* I'm going home to hose down. I'll see y'all in the morning."

The surge of disappointment that hit him when she left startled Jack. Maybe pollen had clogged his brain. He had no business getting emotionally attached to any of these people. He jammed his time card into the machine and moved aside for Herrera.

Twenty minutes later he was roaring down I-30, when he passed a powder-blue classic Mustang stopped on the side of the road with its emergency flashers blinking. He nearly wiped out when he saw a big yellow sunflower sticking out of the open window.

Taking the next exit, he circled back around and parked behind the Mustang. By now Meg had gotten out of the car and was bent over with her head under the raised hood.

He tucked his helmet under his arm and got off the bike.

"Fine spot for a picnic, St. John," he said, peering into the bowels of the engine, "but maybe you could find a place with a little more ambience."

She gave a startled squeak and banged her head on the hood. "Ow! Torres, will you quit sneaking up on me?" Traffic whizzed by, all but drowning out her words. She rubbed the back of her head. "I was just going to call my dad."

"Want me to take a look?"

She shook her head. "It's just a bump on the head."

He laughed. "Not at you. The real patient." He patted the slick fender of the car.

"Oh. I knew that. Sure, knock yourself out."

Resisting the obvious comeback, Jack leaned over again to poke around. "Crank it and let me listen."

A minute later he signaled for Meg to get out of the car again. "It's an idler pulley," he told her. "Locked up and threw off a belt. You know somebody who can tow it for you?"

"Oh, man! Daddy's gonna croak. He wants me to get rid of this thing and get a new SUV."

"No way!" Jack said, horrified. "This is a great car. Just call a tow company, and I'll take you home."

She leaned around her car to peer at the motorcycle. "On *that?*"

"You'll be safe. I've even got an extra helmet."

"Well…okay." She shrugged. "We're not far from my dad's office. If you can get me that far he'll take me home." She reached into the car and extracted her cell phone.

Jack enjoyed watching Meg's gray-green eyes widen as she walked around the antique bike. The black-and-silver console was scratched, but he'd recently had the seat recovered. He didn't know many women who understood the appeal of a bike.

"My brother's drooling over Harleys," Meg said, running her hand over the long, butter-soft black leather seat, "but his wife won't let him have one."

"Exactly why I don't have a wife." Jack put on his helmet and unstrapped a second, smaller one from the back.

Meg allowed him to settle it on her head. "But you have two helmets."

"Ah, the lady can count." He slung his leg across the seat, pulling a set of keys from his pocket. "Hop on."

She hesitated, then placed a warm hand on his shoulder. He could feel it through the cotton of his T-shirt, all the way to the skin. He tensed at an unexpected jolt of pleasure as she settled behind him. She smelled faintly of vanilla and honey-suckle. With a slight hint of sunflower pollen.

Chapter Four

Torres pulled into the parking lot of her dad's pediatric clinic, and Meg relaxed her awkward hold on his midriff. Good thing a residue of chivalry existed somewhere in all that grungy masculinity. When he cut the motor and removed his helmet, she slid off the seat. She studied him as he strapped her helmet back in place. He seemed to have quickly become a presence in her life, whether she wanted him to or not. *Bad boys,* she thought, watching the tattoo on his arm flex.

"Thanks for the ride, Torres—you're a lifesaver." She stepped back onto the sidewalk.

"I couldn't leave you on the side of the road, could I?" He hesitated. "By the way, how's your head?"

She lifted her hand to the small bump, which was sore to the touch. "I've got a pretty hard head." His concerned expression threw her off-kilter. "Do you think my sunflower will be okay?"

He grinned. "I'm pretty sure it'll be dead by tomorrow. Don't worry, though, there's plenty more where that came from."

"That's true." There was an awkward pause. "Would you like to come in and say hello to my dad?" she blurted.

My dad? she mentally echoed in horror. What was she, ten? Could a knock on the head make your tongue take off without you? Maybe she had a concussion after all.

His face blanked. "Uh, no. No, I have to get going."

"No, right, of course you do. Well…thanks again for the ride." Meg hurried into the office building without looking back.

She went straight to the ladies' room, locked the door and stood staring at her pink face in the mirror. *Whatever possessed you to do that? Torres probably thinks you're pathetic.*

But she couldn't help wondering where he had to go that was so all-fired important. What did he do with himself when he wasn't watching cartoons and rescuing damsels in distress?

She turned on the cold water and splashed her face.

"Get a grip, Meg," she told herself. "You do not care what Torres thinks, and it's none of your business how he spends his free time."

And it was a good thing he'd had better sense than to come in with her. Her dad would have had a stroke.

"I'm sorry," mumbled Dr. George St. John to Meg as he scribbled a prescription. "I thought I heard you say you left your car on the interstate." He smiled vaguely at his daughter, then wandered toward the exam room across the hall.

"I did." Perched atop a gleaming stainless steel table that held a baby scale and a clutter of thermometers and other medical paraphernalia, Meg sheepishly bumped the soles of her feet together.

Peering over the top of his reading glasses, Dr. St. John paused with the sliding door half open. "Don't go anywhere, Sweet Pea, I'll be right back."

She sat there listening to the familiar sounds of the clinic: carts rattling, a baby screaming, cartoons from the waiting

room TV. From the X-ray room at the end of the hall she could
hear Elliot Fairchild's booming bass voice. She hoped he
wouldn't come out and discover her here. She liked her father's young partner, but she wasn't in the mood for pediatric jokes.

To her relief, Elliot stayed out of sight, and her father returned. "Last patient for the day." George waved at the pre-
schooler trotting down the hall, licking a blue sugar-free sucker.
He turned back to Meg, frowning. "Why do you look like
you've been rolling around in chalk dust?" He pulled off the
stuffed koala bear clutching his tie and tossed it onto the table.

Meg sighed. "It's a long story."

"Hmm. Well, I'm meeting your mom at the Hong Kong
Kitchen for supper. Why don't you join us, and you can fill
us both in."

Thirty minutes later they occupied a booth in the family's
favorite restaurant on the Bluebonnet Circle. While waiting
for her mother to arrive, Meg gave her father a rundown of
her adventures since Friday.

Sipping his sweet tea, George regarded his daughter with
raised brows. "Boy, it doesn't pay to go out of town for the
weekend. Look what I missed."

"It's been interesting. But the good news is, the Silver Hill
project is my chance to move into the office."

"And the bad news is, nobody in their right mind would
take it on." George scratched the back of his silver head.
"Honey, I've seen that place. These people are taking advantage of you by making the conditions so tight."

Meg folded her arms. "Well, you know what? I'm pretty
sure you're right."

Her father gave her a quizzical look. "Then why did you
agree to do it?"

"Dad, when you were in residency, who got all the long, stinky shifts and peanuts for pay?"

He had to laugh. "That's different. Residents *expect* to be treated like the lowest of life-forms."

"And why should I be any different? Concert pianists don't get paid to practice." She grinned. "You know I like a challenge." As alarm built in her father's expression, she added quickly, "And you have to admit it's the best opportunity I've had so far."

He shook his head. "What you really ought to do is start your own company."

"I want to do that someday, but I've still got a lot to learn. Besides, I can't afford it right now."

He smiled like a pirate. "Want an investor?"

"Now, Daddy—"

"No, think about it. You'd have to have some capital to start up, and I've been looking for a promising company to invest in."

"That would be...nepotism, or something."

"It's been done since the beginning of time. My parents gave me a loan when your mom and I decided to go to med school."

Meg shook her head. "You already paid for my education. This is business. I want to do it myself—or not at all."

"How many times have I heard that one? 'I do it *myself,* Daddy!'" George mimicked, rolling his eyes. "All right, if you won't take my money, will you at least take my advice?"

Meg gave her father a wary look. "Free advice is always a good deal, because you get what you pay for."

"Move back home, Sweet Pea. You'd be safe, and you could save up for that business."

Meg could hardly bear the gentle pressure of her father's deep gray eyes. "We've had this discussion a million times, Dad."

"Listen to me. I appreciate your independent streak, but

hat neighborhood you and Benny live in is atrocious. Your mom and I worry about you every day."

"It's close to the seminary where Benny's classes are, and 's close to our church. Neither one of us is the least bit cared." Meg's eyes pleaded with her father to understand. *You're* the one who taught me to get out of my comfort zone nd look for where the Lord's working. For me that's south-vest Fort Worth."

"Yeah, but I never thought—" The tips of George's ears eddened. "Bernadette is the one training for the mission field. know you two are like sisters, but—"

"Daddy, don't worry so much." Meg touched her father's aand and repeated something her mother said often. "The Lord takes care of the sparrows and we're—"

"Worth a boatload of sparrows." George blew out a breath. 'I know, you're right. The landscaping itself is fine, but it scares me when you go off on these…these tangents." His smile was gentle and rueful. "We just want what's best for you."

"I know you do, Dad." Meg felt her throat tighten with tears. He did want the best for her. Even if he was a little overprotective.

Then she saw her mother coming through the door of the restaurant, followed by a hulking, curly-haired young man with a white lab coat over his arm.

Meg leaned over the table. "Daddy," she hissed, "you didn't tell me you'd invited Elliot."

"It was your mother's idea," he said, looking guilty.

"Sure it was." She smiled at him. "But don't be surprised if that Enya CD Mom 'lost' suddenly turns up."

He sat up straight. "You wouldn't."

"Yes, sir, this place is a dump," Jack told Carmichael, "but there's a big community of seasonal workers here. At least I'm

close to the action." With the phone receiver hooked betwee
his shoulder and ear, he threw a tennis shoe at the third cock
roach he'd seen in an hour. He missed.

"All right, son," Carmichael's measured drawl rolled acros
the line. "Sounds like you got it under control. Just keep m
posted, all right?"

"I will." Jack hung up.

Under control. That was a laugh. He rubbed his forehead, try
ing to pretend the air-conditioner window unit was putting ou
more than a lot of noise and a steady drip onto the carpet. Th
Starlight Inn, which ranked just one notch above Folsom Priso
in terms of comfort and amenities, was infested with dope ped
dlers, hookers and petty thieves. He'd parked the Harley inside
the room so it wouldn't be carted off and fenced while he slept

Sighing, Jack elbowed his feather pillow, one of his few
personal possessions, into a more comfortable position. He
refused to sleep on the brown-stained item he'd relegated to
the underside of the bed.

He wished he could as easily discard the dissatisfied and
achy feeling that had settled in his gut when he left Meg
standing on the sidewalk in front of her father's clinic.

A doctor's daughter. College graduate, probably a master's
degree, if her vocabulary and job level were any indication.
What would she say if she knew he had a college degree of
his own, that he spoke four languages and had been invited
to dinner with the governor of Texas?

Those big sea-green eyes had held a message difficult to
interpret. Clearly she'd regretted her awkward invitation to
come inside to meet her father the minute it was spoken. As
things stood, there wasn't a chance in the world of taking her
out for dinner or a movie or any of the other mundane things
nice women were fond of doing.

You've got a job to do, Torres. Don't get distracted.

He rattled the phone in its cradle. Maybe he should call and make sure she'd gotten home all right. This morning he'd entered Warner's office before anybody else got there. He'd only had time to examine a few personnel files, but he'd memorized Meg's phone number.

Call her.

Don't call her.

Grimacing, Jack released the phone and picked up the German Bible he'd bought in an antique store about a month ago. He loved languages and had met Christ while reading a Spanish New Testament given to him by his late partner.

"Here, *amigo,*" Rico had said one night, handing Jack the little book as they stood in a convenience store drinking coffee. "Put this in your pocket and see if it'll answer some of the dumb questions you been asking me."

"Dumb questions—?" Jack had spluttered.

Rico laughed. "I know you aren't looking for real answers. You just want to give me a hard time. But read it anyway and tell me what you think. Start with John."

Because his baptismal name was John, that struck Jack as funny, and he took Rico's instruction literally. That night—really the wee hours of the next morning—he began with "*En el principio era la Palabra…*" "In the beginning was the Word…"

Somewhere along the line he'd come across John 3:16. But reading the familiar words in the language of the barrio he'd grown up in gave them a new freshness. He finally "got" the idea that God loved him personally.

Now, in spite of everything, he still believed that.

What he couldn't believe was that God intended for His children to sit around whining about what happened to them.

Choices. You always made choices that set you up for further choices. A year ago, on a muggy summer night on the border, one of Jack's choices had blown his life apart.

You reap what you sow. How many times had his first border patrol mentor drummed the phrase into his brain? People who made excuses were delusional.

And John W. Torres was nothing if not rational and realistic.

By five o'clock Wednesday afternoon when the crew pulled in, Jack's new uniform shirt was soaked with sweat. He parked the equipment truck and got out, his face stiff with dirt and a gritty coating of Texas clay covering his forearms. He'd spent the day tramping around behind Meg, tying orange flagging tape around the trees she wanted to save. Her excitement was contagious. She really thought she could finish in less than three months. But he couldn't help wondering what was going to happen to her when her bosses went to jail.

Before starting to unload, Jack took time to stretch, involuntarily looking around for Meg. He frowned when he saw her in the parking lot, towing young Tomás along by the sleeve. The boy backed up against her truck with both hands behind his back, his usual quick smile replaced by flat-lipped apprehension.

Jack watched Meg put out a hand, palm up. "Let me see it, Tomás. I promise I won't hurt you." When the boy jerked his head back, Meg said more gently, "Come on, give me your hand."

Moving closer, Jack saw brown splotches all down the front of the boy's shirt and pants. Blood.

Tomás glanced up and saw Jack. "*Lo siento,*" he said. "*No quería hacerlo.*" *I'm sorry. I didn't mean to.*

Meg looked around. "Torres! Tomás cut his hand with the

machete whacking down those sunflowers this afternoon. Would you ask him why he won't let me look at it?"

"He thinks you're mad at him," Jack explained.

"Why would he think a crazy thing like that?"

"Because you look like a boss who's just had some equipment bled all over."

"I do not!" she exclaimed, then blinked. "I do? Okay, then would you please tell him what I said?"

Jack approached Tomás, explaining that the *señorita* wasn't angry; she was simply concerned about his cut. "Let's see it, kid," Jack added, holding out a friendly hand.

Tomás reluctantly held up his grubby paw for Jack's inspection. There was a ragged gash in the web between the thumb and forefinger. It was deep, angry and dirty.

Jack held the boy's bony wrist with a matter-of-fact, impersonal touch. "Why didn't you say something?" he continued in Spanish.

Tomás shook his head, looking pasty-faced. "I can't afford to go home early."

Jack turned to Meg. "St. John, where's the first-aid kit?"

"In the truck. That's why I brought him over here. But we've got to wash it off first."

"A little peroxide'll do the job."

In short order Jack was leaning against the cab, arms folded, watching the operation. Tomás sat on the running board of the truck, letting Meg doctor his hand, wincing as the hydrogen peroxide fizzed over the wound.

Crouched beside him, she wrapped the hand in sterile gauze, then taped it neatly. "When's the last time you had a tetanus shot?"

The boy looked at Jack. Jack translated, laughing when Tomás's brown eyes widened.

"No shot!" said Tomás. "Tell her I said thank-you. She is a nice lady. I'd better see if Manny needs me." He jumped up and hightailed it.

Jack extended a hand to pull Meg to her feet. "That is one hardworking kid."

Meg replaced the peroxide and gauze in the first-aid kit. "They're a great family. I wish I could do more for them."

He could see she meant it. "I don't know what else you could do. They work hard, seem to have clothes and food and a place to stay."

Meg bit her lip. "Did you know the rest of their family is in Tijuana?"

Jack shrugged. "That's pretty typical."

"I know, but can you imagine being on your own at sixteen?"

Jack had last seen his own mother lying lifeless on a metal stretcher, being hauled out of their apartment by a bored paramedic. He'd been about eight at the time. "At least he's got his brother and his uncle."

"He hardly ever eats a decent breakfast."

"I grant you he's skinny, but he seems healthy as a horse."

"Yeah, but—"

"St. John, you're not his mother. Give it a rest."

She sighed and leaned into the truck to put away the first-aid kit. "Okay, but I'm keeping an eye on that hand."

"You do that." He started to walk off, but he caught her looking at him in that intent, past-the-surface way she had.

"What's the matter now?" he asked, goaded. She'd kept her distance since Monday afternoon, staring at him when she thought he wasn't paying attention.

"I was just wondering if you've got *things to do* tonight."

"Yeah, I've got tentative plans. Why?"

She tilted her head. "You're such a good translator."

"I should hope so," he said. "I spoke Spanish before I learned English." Jack knew he sounded defensive, but he couldn't figure out where she was going with this conversational tack. "What are you up to?"

"Nothing, I just thought you might be interested in helping with an ESL class sponsored by my church."

"English as Second Language?

"That's right." Meg leaned against the truck next to him, her shoulder brushing his elbow. Removing her cap, she gave him that *look* again. "You'd be great at it."

For a tense moment Jack felt as transparent as a crystal vase. *She's not at all afraid of me. She knows I'm a Christian. She knows I'm a cop.*

But from what he'd seen of her, Meg was far too naive to know any such thing. She didn't know him at all. And he'd better keep it that way.

"Sorry, Spanky, not my idea of a good time." He gave her a wink to soften the blow and pushed away from the truck. "But let me know if something else comes up."

Meg skirted a series of metal outbuildings behind the office and entered the one farthest back on the property, which served as a combination repair and storage building. There she found Sam sitting at a work table, poking at the disassembled pieces of an auger with the fierce concentration of a little boy stationed in front of a pile of Lego blocks.

"Sam!" Meg skipped across the open floor of the warehouse and skidded to an awkward halt in her unfamiliar three-inch-heel sandals. "Sam, guess what? Mr. Crowley approved my preliminary design!"

Sam continued bolting a blade in place. His bristling mustache twitched in what, for him, passed as a smile.

ᴵpatient, Meg leaned on the end of the table and peered at the shambles of metal parts and rubber gaskets strewn across the table. Sunset had a mechanic whose sole responsibility was keeping the machines functioning, but Sam claimed he could think better with dirt and grease on his hands.

Wiping his hands on a rag, he removed his goggles and looked at Meg. "Well now, don't you clean up nice?"

She twirled, making the gored hem of her forest-green skirt swing. A matching tuxedo jacket and ivory lace shell completed the only dress-for-success outfit in her closet. "You think Mr. Crowley noticed it's the same thing I wore for my interview last year?"

Sam snorted. "Not likely. So you showed 'em how to make a silk purse out of a sow's ear, huh?"

"Yep. I thought Mrs. Grover-Niles was going to swoon when I showed her what the carriageway would look like with clematis dripping all across the arch. Do you know how many hours I spent in the newspaper archives, researching historic plant material?"

"Too many, I expect," Sam said dryly, "but I'm mighty proud for you. Why don't you take the rest of the day off to celebrate?"

Meg frowned. "Take the day off?" For reasons she wouldn't admit to herself, much less to Sam, that idea held no appeal whatsoever. "There's too much work to do! I have to get started choosing plant material for the front beds. Where's Manny and the rest of the crew?"

"I sent 'em to do that midtown median job while you were occupied this mornin'." Sam tilted his head back and gave her a narrow look. "Why?"

She took a sudden interest in her Spanish design jade bracelet. "Just wondering."

She'd spent a good bit of prayer time this morning agonizing over her fumbling attempt to get Torres hooked up with her pastor, Ramón Santos, who led the ESL class. Jack probably thought she'd been angling for a date. *That* was an embarrassing thought. She didn't know what else she could do, but the more she tried to put him out of her mind, the more he insisted on camping out there.

She wanted to know where he lived, what he liked to do in his spare time, what had happened in his past to make him so self-protective.

Sam probably wouldn't tell her, but it wouldn't hurt to ask.

Meg lined up a jade cross carefully alongside its neighbor. "Sam, if you knew something dangerous about one of my guys, would you tell me?" She risked a look at him.

"Anybody bothers you, I'll kill him." He said it so flatly that a chill walked up Meg's arms.

"Oh, no!" she said, alarmed. "Nobody's even looked at me funny." Well, if you didn't count Warner. He was out of Sam's province. "I was just...wondering about Torres," she said in a rush.

"Mmm." Sam had a way of humming when he was considering what to say. "You were wonderin' about Torres, huh?"

"Yes."

"I'm thinking he deserves a chance, Meg."

Meg stared at Sam. If he confirmed her fears, everything would change. But she had to know. "He's been in prison, hasn't he?"

Shaking his head, Sam picked up a screwdriver and tapped the handle on the work table. "You'd better ask him."

"I did, but he wouldn't answer me."

"Well, then he doesn't want you to know." Sam's brown eyes bored into hers. "You get my drift, missy?"

Disappointed, she nodded.

"Good." Sam dismissed her with a wave of his hand. "Now go get you some lunch and leave me alone so I can get this piece of junk fixed."

Meg shook her bracelet back into place and backed away. The enigma of Jack Torres bothered her like an itch between the shoulder blades. She was going to figure out a way to scratch it if it killed her.

Chapter Five

"**M**ost doctors don't make house calls these days," Elliot Fairchild said to Meg Saturday morning as he turned his gray SUV onto a deserted street not far from her house.

Meg glanced at her cranky chauffeur. Maybe she should have taken him for coffee first. "I know," she said, "but these people are proud, and they'd never come to the free clinic."

A piece of paper blew against the windshield just long enough for Meg to read the advertisement for a bar down the street. The paper scuttled away, drawing Meg's attention to cracked sidewalks and beer bottles rolling against the storm drains. At one time, this had been the business section of an upscale neighborhood. Over the years it had deteriorated into a fusion of graffiti-painted walls and dusty plateglass windows fronted by iron bars.

"When your dad finds out I brought you here he'll fire me," Elliot said unhappily.

"He can't fire you. You're his partner."

Elliot winced as the SUV bounced into a pothole deep enough to plant a tree in. "Still. I don't like it. You should've let me come by myself."

Meg regretted involving her father's good-natured young partner in an escapade that obviously made him uncomfortable. Benny would have been better company, but she was studying for finals; besides, Elliot was the one with MD after his name.

"The Herreras don't know you, and I had to bring the food." Meg checked the two gallon-size Ziploc bags between her feet to make sure sixteen-bean soup wasn't leaking onto the carpet.

"I could have—"

"Elliot, I *wanted* to come, all right? The Lord told me to do this."

Elliot gave Meg his patented wrinkle-browed look. "The Lord says weird things to you, you know that?"

She made a face at him. "If you'd seen Tomás's hand...it was starting to get those red stripes out from the cut. That means trouble, right? He kept breaking it open and getting it dirty."

Sighing in defeat, Elliot went into doctor mode. "How old is this little boy?"

"He's sixteen." Meg leaned forward. "Turn in here."

"*This* is it?" Elliot braked with a jerk.

The parking lot of the Starlight Inn spread out on their right like a vast asphalt desert. The hotel itself was a staggering pile of cinder block and iron, with a neon sign flickering above a canvas overhang that looked like it might collapse in the next strong wind.

"This is the address Sam gave me," Meg said. She neglected to mention that Sam had forbidden her to set foot in the neighborhood without an armed guard. "Just—" she gulped "—park under the overhang, I guess."

"Meg, I can't leave my car here! It'll be stripped in five seconds flat."

"Okay, well—" She noticed a group of young men playing basketball in a schoolyard down the street. They were all dressed in shorts and sleeveless T-shirts, but one towered several inches above the others. "Hey, that looks like Jack Torres!" Giddy with relief, her voice rose. "And there's Tomás. Drive on down there."

"This is a bad idea," Elliot muttered. "Looks like a gang."

He crept down the street, dodging craters with tight-lipped concentration. Before he'd come to a complete stop in the circle drive, Meg had already opened the door.

"Wait!" Elliot protested. "Let me go first."

But Meg jumped out and crunched across broken glass, rocks and crabgrass toward the basketball court, a chain-net backboard leaning drunkenly in the corner of the parking lot. The game in progress was fast, rambunctious and noisy. Meg had a feeling her Spanish swear-word vocabulary was increasing by the moment.

She put her fingers to her lips and blasted out one of the earsplitting whistles her brother had taught her. The action on the court stopped. Distracted, Tomás let a boy twice his size shove him onto his rear, and he rolled over with a grunt of pain. Torres, who had the ball, turned around with a quizzical look.

Meg waved. "Hey, y'all. Are girls allowed to play?"

"I'm not believing you brought her into this neighborhood in a *Lexus*," Jack said between his teeth. He leaned over Tomás's shoulder to watch Meg's friend sew up the boy's hand. Tomás had reluctantly agreed to sit on the car's gleaming hood to have his cut examined, while the game continued.

"I would have brought the limo, but my driver's on vacation." The young doctor glanced up, his brown eyes myopic but shrewd behind a pair of Buddy Holly glasses that tempered his Lurch-like voice and build. "Have *you* ever tried to talk Meg out of something she's dead set on doing?"

"My car's still sitting in the driveway because Dad can't find the right part for it," Meg volunteered, "so we *had* to bring Elliot's car." She peered around Fairchild's arm, wincing in sympathy as the needle flashed in the sunlight. "Hang in there, Tomás, it'll be okay."

Tomás tried to smile, looking slightly green from the shock of three shots—tetanus, antibiotic and local anesthetic—not to mention the visual impact of being sewn back together.

Jack sighed in exasperation. "St. John, you shouldn't be here at all. How'd you even know how to find this place?"

"I can read a map."

"I meant—" He met the doctor's amused gaze. "Never mind." Jack knew how he'd found *her* phone number. Would someone that innocent-looking go snooping through employee files?

Meg's persistent kindness reminded him of Dottie Rook, his third-grade teacher, who'd been the closest thing to a mother Jack had ever known. He couldn't remember ever thanking Dottie for trying to set him on a straight path. Ashamed that he hadn't seen to Tomás's injury himself, Jack felt his own spiritual lack. How long since he'd done more than ask God for help in emergencies? He hadn't even been to church since Rico's funeral, over a year ago.

Seeing Meg here, away from the context of work, threw him off balance. Wearing a peach-colored knit top and denim shorts that showed off long, tanned legs, she observed the operation with the tip of her tongue caught between her teeth. She looked fresh, sweet and utterly out of place.

For her own safety he had to send her back where she belonged.

As Elliot Fairchild knotted the last suture, Jack picked up the boy's hand and examined the neat row of stitches. "Good job, Doc. Sometime when you're not busy, I've got a button off a shirt." He spoke to Tomás in Spanish. "Now you're put back together, I'll treat you to a game of Time Crisis down at the laundromat." Trong's Coin-Op Laundry was the boy's favorite hangout.

"Okay." Tomás gave Meg an uncertain look, mumbled "*Gracias, señor,*" to the doctor, and slid to the ground.

"Wait, I brought you some soup," said Meg, thrusting two plastic bags of something squishy at Jack. "You need to put it in the refrigerator."

"Thanks." He reluctantly took the bags and looked down at Meg's hopeful face. He could tell she wanted to be invited to stay. Steeling himself, he gave Tomás's shoulder a friendly thump. "Come on, dude. We'll share the wealth with Mr. Trong. See you Monday, St. John." With a wave to Meg over his shoulder, he led the way toward the laundry.

He could feel Meg's gaze all the way.

Meg studied the board, looking for a place to use an X, a C, two G's and three E's. Benny's last score had been forty-two, so it was no surprise Meg was suffering a dismal loss. "It's a wonder anybody will play this game with you," she grumbled.

Benny looked amused. "Roxanne can still beat me."

"I bet." Meg grinned. Benny's eighty-year-old adoptive mother was still sharp. "When are you going home again?" She put her X underneath an O and made "ox."

"Maybe Fourth of July. There's a big family reunion." Bernadette twisted a dark curl around her finger and gave Meg a cajoling look. "Why don't you come with me?"

"I'd go farther than Mississippi for some of Roxanne's homemade ice cream," Meg said, smiling. "But Ramón's planning that big church party for the Fourth. Remember?"

"Oh yeah." Disappointment pulled down Benny's full mouth. "I wanted you to meet my brother Grant. He really needs a wife—"

Laughing, Meg upended Benny's rack of tiles. "And he's so desperate you think he'll fall for me?"

"Oh, you knew what I meant!" Benny reracked her tiles and studied them. "You've just been sort of restless lately. I thought it might be a dearth of romance. *Dearth!* Hey, that works right here."

Rolling her eyes, Meg added up thirty-five points for her roommate. "I concede, O great Scrabble Queen. Do you think a dearth of romance is my problem? Maybe I should cave in to my parents and toss my cap at Elliot."

Benny snorted. "You've been reading too many historical romance novels. Why Elliot?"

"He went with me out to the Herreras' this morning. Almost hyperventilated when his Lexus bottomed out one time, but he got over it and behaved like a champ. Sewed up Tomás's hand, and he was even nice to—" Meg stopped. Elliot and Jack had eyed each other like a couple of junkyard dogs.

"Nice to who?" asked Benny, a curious gleam in her eyes.

"Nobody."

Nobody with gleaming muscles and long, sweaty black hair and exotic eyes. Meg grimaced. *Dearth of romance indeed.*

The doorbell buzzed, and Gilligan started barking. The roommates gazed at each other in dismay. At nine o'clock, Benny was already in her pajamas. Meg had on a lime-green tank top over her rattiest pair of cutoffs, with the Elmo slippers her nephews had given her for Christmas on her feet.

"Are you expecting company?" asked Benny.

"Nope. Maybe it's one of your seminary friends."

"Maybe," Benny said. "I'll go throw on some clothes while you answer the door."

"Okay." Meg got up and tossed an afghan around her shoulders for modesty. "Shut up, Gilligan," she scolded the dog, who followed her to the door without noticeably lowering the decibel level. Looking down at him, she flipped on the porch light and opened the door. "I said, shut *up!*"

"Can't you just feel the love," said Jack Torres.

Jack stood on Meg's tiny porch, looking down into her lamplit face. In spite of the fact that it was eighty degrees outside, she was draped in a blanket, her hair loose around her shoulders.

"What are you doing here?" Meg picked up the dog, but it continued to growl, hackles raised.

"I come bearing gifts."

She looked down at the greasy towel-wrapped item in his hand. "What *is* that?"

"You brought me lunch today, so I brought you—" he flipped the towel back "—an idler pulley."

She wrinkled her nose. "It sure is dirty."

"The laundromat was closed."

"You don't put car parts in the—oh. You're kidding." She tugged the multicolored afghan higher on her shoulders. He watched her gaze flicker to the dark yard behind him and back to his face. "If that goes in my ol' car, you went to a lot of trouble. Want to come in?"

It had probably been a bad move to come here. After Meg

had left the neighborhood this morning, he'd done some looking around and found the idler pulley in a salvage yard. It cost more than it was worth, but he'd thought—

Well, what *had* he thought? That he was going to win the princess's favor with a used car part?

"Nah, I'm going." He set the lumpy towel down on the porch. "Thanks for bringing the doctor out this morning. The kid's hand is better already."

"I'm glad." Meg smiled and opened the door wider. "Please, come on in."

"Who is it, Meg?" called a low-pitched female voice inside the house.

Meg turned. "Jack Torres from work."

"Who?" A young woman with wild black hair and café-au-lait skin stood on tiptoe to peer over Meg's shoulder.

"Jack, this is Bernadette. Benny, Jack is the one who rescued me from the interstate the other day."

Jack gave Meg's roommate a quick once-over. Even in baggy overalls she was fragile as an orchid.

"Jack brought me an idler pulley. Isn't that sweet?" Meg elbowed her roommate.

"Yeah." Benny folded her arms and rolled her big, dark eyes. "Give him a gold star." But she moved aside to let Jack in.

He flinched when the dog snarled.

"Be quiet, Gill," Meg said, sending Jack a teasing look. "I'll let you know when to attack." She dumped the dachshund in a big wicker chair, then backed toward the hallway. "I'll just, uh—I'll be back in a minute." With one more wide-eyed glance at Jack, she ducked away.

Jack shoved his hands in his pockets and looked around, avoiding Benny's measuring gaze. The house was built in 1930s shotgun style and, judging by the cracks in the corners, had serious foundation problems. The hardwood floors were old and scuffed, but swept clean. Inexpensive bamboo furniture with flowered cushions gave the room a homey feel.

There were potted plants everywhere; he recognized a peace lily, ivy spilling out of a black ceramic pot on a brass-bound trunk, and a schefflera on a wooden plant stand near the front window. Like Meg herself, nothing exotic, but healthy, vibrant and alive.

"Why don't you sit down," said Benny. "I'll go fix us a Coke."

Jack could tell the roommate didn't like his looks. Well, tough. "No, thanks, I'm not—"

But she'd already slipped out of the room. Left alone, he walked over to look at a pen-and-ink drawing hung above the scroll-top desk. When he got too close to the Papasan, Gilligan let him know it.

Jack frowned at the dachshund. "Look, squirt, you and I gotta come to terms here. You no touchy me, I no touchy you. Got that?"

Gilligan's upper lip lifted to reveal a set of needle-sharp canines. He laid his head back down, rolling one eye as if to say, *Okay, buster, but I'm watching you.*

Jack turned his back on the dog to examine the drawing. Framed in black lacquer, it was a portrait done in finely executed stippling: a skinny young fellow with glasses and a bulbous nose, wearing a fishing hat with a lizard dangling from the brim. Just looking at it made Jack grin. It was signed with a blocky *MSJ* in one corner.

So Meg was an artist. Well, maybe a cartoonist. He was looking around to see if there were other pictures, when Meg returned. She'd ditched the afghan in favor of the outfit she'd worn that morning, but her hair still rippled like creek water around her shoulders. She was barefoot.

He jerked his eyes off those slender, high-arched feet.

"That your boyfriend?" he asked, nodding at the drawing

She grinned. "I had to take commercial art in college. It's just a magazine ad I thought was funny, so I copied it." She glanced at the picture. "Benny likes it, so she had it framed."

"Benny has good taste," said Benny, returning from the kitchen with three jelly jars balanced on a metal tray. "It'll be worth something one day, you watch." She set the tray on top of the Scrabble board. "Here ya go. The real thing."

She hooked one bare foot around the leg of a small rocking chair to pull it forward, while Meg curled up in the Papasan with the dog in her lap.

Jack took a glass and sat down on the love seat. "Sorry I interrupted your game. Who was winning?"

"Benny *always* wins," Meg said. "Her vocabulary's bigger than Noah Webster's."

Which meant that she was one of those intellectual women who enjoyed feasting on the unsuspecting male ego. Jack flicked a glance at Benny, expecting her to demur with false modesty.

Instead she gave him an eager thousand-watt smile. "*¿Quiere usted jugar, Señor Torres?*"

Jack laughed. "No way, lady. You'll have to find another victim." He looked at Meg, suddenly comfortable with these two sweet-faced young women. "Do you want me to install that pulley for you?"

Meg's mouth fell open. "You mean you can do that, too?"

"Sure. I'm a Jack of—"

"All trades," Meg finished with a groan. "That's terrible."

Jack grinned. "Yeah, puns are us."

"Have you ever lived in Connecticut?" Benny asked out of nowhere.

Jack could feel the back of his neck heat. "Why do you ask that?"

"The way you said 'are' just now. Flat like a New Englander." Benny rocked placidly, but her eyes measured Jack. "Or if not Connecticut, maybe New Hampshire."

Meg shook her head. "Benny analyzes everybody's accent. She's a language expert."

Jack suddenly realized that Meg St. John, guarded as she was on every side by the people in her life—from her co-workers to her family to her roommate—was about as accessible as Rapunzel in her tower.

Alarm bells clanged at the direction of his thoughts. He turned to Meg. "So is tomorrow a good day?"

"For what?"

"The idler pulley."

"Well, there's church…"

"Do you go to church somewhere, Jack?" Benny seemed determined to interview him.

Jack began to get irritated. "I just moved to town. I haven't had time to look for a church."

He should have seen it coming. Meg beamed. "Good! Then you can come with us."

"I don't have the right clothes," he said, looking down at his only pair of jeans. The right knee was almost out, and he owned nothing else but uniforms and T-shirts.

"Oh, we're not a dress-up kind of church," Benny assured him.

Jack hesitated, rattling the ice in his glass. He felt as touchy as that snarky little dachshund, wanting Meg to think well of him, but reluctant to back down from her needle-eyed roommate.

"Benny—" Meg began, evidently aware of Jack's discomfort.

"Don't worry," Benny said, looking thoughtful, "I won't carve him up on the spot. I just can't help wondering—"

Jack set his glass on the tray and got up. "I'll pass on church for now. Just let me know when I can come work on your car."

Benny continued to rock, while Meg jumped to her feet to let Jack out. "I'm sorry," she whispered.

He had an insane urge to lean down and kiss the worried look off her face. "Good night, St. John," he said instead and stalked toward the motorcycle parked beside her Mustang.

Bad idea to come here. Bad idea.

"Benny!" Meg leaned back against the door, frowning at her roommate. "You just embarrassed him."

"He seemed to be man enough to take it." Benny picked up the tray of drinks and carried it into the kitchen.

Meg followed. "But what got into you? Couldn't you tell—"

"Meg, he never answered any of my questions."

"So?"

"He's hiding something." Benny's brows drew together, her eyes piercing with skepticism. "What do you know about him, besides the fact that he's built like a Greek statue?"

"Benny!" Meg seemed destined to spend the evening gasping out her roommate's name. "You never notice stuff like that."

"I've got eyes in my head. And you better answer my question, my friend. Who is this guy?"

Meg thought about the expression on Jack's face as he'd left her, and her knees buckled. "I don't know," she mumbled. "I think he may be an ex-convict. Or something."

Benny's eyes widened. "You're kidding, right?"

Meg felt like crying. It had been a very long day. "I didn't *ask* him to bring me that car part, but I thought it was a nice thing for him to do."

Benny looked grim. "Unless he's got some ulterior motive. Don't you dare let yourself get caught alone with him. You hear me?"

Meg sighed. "Yes, mother."

Kenneth Warner picked up Manny Herrera Saturday night at the bus station in downtown Fort Worth.

"Let's get out of here before we get knifed," Warner muttered, gunning the Beemer before Herrera had even shut the door. "Are your shoes clean?"

The Mexican smiled faintly. "What is the problem, Mr. Warner?"

Herrera's politeness and meticulous English got on Warner's nerves.

"It's more in the nature of an avalanche than a *problem,*" Warner snapped. "The Wolf is pumping me for money on one side, customers in Illinois screaming for workers, and the overhead on this operation is killing me. I thought you said you had a load of illegals lined up to come north last week."

Herrera looked out the darkened window for a moment without answering. Neon signs in the windows of bars and clubs along the street lit his scarred face in flashes of red and blue.

"Well? What happened?" prompted Warner.

Herrera stroked his heavy mustache. "I don't know. My cousin Efrin has been organizing the coyotes. He'll be here tomorrow."

"If he can't do the job, then get somebody else." Warner paused. "And if *you* can't do the job, *I* get somebody else. *Comprende?*"

Herrera was silent.

Annoyed, Warner ran a yellow light. "I've heard rumors that Torres has connections on the border."

"Rumors...sometimes there's truth in them, sometimes not."

"What do you know about him?"

"My little brother likes him."

"Oh, well, *there's* a fine recommendation." Warner snorted. "See what you can find out. Maybe he's interested in a little extra income." He turned to make the block back to the bus station. "Because if we don't get rolling again, the whole thing's going to blow up. And we can't have that, can we?"

"No," Herrera sighed, "we can't have that."

Chapter Six

Mowing a lawn the size of Silver Hill gave a man plenty of time to think—almost as much time as sitting in a truck waiting for illegal aliens to slip out of a dark river.

A month ago Jack would have spent the time meditating on how much he missed his partner. And devising plans for bringing the killer to justice. Now, as he drove the bush hog round and round in the sweltering afternoon sun, his thoughts kept sliding into images of chestnut hair and green eyes. And a warm laugh. Music and funny pictures. Meg.

Lulled by fantasies of kissing that teasing smile, Jack suddenly felt the tractor jar. He killed the motor and got off to investigate.

Crouching, he pulled the weeds aside and let out a low whistle of surprise. A black marble sundial on a concrete base lay half-buried under a clump of crabgrass, the Roman numerals etched in its square face almost obliterated by dirt. If he'd driven another inch, the mower would have flattened the upstanding bronze triangle in the center.

Meg would go berserk over this thing.

He headed toward the carriage house, where Meg had been all morning, sorting through multiple generations of junk.

The carriage house windows had been cranked outward, the broad double doors propped open to catch the breeze. As he crossed the drive, he listened for Meg's rather unsteady alto; she loved to sing as she worked. He wondered if she ever got depressed about anything.

As he got closer, he heard male voices from inside, conversing in Spanish. He stopped short when he heard the word "coyote"—the Mexican term for a border-crossing guide— and hurried to flatten himself against the building.

"You should handle this on your own, cousin," said a quiet, measured voice Jack recognized as Manny Herrera's. "I don't have time to worry about your mistakes."

The answering rapid-fire whine belonged to Efrin, yet another member of the Herrera clan who had signed on to the crew Monday. Efrin was walleyed, whippet-thin and greasy of hair. To his credit, though, he seemed to be a hard worker.

"*My* mistakes?" Efrin echoed. "No, no, this rotten cheat takes the money and disappears, leaving the *pollos* in plain sight. They're picked up and sent back, and there I am without a cent to show for my trouble."

Jack froze. Pay dirt.

Efrin's excuses seemed to test Manny's legendary patience. "You think you got more troubles than anybody else? Huh? The chickens don't get delivered, nobody gets paid. Not you, not me, not *El Lobo*."

"I'm sorry, Manuelo—"

"So this coyote is bad," Manny interrupted. "Don't you know any more?"

"I know them, yes," Efrin admitted, "but trustworthy is another matter. A useful coyote must be strong, wily as a fox and able to think on his feet without running scared at the first bark of the dog."

Still crouched under the window, Jack smiled. He knew what he was going to do.

Suddenly he heard off-key singing.

"It's a beautiful day in the neighborhood, a beautiful day— Torres! What are you doing?"

Jack jerked around to find Meg standing at the corner of the building. In her hand was a plaster statue that looked like a naked troll. He'd forgotten all about her. The conversation inside the building had, of course, abruptly ceased.

He scrambled for a logical reason for skulking beneath a window in broad daylight. "I was looking for you," he said. "You'll never believe what I found in the front yard."

Curiosity chased away Meg's suspicious expression. "What?"

"I'll have to show you. Come on." He set off the way he'd come, relieved when she fell into step without arguing.

"Did you finish the mowing?" she asked, tucking the statue under her arm. "I can't wait to see what it looks like without all the weeds."

"Just about," he said, peering at her ugly artifact. "What *is* that? It looks like an extra from *Lord of the Rings*."

She laughed. "Vintage garden art. He may not be pretty, but he'd be worth a few hundred dollars on eBay. I'm gonna put him in charge of the rose garden."

"Oh yeah?" Jack grinned at the idea. "Well, see what you think of this." He stooped to pull the weeds away from the sundial.

Meg's eyes widened with delight. "My sundial! You found my sundial!" She thrust the troll at Jack, cast herself on her knees and eagerly began brushing dirt off the face of the clock with her hands.

"Just call me Indiana Jones." Jack grinned at her excitement. "I wish I'd known you were looking for it. I nearly ran over it."

She beamed at him. "Mrs. Grover-Niles is going to be thrilled when I tell her we found it. She showed me a newspaper article about it last week. It's purbeck marble, brought all the way from Cyprus in 1927. See the design cut in the gnomon? Hand-forged bronze."

"*No-min?*" Jack repeated the unfamiliar word. "What's that?"

"G-n-o-m-o-n. The metal part that casts a shadow so you can tell the time."

"You learn something new every day," Jack said, impressed with Meg's attention to detail. "You want me to move it to the shop, get one of the guys to clean it up for you?"

"No!" Meg looked alarmed. "A sundial is specially designed for the exact spot it's located in, so the time will be accurate. We'd never get it back in the right place if we move it. I'll get Manny to flag it so we won't risk running over it again." Meg wrinkled her nose. "You know, I never would have pictured him as a chicken farmer."

Jack was startled into laughter. "A what?"

She looked at him uncertainly. "Doesn't *pollo* mean chicken?"

"Well, yeah," he said. "What makes you think—" Oh. The conversation between Manny and Efrin in the carriage house. Meg had evidently understood at least part of it.

"I probably shouldn't eavesdrop," she said, "but Manny's been worrying me lately. He always looks serious, but lately he's been cutting out of here the second work is over. I can't help wondering what's wrong."

Trying not to show how deeply her tenderheartedness affected him, Jack put out a hand to help Meg to her feet.

"Manny and Efrin were probably just making plans for supper." He handed her the statue. "Will you be home tonight? I thought I'd come install your idler pulley."

"No, we have our ESL classes on Wednesdays. I'm sorry."

Jack swallowed disappointment. "No problem, just leave the keys under the seat, and I'll take care of it while you're gone." He climbed back on the tractor.

Meg's eyes lit. "I've got an even better idea. Tomás wanted to come to the class, so why don't you bring him to my house, and work on the car while we're gone? When you get done, you can come pick him up. We'll be at Wedgwood Elementary School."

"And...?"

"And what?" Meg pulled her sunglasses off the top of her head where they'd been resting, and slid them onto her nose.

"You think I just fell off the turnip truck? You're trying to rope me into helping with that class."

Meg smiled. She lifted the statue in front of her face. "Master is too smart for us," she said in a familiar exaggerated whine. "Gollum hopeses Master will go out for ice cream with us after class. We has somebody we wants you to meet."

"Ice cream, huh?" He gave her a suspicious look. "You're not trying to set me up with somebody, are you?"

"As if!" Chuckling, Meg lowered the statue. "Ramón's a seminary student who pastors our bilingual church. He's the one who started the ESL class."

Jack studied the hopeful wrinkle between Meg's perfect brows. She was going to dog him to the ends of the earth until he agreed to show up at one of her classes. On the other hand, there was no telling what kind of information he could pick up from the Mexicans in the class tonight—if he played it right.

"All right," he said on a long-suffering sigh, "you win. I'll bring Tomás to your house at six, then after I fix your car I'll come by the school. But you'll owe me a double-dip butter pecan waffle cone with chocolate jimmies."

Meg's smile shone brighter than the afternoon sun. "Yesss, Master, we hears you. We is good Gollum!" She saluted and turned toward the carriage house, swinging the statue by its bare feet. Just before Jack replaced his earplugs, Meg called over her shoulder, "Make sure Tomás eats supper before he comes, okay?"

Shaking his head, Jack waved and cranked the tractor. Might as well bow to the inevitable.

The inevitable turned out to be not quite what Jack had expected. Elementary school apparently wasn't the safe place it had been in his day. The chain on the handle rattled as he opened the front door, and iron bars guarded every window.

Still, waves of pleasant memories washed through him as he encountered the old-fashioned smells of chalk, wax crayons and pine cleaner. Made him think of Dottie Rook—sweet-faced, smiling Mrs. Rook, who comfortably squished when you hugged her. She wasn't afraid to get hugged by little boys who didn't take a bath often enough. She'd made him love reading and corrected his grammar. No Ebonics or Spanglish allowed in her classroom.

Miraculously, she'd taken an interest in Jack that lasted all the way through high school, and because of her he wound up in college on a military scholarship. She'd even talked her husband into giving Jack a reference for his application to border patrol academy. Though they'd never been stationed in the same city, he'd managed to stay in touch up until about two years ago. It was about time to give them another call.

Jack turned to the right, glancing into empty classrooms as he followed the muted sound of voices coming from the end of the hall. He understood the rarity of a life like Dottie Rook's, a life where spirituality had permeated everything she did. It was the same kind of spirituality he saw in Meg St. John.

Jack supposed he was in a precarious position, exploiting her goodness for his own purposes. It was doubtful she'd forgive him when she inevitably found out what was going on. But if he'd tried for a year he couldn't have picked a better liaison between administration and labor in this dirty company. In spite of Warner's jealousy, Meg was in favor with the big boss, Crowley. And the Mexicans treated her like the Queen of Sheba.

A burst of childish laughter drew him to the end of the hall. Stopping in the open classroom door, he found a bunch of dark-haired, brown-skinned children, all shapes and sizes, lined up across the front of the room.

And one nut in a six-foot cucumber costume, singing at the top of her lungs: "Oh, whe-e-e-ere is my hairbrush?" The song continued, the children giggling at the cucumber's operatic twang and comical gestures.

Jack leaned in the doorway, watching the children mimic the words and actions—having a blast learning English. When the song ended in a strident screech, the children rushed to hug the big, fuzzy costume. The cucumber staggered under the onslaught of squirming little bodies.

Grinning, Jack sauntered in. "St. John, your talents never cease to amaze me."

The cucumber gave a startled squeak and toppled under a pile of children.

* * *

"I told you you'd have a good time," Meg said, spooning a blob of root beer and ice cream into her mouth.

Jack saluted Meg with his loaded waffle cone and winked at Benny, who was daintily sipping a milk shake. "I confess I had to see who was inside the cucumber. Your cheeks look like traffic lights, St. John."

Fanning her still-hot face with a paper napkin, Meg smiled at the sight of Tomás using his tongue to chase a dribble of chocolate syrup down the side of his cone. "Dad rented the costume for a Bible School gig at church and let me borrow it tonight. He forgot to warn me old Larry-Boy might give me heat stroke."

Meg had expected Jack to pick up Tomás and head the motorcycle straight back to the *barrio*. Instead he'd sauntered into her classroom, picked her up off the floor and asked for an encore. When she'd towed him across the hall and introduced him to Ramón and Connie Santos, the pastor had set Jack to pouring punch with Benny.

And Jack had kept his promise of joining the trip to Braum's after class.

"We appreciate you pitching in to help, brother," said Ramón, a swarthy, goateed young man whose smile seemed to swallow his dark eyes. He gave Jack a bone-bruising whack on the arm. "You're a natural-born teacher, man."

Meg watched Jack shrug off the compliment. Because of her friendship with Benny, she knew there could be multiple reasons a person would be uncomfortable with attention. She couldn't help wondering what fed Jack's reserve.

"We need all the help we can get," said Benny, giving Jack one of her measuring looks. "Immigrants stand a better chance at good jobs if they can speak English." Meg knew her roommate was trying to be fair, even while reserving judgment. Benny threw the remains of her milk shake into a nearby garbage can. "Meg, we'd better head toward home. I've got an early class in the morning."

"Me, too. But let's pray before we go." Ramón leaned forward on the table. "Got any pressing needs?"

"My dissertation's in disarray at the moment," said Benny, grimacing. "My professor says I need more research."

"Okay, we'll cover you. Meg?"

"Oh, work, I guess," she said on a sigh. "I'm still picking up weird vibes from Mr. Warner every time I'm around him."

Jack frowned. "What do you mean?"

Meg immediately wished she'd kept her mouth shut. What if he decided to make trouble with her boss? Who'd have thought he'd be so protective? "It's nothing major," she assured him, glancing at Tomás, who was enjoying his ice cream, oblivious to the adult conversation. "Anyway, we need to pray for the guys on my crew." She was pretty sure Tomás was close to accepting the Lord.

"Okay." Ramón nodded. "And Connie and I need you guys to pray for Valentina's eyes. We have a doctor's appointment next week." He smiled at Jack. "What about you, Torres? Now's your chance."

Jack looked taken aback. "I don't pray out loud."

Ramón's eyes twinkled. "You don't have to. Just tell us how we can lift you up."

Jack's gaze homed in on Meg's. "Work issues for me, too."

Ramón nodded and took his wife by the hand. "Let's pray."

Meg bowed her head, wishing she knew exactly what was bothering Jack.

Jack hustled Tomás out of the ice-cream shop, shaken by the experience of being prayed for. As far as he knew, it was the first time since Rico's death. Jack prayed often, alone in his room or on Sunday mornings when he knew he should be in church, with a notable lack of response from on high. But this corporate besieging of heaven almost made him believe God hadn't abandoned him after all.

He'd opened his eyes once to look at Meg, watching her pray with her eyelashes damp and fingers curled upward as if to receive a blessing. His heart had cracked a little. Rico used to pray like that, bold and unembarrassed, whether they were with his family, alone together in their border patrol truck, or in a wide-open public place like a restaurant.

He wondered what Tomás thought about the whole thing. The boy had listened wide-eyed to the conversation, apparently too shy to try out the English he'd learned at the ESL class.

Jack mounted the Harley and waited as Tomás strapped on the extra helmet. They both watched Meg and Benny get in Benny's little Toyota and back out into the street.

"That is two good-looking ladies," Tomás commented on a gusty sigh. "Which one you gonna ask out?"

Jack cocked an eyebrow. "Down, boy. Neither one of 'em's exactly in my league."

Tomás's look was incredulous. "You gotta be kidding. The *señorita*...Meg, she looks at you all the time."

Despite a strong urge to pursue the nature of Meg's "looking" at him, Jack knew he'd better squelch this conversation. "Look, can you see me doing the religious thing for more than five minutes?" Jack shook his head. "I don't think so."

"All women are religious. You just gotta learn to deal with it. Play the game." Tomás gave him an exaggerated leer.

"Since you're the expert, why don't *you* ask her out?"

Tomás puffed out his chest, all teenage hubris. "Maybe I will." Ignoring Jack's snort of friendly derision, he jerked a thumb over Jack's shoulder. "Hey, do you know that guy over there in the red truck?"

"Where?" Jack followed the direction of Tomás's pointing finger. "I don't recognize it. Why?"

"He's been watching us in his mirror ever since we came out of the store."

"Are you sure?" Peering into the darkness, Jack removed his helmet. He could just make out the shadowy silhouette of the driver of the truck, which was parked under a light about ten yards down the street.

"Yeah," said Tomás. "He's adjusted the side mirror a couple of times when you moved."

As Jack hesitated, deciding whether to confront the man or make a run for it, the driver's side door of the truck opened and the man got out. He was about six feet tall with a burly build—despite the heat, he wore a dark jacket and cream-colored Stetson.

"Keep your mouth shut, Tomás," Jack muttered and waited for the man to approach.

Tomás gulped. "Okay." He shrank into the shadows.

As soon as the storefront light hit the man's face, Jack was glad he'd sent Tomás out of earshot. He blinked to make sure he wasn't hallucinating. "Of all people to run into right now," he muttered. Swallowing his dismay, Jack got off the bike and slouched forward. "Vernon Rook! Long time no see."

His former mentor stared at Jack with a strained smile that incorporated a peculiar mix of gladness and challenge. "Well, if it ain't the scourge of the West. How are you, boy?"

Jack shook Rook's hand and found it just as hard and callused as it used to be. That was a relief. There was a certain slackness in the man's face—a weight of skin around the eyes, jowls at the chin, thinness of the lips. Older, of course. Five years was a long time. "I thought you'd retired."

"They'll have to peel my gun out of my cold dead hand," Rook deadpanned. His craggy features creased as he surveyed Jack's long hair and scruffy attire. "You're off duty, I see."

Jack shrugged and glanced at the shadows where Tomás had disappeared. "I'm out completely."

Rook nodded. "I heard about that fracas with your partner down in Eagle Pass."

Fracas? Rico's murder was a *fracas?*

"It's been a rough year," Jack said.

"Dottie wanted to come down and see to you, but I wouldn't let her—her health ain't so good anymore." Rook's look was accusing. "You could have called her."

Jack looked at this man who had sponsored his border patrol career. And who hadn't returned a phone call, letter or e-mail in more than three years.

"I'm sorry, Vernon. Now that I know you guys are in Fort Worth I'll give Miss Dottie a call." It would be tricky, but Jack owed a lot to Dottie. Vernon, too, for that matter.

"You do that." Rook slapped Jack on the shoulder. For an old guy, he'd always had more strength than he realized. "Where you staying?" Rook smiled. "You know Dottie's gonna ask."

"Other side of town," Jack said. He slid his helmet over his head and backed toward the motorcycle. "Listen, I've gotta go. Tell Dottie I'll be in touch."

"Will do." Vernon walked off, then turned. "It's good to see you again, son."

"Yeah, same here." Jack half saluted and cranked the bike. He beckoned Tomás, who'd been leaning against the wall at the corner of the building. As they roared off down the street,

Jack wondered how much of the English conversation Tomás had heard.

Most of all he wondered what Vernon Rook was doing staking out an ice-cream store in midtown Fort Worth.

Chapter Seven

Meg looked up as the cantina-on-wheels affectionately known as the "Roach Coach" rattled up to Silver Hill's front sidewalk, stopping with a squeal of brakes and a jaunty horn-honk. Relieved that Friday afternoon had finally arrived, she radioed Jack to call the crew to lunch. Manny had taken a week off to go back to Mexico, leaving the crew shorthanded.

"*¡Hola, amigos!*" caroled Raffi Garcia, entrepreneur and chef extraordinaire. He hopped out of the brightly painted vehicle accompanied by a burst of music from a salsa radio station. "*¡Espero que todos tengan hambre!*" He flipped open a row of locks to reveal his wares with the élan of a television magician.

Diego Herrera, plucking a plastic-wrapped mystery-meat sandwich from the stack, said something to Raffi in Spanish, making the other men laugh. Meg tried to work out the unfamiliar words, but her Spanish wasn't quite up to the translation.

She felt a tug on her braid and looked up to find Jack smiling down at her. "Raffi said he hoped we're hungry, and Diego wanted to know if Raffi does his shopping at the goat farm."

"Oh, gross." But she laughed, absurdly pleased that Jack had bothered to explain the joke.

With a slight smile he stepped away to take a sandwich from the cooler. She noticed he put his mirrored shades back on and stood jabbering in Spanish with Raffi.

When the cantina had scuttled off to the next site, the whole crew moved to the shade of the carriage way, where Meg's pickup and the equipment truck and trailer were parked. She sat down on the tailgate of her truck and opened her sandwich, praying it wasn't somebody's pet goat.

After distributing a stack of five-gallon buckets for the men to sit on, Jack plunked down beside Tomás. They were soon engaged in conversation, while the other men finished eating and sprawled in the grass for a short siesta.

Meg opened her copy of *Spanish for Gringos* to review as she ate. After a moment she realized she'd read the same page twice; she kept glancing at Jack and Tomás. Tomás had taken to wearing his long hair tied back, a bandanna twisted around his head. An earring had appeared in one earlobe, too.

Just like Jack. Meg smiled. Tomás seemed to be growing taller every day.

Jack caught her staring. "I was just asking Tomás if he'd heard from Manny," he said without any noticeable discomfort.

Meg brightened. "Has he?"

Tomás smiled and tried out his English. "My brother is now home."

"Mi hermano ha llegado a casa," Meg echoed. "Right?"

Jack applauded. *"Tú eres una joven muy brillante."* When Meg wrinkled her forehead, trying to decode the unfamiliar word *joven,* Jack translated with a laugh. "Such a brilliant young lady. Tomás said Manny called last night."

"That's good." Meg pulled her legs up to sit cross-legged. "Is everything okay?"

Tomás understood her simple words and answered in English, "Okay. Mother is good. Baby is good." He held his hands in front of his stomach, pantomiming pregnancy. "I am another uncle soon."

"No wonder Manny wanted to go home!" Meg exclaimed. Jack looked thoughtful. *"¿Tienes otros niños?"*

"Sí, tres."

So Manny had three other children besides the baby on the way. This was the most Meg had discovered about the family of her lead man since she'd met him two years ago. Jack lounged on his bucket as if the last thing on his mind was interrogating a sixteen-year-old Mexican youth, but something of the Terminator look gave Meg a shiver of awareness. There was something going on here below the surface.

Jack rattled off something else in Spanish, and Tomás shook his head. *"Tengo catorce años."* Then the boy's eyes went wide with dismay.

Meg knew her Spanish numbers. Her young friend was out of school doing backbreaking labor at the age of fourteen. She opened her mouth, then shut it when Jack shook his head warningly.

Tomás jumped to his feet and mumbled something about getting back to work.

Meg stared after him. "There's no way he's legally in the United States working at that age."

"St. John, it would be best if you kept your mouth shut."

She looked around. Diego Herrera opened one eye sleepily, then closed it again. Meg lowered her voice. "I thought he was at least sixteen."

"Come here." Jack pulled Tomás's abandoned bucket

closer and waited until she moved to sit on it. He leaned his elbows on his knees. "You know you can't report him," he said quietly.

Clearly Jack considered himself one of *them.* Caught by the palpable air of mystery that surrounded him, Meg tried not to notice the close proximity of that hard muscled arm.

"Why not?" she whispered. "It would be for his own good. He's too young—"

"Have you ever seen the villages along the Mexican border?" Jack held her gaze. "Manny's baby is probably going to be born in a cardboard house."

Meg shut her eyes, but the image wouldn't disappear.

Jack leaned his shoulder into hers. "You can't report him," he repeated.

Meg bit her lip. "I'll pray about it." She glanced at Jack and stood up. "Mr. Warner's rounded up some guys to help us throw sod tomorrow. We won't be ready if we don't get back to work."

Looking unhappy, Jack stood up and moved around, nudging the crew back to life.

Meg knew she had just waded into deep water, following right behind Jack. She couldn't decide if she felt scared or exhilarated.

"I'll think about it tomorrow," she muttered as she yanked her gloves out of her back pocket.

Saturday morning, Jack stood in the back of a flatbed truck loaded with grass pallets, surveying a clutch of nervous and ill-dressed Hispanic men. They had been processed for employment that morning, and he and Meg were to orient them to the basic tasks of a landscaping crew. Kenneth Warner, though generally stingy about approving overtime, obviously wanted to take full advantage of these poor fellows while they waited for transportation north.

Jack took in the colorful array of polyester pants, plaid dress shirts and rubber sandals. He doubted any one of these *pollos* had been in the United States longer than forty-eight hours. The odor of travel, privation and fear was enough to shout their illegal status. Jack could take them to a detention facility any time he chose, of course. But he wanted the boss who'd brought them here, the man called *El Lobo*. He wasn't about to blow his cover for such small game.

"'*Dias, amigos*," he said, continuing in Spanish, "today you're going to learn to throw sod. Bonuses if we get done by noon."

A murmur of appreciation passed through the men, hunger and relief in their faces. They would earn more today than they could earn in a month down in Mexico; at the same time Jack would shore up the foundation of trust in his cover. A win-win situation.

Jack jumped to the ground and began to explain the finer points of the most menial of landscaping tasks.

A couple of hours later, taking a breather in the shade of a gigantic oak tree, Jack watched Meg haul an armload of grass across the driveway.

She seemed unaware of the crew's surreptitious gazes following every step she took. She wasn't dressed for seduction in overalls and a sleeveless top, but her dewy, slightly sunburned skin still drew the eye. A Texas Rangers baseball cap protected her face, but her shoulders were getting pink. If he were the boss, he'd make her sit down and take a break.

Jack noted the progress of the grass that was filling in the landscape with emerald color. More than half done. The men were working hard, taking direction well, and beginning to relax and joke around a little. When the job was finished, they'd all be taken to a holding house that would make the

Starlight Inn look like the Waldorf-Astoria. It was virtual slavery, and he deeply regretted his part in it. He briefly closed his eyes.

Lord, forgive me.

He realized Meg was leaning around the trunk of the tree, her nose crinkled.

"Torres, I think a couple of these guys worked for us before."

He tensed. "Probably. They move around all the time."

"No, I mean—I think they were on a crew that the INS busted back in April." She whispered, "The ones that never came back."

She was naive, but she wasn't stupid. And she had a conscientious streak a mile wide.

"St. John, we've been over this. They have documents. Now leave it alone."

She studied him, lips pursed. "I don't know what to think about you."

He wiped the sweat out of his eyes with his fingers. "Let's just get this finished so we can go home."

She backed away from him, shaking her head.

Jack sighed. It was getting harder and harder to keep straight who he was and who he wanted to be.

Meg staggered away from the trailer with three blocks of grass clutched against her stomach, and headed for the area of new lawn along the porch shrub bed.

She'd spent her first summer internship slinging sod, and she was a pro at lining up the cut edges so that they seamlessly matched. It was a point of pride to teach this new crew to follow her example.

Still, she planned to call the INS Monday morning and tell

them she suspected her company had been fudging on documentation papers.

On the other hand, these poor men weren't hurting a soul. If Warner found out she was the one who reported Sunset's violations, she'd lose her job. And nobody else in the industry would trust her again.

Jack had asked her point-blank not to tell. If she did, he'd never trust her again, either. That was a sobering thought because, for whatever reason, she valued his trust.

Obedience or compassion? *Lord, what should I do?*

It was a measure of her preoccupation that a trail of fire ants had marched out of the sod, around her waist, and into the opening of her overalls as inexorably as the Israelites conquering Jericho before she felt the first bite. Meg let out a scream that undoubtedly startled the steers in the Stockyards twenty-five miles away. Sod flew in all directions.

The new crew dropped what they were doing and came running, forming a circle of sympathy and curiosity around the crazy Anglo lady, muttering to one another in anxious Spanish.

"*¡Mueva al revés!*" Meg panted, hopping up and down. "*¡Por favor!*" She couldn't reach in and grab bugs with all those male eyes on her.

The men exchanged looks and took a couple of steps backward.

Meg groaned, forgetting most of her Spanish. "No!" She twirled one finger in a circle. "*Mueva*—turn-o around-o, *comprende?*" The men looked puzzled and mildly fascinated. She bowed to the inevitable. "Jack!" Her scream spanned two octaves. "Get over here! *¡Caramba! ¡No me gusta!*"

Jack appeared from behind the other men. "Hey, St. John, did you see a roach?"

He grinned, and she was so glad to see him that she decided to let him live. For the moment. "Tell these men to turn around!"

"I'd get my money back on *Spanish for Gringos,* if I were you. You told 'em to move backwards."

"Please, hurry! I've got fire ants in my pants, but they're looking and I can't—"

"*¡Hombres, dense vuelta ahora!*" he ordered in rapid Spanish. "*¡Salgan de aquí!*"

The men scattered in the direction of the truck and trailer, while Jack stood there frowning at Meg in concern.

"You, too!" Meg shivered and hopped in agony.

"Oh, yeah." Jack did an about-face.

Because there was nowhere else to go, Meg stayed put and yanked off the straps of her overalls, then began to frantically scoop and fling ants to the four corners. By the time she got rid of them all, she was sobbing in humiliation and pain.

"Meg," Jack said cautiously, "can I turn around yet?"

"No!" she wailed. She examined the fiery welts around her midsection. She was going to need some medicine fast. Gingerly tugging her top back down and holding her pants at her waist, she stumbled toward the truck and the first-aid kit.

She found the crew clustered around the water cooler. An older man in a Blue Bell Ice Cream T-shirt handed her a cup of water. He respectfully avoided her eyes, for which Meg was grateful. She'd never been so embarrassed in her life.

"*Gracias,*" she said with a grimace of a smile. After gulping down the water, she yanked open the passenger door of the truck and leaned in to root through the glove compartment.

"It's under the seat," Jack said from close behind her.

Meg sent a glare over her shoulder. "You looked!"

"I swear I didn't." He stepped back, hands in the air. "Come on, let me help."

She shook her head and sat down in the open doorway of the truck, the white metal box open on her knees. "You think this is funny."

"Fire ants are no joke." He leaned in with an elbow on the door. "Are you allergic?"

She found the antihistamine lotion and peeled her shirt up a modest couple of inches to dab it on the bites. "Since I'm not having a seizure, I guess not." She looked up. Jack had propped his sunglasses on top of his head, and his dark eyes were fixed on her stomach, which promptly did a somersault. "I wish you'd go away."

"I'm sure." There was humor and concern and amazing tenderness in his expression for just a second, then he took the tube of ointment. "Turn around. I'll get your back."

Meg swallowed her objections and obeyed.

"You need to have your dad look at these bites. He might want to give you an antibiotic." Jolted by the gentle touch of Jack's rough fingers on her skin, Meg found herself incapable of anything but a weak little grunt. He smeared on more lotion. "Did you know that *caramba* means 'wow'? Interesting segue into 'I don't like it.'"

She gave a weak chuckle. "I did—ooh—the best I could under duress." The sting of her bites was beginning to ease. "Thank you. That's better." She turned around, surprising a peculiar expression in Jack's eyes. "What's the matter?"

"Nothing." He capped the ointment and tossed it into the box. "Sit here and rest while we finish up. Fifteen minutes ought to do it. Can you stand it that long?"

He stood close to her, one long arm draped across the open door of the truck, the other propped on top of the cab.

She felt protected and cherished by a man who threatened her in many ways.

She nodded. "I'm fine."

But as he walked away with that swinging swagger of his, she knew she wasn't anywhere close to fine.

Jack wouldn't have remembered it was Father's Day if Meg hadn't mentioned that she was going to church with her parents on Sunday. She'd reminded the crew that worship at the Spanish church started at nine o'clock, and Pastor Ramón would love to see them there.

Jack considered going, but decided he'd better follow up on the document he'd pulled off Warner's computer yesterday morning. It was a list of company CEOs open to hiring large shipments of workers. Amazing that it had turned up in Warner's computer so quickly.

Last night he'd reported in to Carmichael, who told him that the rising number of illegal crossings at the border over the last two weeks made the timing of Jack's investigation critical. Escalating activity meant big money changing hands. Money that funded drug traffic as well as illegal immigration. A Senate oversight committee was foaming at the mouth to know who was at the root of this cartel. Bottom line, it had to be stopped.

Jack made his phone calls and Internet searches. Restless, he picked up the guitar he'd bought in a pawnshop the other day. The instrument had a mellow resonance that pleased his ear and mitigated the loneliness that had hounded him since he'd crossed paths with Meg.

He remembered most of the chords Rico had taught him. Jack could carry a tune, but it wasn't pretty; Rico had been the singer. He found himself playing "Amazing Grace," finger-picking a soft pattern that came back to him with increasing fluidity. It was Rico's wife Isabel's favorite. Three-year-old Danilo had always wanted to sing "I'm in the Lord's Army," marching and shouting out "Yes, sir!" at the top of his lungs at the end of every line.

Jack switched to the children's march, smiling in spite of the ache. He wished he could pull Danilo onto his lap and hold him for Rico. A little boy needed a daddy, especially on Father's Day.

He hadn't talked to Isabel in several months. It was too awkward to get past the cavity of Rico's absence. But if somebody had made an effort to fill in the father gaps when Jack was small, maybe he wouldn't have wasted so much time proving he didn't need a dad. That he could get along just fine on his own.

Jack began to pray that somebody would do that for Danilo.

Father's Day. He lay back on the bed, cradling the guitar. He hoped Meg was enjoying the time with her family.

Meg was considering putting herself up for adoption. She picked up a junior-size bowling ball, sticking her fingers into its chipped holes. It barely weighed enough to roll to the end of the lane and knock over a pin, no matter how hard you threw it. But at least she could control it.

Which was more than she could say for about ninety-five percent of her life. In honor of Father's Day, she'd given her dad carte blanche on the afternoon's entertainment. Bad mistake.

That's what I get for finding Enya, Meg thought as she watched her ball slide into the gutter without so much as breathing on a pin. Control. Yeah, right.

"Remember it's like a waltz, Meg," said Benny, getting up

o squeeze a resin bag against her palms. "One, two, *three!* And roll the ball while you're on your left foot."

Meg put her hands on her hips. "I know *what* to do, I just can't *do* it." Rubbing her temple, she plopped down beside Elliot Fairchild, who'd been invited by her matchmaking parents. The noise of the alley, combined with worry about Jack and those Mexican men she'd worked with yesterday, had given her a throbbing headache. Or maybe it was the ant bites. She gave Elliot a beseeching look. "Have you got an aspirin?"

"You need something to eat." Elliot gently pulled her eyelid up with his thumb and peered into her eye. "A low insulin level will give you a headache."

"I'm not hungry," Meg grumbled, resting her head against the hard plastic seat back. She crossed her outstretched legs at the ankle, bumping the maroon-and-green rubber-soled shoes together. There was a certain perverse satisfaction in wearing something that ugly.

While Benny took her turn, Elliot leaned close to Meg's ear. "Hey, do you think she would go out with me if I asked her?" When she raised her brows, he gave her an astute half smile. "You aren't going to give me the time of day, and we both know it. But Benny's really sweet."

"And I'm not?" She grinned when Elliot rolled his eyes. "Go for it, I say. What have you got to lose?"

"Maybe the remnants of my pride," he murmured, watching Benny's balletlike glide and release of the ball. Nine pins fell down, and she turned around with a disappointed huff.

Meg hid a smile. "Elliot," she said, "if you suspected something that could get a bunch of innocent people in trouble, would you tell?"

He gave her a cautious look. "I ratted on some people who

stole an anatomy test in medical school. Fair is fair, right right, wrong is wrong."

"Okay, but did you know for *sure* they did it, or were yo just guessing?"

Elliot looked alarmed. "This sounds like something yo should ask your dad."

"I know what he'd say." Meg bent forward and retied on of her shoelaces. "I'm taking a poll here."

"Well, let's see." Elliot licked a finger and stuck it in th air as if testing the wind. "Definitely you should tell."

Meg scowled at him. "Some help you are. This is serious.

"Then do what your dad would say." Elliot poked hi glasses up on his nose. "He's the wisest man I know."

Leaning her elbows on her knees, Meg looked up at Ellic with dawning respect. "And I think *you* make a great partner. She watched Benny pick up her spare with deadly accuracy

Right was right, wrong was wrong, huh? Was her dilemm really that simple?

Chapter Eight

Meg shut the door of Silver Hill's newly renovated powder room, checked to make sure she was alone, then perched on the end of a burgundy velvet chaise longue. The interior designer had done a good job of blending the paint, wallpaper and fixtures with the age of the house. This was one advantage of being the lone female on the crew. The rest of the guys still had to use that stinking portable facility out by the street.

Taking her cell phone off her belt clip, she thumbed in the number of the Dallas Immigration and Naturalization office and waited, foot tapping, for the automated system to transfer her to the correct department.

You're doing the right thing, Meg. Dad thought so. Benny thought so. Even Elliot thought so.

Another recorded voice answered.

"Oh, good grief." She'd hoped to talk to a real person. How was she going to explain her vague suspicions to a machine? She was going to sound like a paranoid nut. Flustered, she hung up.

Gathering her thoughts, jiggling the phone, she rehearsed her speech.

"Good morning, I'm yada-yada and I work for one of the most influential landscaping companies in the Metroplex. I've noticed lately that every time a green truck drives by, half my crew heads for the hills—" Bad, bad. *I'm not a speaker, I'm a landscaper.*

Before she could change her mind, she hit Redial and listened again to that maddening chain of recordings, pausing to punch in whatever number they told her to. Finally she got the last one.

And somebody pounded on the door. She jumped, and the phone clattered to the floor.

"Meg! You okay in there?"

It was Jack. Fumbling to recover the phone, she looked at her watch. Yikes, break time had been over for fifteen minutes. "I'm fine, I just—"

"Please leave your message at the sound of the tone," said Rachel Record-o-Voice.

"I'll be right there!" she shouted at the door, louder than she meant to.

"Manny got back from the nursery and wants to know where you want this stuff," Jack said.

"Okay, okay, I just—" *Beep!* she heard in her ear. She turned her back to the door and muffled her voice with her hand. Maybe it would be best to remain anonymous. "Um, I want to report that there may be…uh, illegal aliens working for Sunset Landscaping in Fort Worth. I'm not sure, but you can kind of tell, you know?"

"Meg? Did you run into man-eating ants again?" Jack sounded concerned.

"No!" She lowered her voice and said into the phone, "I mean, okay, that's all, but if you need me you can—" *Don't give them your number, dummy!* "Anyway, I hope you can take care of the problem," she finished. Rats, she sounded like she was reporting roaches in her kitchen. "Goodbye." She pressed the "end" button, stuffed the phone into her pocket and yanked open the door. "Can't a person have any privacy around here?"

When the Wolf called, Warner was surfing the Internet looking for gym equipment. His wife, Jeri, had been bugging him for a month about wanting to lose weight. Anything to keep her happy.

His study was located above the garage of his split-level brick home in one of the new subdivisions south of Fort Worth. Jeri left him pretty much alone when he was up here, and he'd trained the kids to ring the buzzer outside the door at the foot of the stairs. This gave him time to shut down any inappropriate sites before they came up.

Warner had his values straight.

It was a good thing Sean and Brittany couldn't hear his language when the slow, gruff voice on the other end of the line told him somebody in his company was ratting to the authorities about undocumented workers.

"Who was it?" Warner demanded.

"Whoever called didn't leave a name," answered the Wolf. "The incident report office allows anonymous calls and takes them seriously. They passed it to me because you're in my region." The Wolf paused. "It was a woman."

Warner muttered a curse. "There are only three women in the whole company."

Angel Jimenez was a nineteen-year-old college student who worked part-time as a receptionist. Even supposing she was aware of the documentation discrepancies, her Hispanic ethnicity made it unlikely she would have called in such a report.

Sharon Inge was Ted Crowley's personal assistant. Nominally married, Sharon had been known to go for a drink after work with the men in the office, but never seemed to pay the least attention to the green shirts.

Which left Meg St. John. It would be just like the brown-nosing little prude to get back at Warner for making a pass at her. She could file such a report and never have to go through the hassle and humiliation of a sexual harassment suit.

"I know who it was," Warner said. "I'll fire her tomorrow."

"Well, that'll certainly lower her suspicions," said the Wolf sarcastically. "Look, check your office phone records and do some fishing around before you do anything stupid. Make sure you've got the right person."

Warner hated to be wrong. "Guess you've got a point," he said grudgingly. "All right. I'll call all three of the women in, do a little spiel on company loyalty. Let me know if you hear anything else."

"You can bet I will," growled the Wolf. "Watch yourself, Warner." He hung up.

Warner rose, picked up the antique putter he kept in the corner and whacked a golf ball toward the far side of the office. It cracked against the wall and fell to the carpet with a thud.

He wished it were Meg St. John's sanctimonious little head.

Meg woke up in the middle of the night and lay wide-eyed, trying to figure out if a dream had awakened her, or if she'd actually heard something. The old house had a tendency to creak and groan, particularly when Benny was gone overnight.

Then she heard Gilligan growl. Swishing her feet under the sheet, Meg realized that the dog, who liked to nest between her ankles at night, was standing at the open door of her room.

Moonlight filtered through the blinds, allowing her to see raised hackles and the snarl of white teeth.

Meg sat up and swung her feet onto the braided bedside rug. "Gilligan, what's the matter with you?"

The dog snarled again.

"Come here, Gill."

Gilligan ignored her. She got up and inched toward the door.

Then she heard a faint metal-on-wood clatter from the kitchen. The dog began to bark.

Gooseflesh broke out on her arms. Somebody was in the house, and Benny was in Austin, involved in a prison ministry weekend.

Okay, Meg, think. Don't make any noise, maybe they'll think you're still asleep.

Rats, no way would anyone think that with the dog barking. Maybe whoever had been there had been scared off.

Maybe she should peek in there first, to make sure it wasn't some perfectly explainable noise. It would be embarrassing to tell a policeman she'd been scared by the odd noises of an old house. Or maybe Benny had come home early.

But why would Gilligan bark at Benny?

Some of the houses on the street were barricaded with burglar bars, but break-ins were rare. In fact, Meg couldn't remember the last time a police car had been in the neighborhood for anything except a speed trap. On second thought, maybe that wasn't a good thing.

She picked up the phone to call 911. Would the police get here before something terrible happened?

Okay, I'm not going to get caught in here like a squirrel in a cage. And I'm not charging into the kitchen like some idiot, either.

She tiptoed toward the window and slipped the lock—

or tried to. The window had been painted shut. She sat on the windowsill, panting shallowly and silently, fear roaring in her ears.

This is ridiculous, she told herself. *Some heroine you are.*

Then it dawned on her that Gilligan had stopped barking. He wasn't even growling anymore. He'd found his tennis ball and was noisily gnawing it beside the bed. Whatever—or whoever—had been in the kitchen was gone now.

Meg found the light switch and peeked into the hallway. Dead silence. Except for the hardwood floors creaking underfoot. Flipping on lights as she went, she padded toward the kitchen, Gilligan trotting behind her with the tennis ball.

It finally occurred to her to look at a clock—2:00 a.m.

She looked around for anything out of place. Harvest gold countertops wiped clean. Gilligan's dog dish under the microwave table. Benny's recipe box perched on the ancient refrigerator. Nothing that would have made that noise, except—

Lying on the floor in front of the stove was an enormous butterfly-shaped magnet made out of a clothespin, a pipe cleaner, and a Ziploc bag full of torn construction paper. Her brother's youngest son had made it a few weeks ago at Mom's Day Out. The magnet had been on the ventilator hood, and apparently it had hit the stove on the way to the floor.

She picked the magnet up, laid it on the counter and walked back to the bedroom.

"Gilligan the Wonder Dog," she told her pet in disgust. "Vanquished by a wooden butterfly." She flopped onto her pillow. "Boy, I'm glad I didn't call 911."

But she left the lights on.

The next morning Meg woke to what sounded like Niagara Falls pouring through the wall between her room and the bathroom.

The house's ancient plumbing design made every shower and every flush of the toilet a symphony of hydro-acoustics. Benny loved to joke that little was sacred, and nothing private, in their little corner of the world.

Remembering her fright from the night before, Meg gave thanks for the noise that meant her roommate was home.

Meg staggered into the kitchen for a glass of orange juice, and crammed a Pop-Tart into the toaster. She could have good nutrition on a day when she'd had a little more sleep.

She'd just let Gilligan back in from his morning constitutional when Benny came out of the bathroom, wrapped in her terry robe.

"Meggins, we're going to have to talk about you leaving the door unlocked again," Benny said, rubbing her long hair with a towel.

Meg coughed on a crumb. "But the door was locked just now when I let Gilligan out!"

"Well, yeah. I locked it when I came in about an hour ago." With a disapproving look, Benny looped the towel around her neck. "What were you thinking?"

Meg shook her head. "I locked it before I went to bed. At least I think I did." She started to tell her roommate about her silly scare in the middle of the night, then decided Benny already thought she was goofy enough. "I promise I'll be more careful. So how was the weekend?"

Benny's face lit. "Unbelievable! A hundred eighteen women professed Christ for the first time, Meg!"

"Wow." Meg pushed away her fatigue and lingering fear. "Wish I could've gone. Come on, sit down and tell me about it."

"It's not *my* fault you're hiring illegal aliens!"

Leaning back against the time-clock cabinet, Jack adjusted

the earpiece of the bug he'd installed in Warner's office last week. When Meg had been called in to meet with her boss after work, he'd lingered to "see what he could see."

Meg's outraged comment gave him a strong desire to do the Schwarzenegger thing. Surging through a wall and tearing Kenneth Warner limb from limb seemed like a good day's work right now.

"Did I say it was your fault?" Warner demanded. "I simply asked you if you knew why border patrol would call this morning. They had some pretty embarrassing questions."

"If you didn't do anything wrong, you wouldn't be embarrassed," Meg said reasonably.

Jack frowned. Meg hadn't answered Warner's question. Had she disobeyed his request not to report Tomás's underage employment?

"Ms. St. John." There was a sudden, loud noise—Warner smacking the desk with his hand. "If border patrol starts breathing down our necks again, *everything* slows down. And your little project at Silver Hill will be the first thing to go."

There was a thick, humming silence. "Mr. Warner," Meg said carefully, "did you just threaten me?"

"No," Warner snapped, "I'm trying to get you to be sensitive to the mountain of paperwork it takes in order to man all the jobs we have in queue this summer."

"I'll tell you what I'm sensitive to." Jack held his breath as Meg raised her voice. "I'm sensitive to the fact that I've got a fourteen-year-old boy on my crew who'd let his hand rot off before he'd go to the doctor!"

Jack heard Warner's chair squeak and roll across the floor. "Do you want me to fire him? Is that it?"

Meg seemed to realize she'd just boxed herself into a corner. "Of course not," she muttered.

"All right then," Warner said with satisfaction. "Obviously you have a certain amount of affection for the Herrera tribe. If you have their best interests at heart, we should keep this conversation between ourselves. And in the future, keep your opinions to yourself." He paused. *"Comprende?"*

Jack barely heard Meg's "Yes, sir," before the office door opened and closed sharply. The rapid tap of Meg's boots sounded on the tile of the outer office as Jack slipped out of the closet. He watched her stomp to the front door.

Jack followed. When he reached around to open the door for her, she wheeled. "Leave me—" She took a sharp breath. "Oh, it's you."

Her damp eyelashes tugged at his sympathy. "You don't look so good, St. John. What's the matter?"

She shrugged. "The usual laundry list. Number twelve. Number fifteen."

Jack gave her a searching look. "You want I should go mess up his face?" he asked, only half joking. He'd seen the way Warner looked at Meg.

She gave him a wobbly smile and shoved open the door. "No thanks, Torres. I appreciate your concern, but I'm going to go home and do something constructive, like sort my socks."

Jack rubbed the side of his nose. "Okay, but if you need somebody to sort things out with, you can always get me on my beeper. Anytime, you hear me?"

Looking a bit taken aback, Meg nodded. "I will."

Jack hoped he wasn't coming on too strong, but he didn't like the way that conversation in Warner's office had gone. He couldn't come right out and question Meg without rousing her suspicions.

He slid his sunglasses on and headed for his bike. He would also be interested in what she'd been thinking when she'd turned around and said "Oh, it's you" in that odd tone.

One of these days somebody was going to figure out how to decode a woman's brain and retire as a millionaire.

Girls don't call boys.

It wasn't easy to bypass a dictum her mother had drilled into her since the age of ten, but Meg had been thinking about doing just that since she'd watched Jack roar off toward the interstate in her rearview mirror.

What kicked her over the edge was reaching for the CD wallet she kept behind her driver's seat—admittedly a risky undertaking when you were sitting at a red light at one of the busiest intersections in Fort Worth. She found the padded case under her briefcase on the rear passenger seat.

The car behind her honked. Jerking the car into first gear, Meg tried to think whether she'd moved the wallet herself.

She'd had the same CDs in the car for nearly a month, she was certain. Benny had only yesterday complained about ex-cess bluegrass in her musical diet.

Somebody had been in her car.

The thought was somehow even more frightening than waking up to hear noises in her house. That, she'd been able to explain away.

She pulled into a 7-Eleven and fished in her purse for her cell phone with shaking hands.

Jack answered her page within five minutes, his deep voice

startling her despite the fact that she'd been expecting the call. "What's up, Spanky?"

"How'd you know it was me?"

"Caller ID," he said. There was a fractional pause. "St. John, are you in trouble?"

"I'm not sure."

"Where are you?"

Meg looked around. The convenience store parking lot was crowded and noisy, and a quarter acre of asphalt made the temperature about a billion degrees. "I'm a few blocks from the Water Gardens."

"I'll meet you there in five minutes," he said.

Meg put her cell phone away and started the car. She hoped she hadn't just made the biggest mistake of her life.

Standing thirty-eight feet below street level, Jack stared across a spectacular tiered concrete pit at a thousand gallons of water cascading down a 710-foot wall. The motion of the water surrounded him with cool, swirling sound, softening the space-age starkness that had served as a backdrop for the movie *Logan's Run.* It was a thing of staggering power and beauty, wholly unlike the sleepy Rio Grande.

Yet he couldn't take his eyes off Meg. Barefoot on a flat table in the center of the pool, she twirled like a music box dancer—eyes closed, head flung back and arms stretched wide.

Wishing he had a camera, Jack descended the path down through the water and concrete. When he got close enough to be heard above the noise, he put a hand to his mouth.

"Hey, St. John!" Meg turned suddenly, slipping a little, and he reached to catch her by the elbow. "You thinking about ending it all?"

She made a face and pointed at the water bubbling around

the slab they stood on. "That would be pretty hard to do in two feet of water."

"People drown in their bathtubs all the time." As Meg regained her balance, Jack released her.

"I happen to be a very good swimmer." Looking flustered, she put her hands in her pockets. "You probably think I'm a nut, calling you like this, but—"

"I told you to, remember?" Jack studied her face, noting the fine mist covering her hair, and the little curls loose at her temples. Her uniform was damp, too. "Does this have anything to do with that conversation with Warner this afternoon?"

"No. At least, I don't think so. Warner's a wart, but he wouldn't—" Meg's eyes widened. "Forget I said that."

Jack grinned. "Did you say something?"

"What I *meant* to say was, I'm hoping this is all just my imagination, and you're going to tell me to quit watching scary movies." She looked around as if to make sure they were alone, and blurted, "Torres, I'm scared."

"Scared of what?"

"Something kind of funny happened at my house Friday night—Saturday morning, I mean." Meg stopped and took a breath. "I think somebody broke in my house while I was asleep."

"Did you call the police?"

"No. Nothing was taken or even broken. I know I'd locked the door before I went to bed, but Benny came in and found it open."

"Had the lock been forced?"

"I don't think so. We don't have anything worth that much. Why would anybody do that? Just to scare me?"

Jack shook his head. "I don't know. Maybe." He looked

down at Meg's wet, bare feet. "Is there some reason we're having this conversation in the shower, or can we find a bench somewhere to sit down?"

Meg's toes curled under his scrutiny. "This is where I come to pray sometimes." She turned to lead the way back up to street level. "I've been doing it since I got my driver's license when I was sixteen."

"You've been a Christian that long?"

Meg smiled at him over her shoulder. "I've known Jesus all my life."

Jack was silent. He'd never spiritually catch up to her if he tried.

He watched her stoop to pick up her boots and socks, which she'd left on the lip of the pool, and followed her to a bench. She chose one end, and he sat at the other, turning to stretch his arm along the back. He could have touched her shoulder, but contented himself by letting his gaze follow the curve of her ear, the sway of her earring.

"You want me to come check your house, make sure it's safe?"

"Maybe. There's something else, though." Meg pressed her lips together and slanted a look at him. "I think that break-in wasn't an isolated thing. Somebody's watching me at work."

The hair stood up on the back of Jack's neck. "St. John, you're the only woman on the crew, and you're relatively easy on the eyes. Of course you're being watched."

She wrinkled her nose. "You know that's not what I mean."

"All right. What makes you think it's anything dangerous?"

"It's nothing anybody else would notice." She squirmed. "All last week, when I'd get in my car to go home, I'd find my stuff moved around. I know I don't seem real organized, but I'm pretty particular about my possessions."

Jack nodded. "What stuff exactly?"

Taken seriously, she leaned toward him. "My cell phone. The junk in my glove box."

Jack pushed his hand through his hair, holding it at the back of his skull. "Have you mentioned this to anybody else?"

"No."

"Why not? Your father or Sam, for starters."

"My dad's already paranoid about the neighborhood I live in. He wants me to move home—which I'm *not* going to do," she added when he opened his mouth to comment. "Besides, what if it *is* just my imagination?" She met his eyes. "I just want somebody to stick close for a couple of days. Somebody I trust."

"You're looking for a bodyguard?"

"I figure you're the biggest and meanest-looking person I know."

Jack laughed. "Well, I guess that lets Dr. Lurch out of the picture, huh? Large, but not scary enough."

Meg scowled. "Don't call Elliot 'Lurch.'"

"How do you know *I'm* not your stalker?" he interrupted.

"If you were, I'd never know it. No matter what you want everybody to think, you are not simple."

Jack blinked. IQ notwithstanding, he felt like a man who'd just flung himself off an emotional cliff. No wonder they called it *falling* in love. On the way down he fumbled for a foothold. "So I'm big and mean and, uh, *not* simple."

"That's what you want people to think." She held his gaze, and he couldn't make himself look away.

Drowning, he said, "St. John, I want to know what I'm doing here. Tell me what the rules are so I'll know how to play. How close do you want me to stay?"

The words hung between them as tangible as smoke. Jack

elt like a seventh-grader who had just laid a note on his be-
oved's book bag: *I like you. Do you like me? Check yes or no.*

Meg gave him an uncertain look. "I'm not sure what
ou mean."

"I mean, one of these days you're gonna trust the wrong
erson." Very deliberately he dropped his gaze to her mouth.
le'd been wanting to kiss her ever since he'd laid eyes on her.
le told himself he was going to satisfy his curiosity and teach
er a lesson at the same time.

He should have known she wouldn't respond like a normal
erson. Meg grinned at him. "See, that's exactly what I mean."

His libido came to a screeching halt. "Huh?"

"I *was* kind of scared of you, at first. You remind me of
omebody I used to…" she blushed and looked away. "But
his afternoon, the Holy Spirit prompted me to call you, and
ow I see why. If you were really dangerous, you wouldn't
varn me away."

"Is that right?" he said grimly. Jack laid his palm against
he tender curve of her jaw, resting his thumb beside her
nouth. "I think you've read too many romance novels."

Alarm flared in her eyes. "Torres…"

He sighed. "What exactly do you want me to do?"

"Maybe—" he felt her swallow against his hand "—maybe
you could just stick close to me on the job, especially keep
an eye on Efrin. He pretty much gives me the creeps."

"Efrin the Weasel?" Amused, Jack nodded. "I'll watch him."

"Thanks. It's probably no big deal, but I'll feel better knowing you're—" She clasped his wrist. "Okay, Torres, I get your
point. I won't trust anybody."

He nodded, holding her gaze. "Good girl. Now let's go look
at your car, and you can show me exactly why you think your
stuff's been messed with."

He got to his feet, infinitely relieved that he hadn't give
in to the temptation to kiss her. If he wanted to get Rico
killer, he couldn't afford to get sidetracked by Meg St. Joh
or anybody else.

Chapter Nine

Mary Frances Grover-Niles stood exactly five foot one in her high-heeled designer sandals, but Meg could detect no apparent deficit in self-esteem due to short stature. This confidence in her ability to rule central Texas with wisdom and good taste resulted, Meg surmised, from a lineage traced directly from the cattle barons of the late 1800s.

For three hours now Meg had been trotting around the estate behind the woman with no sign of slowing down—until they came upon the pathway of mosaic tiles Meg had laid in the rose garden.

Mrs. Grover-Niles halted and placed a manicured hand over her lips. "Oh, honey, you are a genius," she gasped. "Really, you are."

Meg blushed with justifiable pride. "I'm glad you like it." She'd spent three days rescuing those tiles from a pile of debris from the old bathroom floor, then cleaning them and laying them in an eye-catching design. At the end of the path, Gollum the troll presided over a birdbath and a wooden bench under a willow tree. A patch of transplanted bluebonnets would pick up the indigo and periwinkle color of the tile. It *was* a lovely spot, and Meg had been bringing her lunch here to enjoy it.

Mrs. Grover-Niles peered at her clipboard. "We'll have Rosalee's bridal photos shot here. Her dress came in yesterday..."

Meg's eyes glazed over as the drone of wedding details continued. She sneaked a glance at her watch. Lunchtime was almost over, and she needed a little time by herself. In conjunction with the church's upcoming Fourth of July barbecue, Pastor Ramón had lined up volunteers for weekend yard work, and Mr. Crowley had agreed to donate some plant materials. Meg had promised to draw up a design for the landscaping and show it to Ramón tonight at ESL.

Ramón was big on people using their gifts for ministry.

Meg wished she could get Jack interested in coming to hear Ramón preach. The two men seemed to have hit it off three weeks ago, but Jack had been evasive about coming to church. He was always "tied up with something else." If he was a Christian, he was an awfully faraway one.

Only to herself would Meg admit why she so hoped his attitude would change.

After the other afternoon at the Water Gardens, it had become harder and harder to keep a professional wall between herself and Jack. He fascinated her in a physical way, but she knew it was much more than that. He seemed to read and understand her better than any man she'd ever known, often anticipating her needs or meeting her eyes in shared humor.

Just this morning, Benny had made Meg repeat three times, "Missionary dating is a stupid idea."

No doubt that was absolutely true.

But it was just as true that Meg had only to look at Jack's

big callused hands in order to feel his thumb resting on her cheek and his palm cupping her jaw. Music ran through her mind. *Bad boys whatcha gonna do...*

Lord, she prayed as she struggled to get her mind back on Mrs. Grover-Niles's Princess Bride, *please help me keep my eyes on You.*

She had to stay focused on doing her job here at Silver Hill, and treating the men under her direction with compassion and integrity.

"So what we need," said Mrs. Grover-Niles with a perky smile, "is a pergola beside the herb garden."

Meg lifted her brows to keep from scowling. Rich, bossy matrons needed love, too.

"A pergola would be lovely," she sighed.

A bank of red and yellow lights nearly blinded Jack as he fired one last time and lowered the gun.

"You got him!" shouted Tomás, pounding Jack's shoulder. "High score for the week! You are so wicked, man."

Jack couldn't help grinning as he stepped away from the laser video machine in the back corner of the laundromat. He supposed there could be worse ways to conduct surveillance.

Letting Tomás take the controller, Jack propped an arm on top of the machine. Ostensibly watching the boy, he kept an ear cocked toward the conversation going on between Manny and Efrin, who sat on a folding table across the room.

Jack could just imagine what Meg would think. She'd worry about Tomás staying out so late, she'd tell Jack he was wasting his time and money, and she'd probably invite him to church again.

He wished he were in a position to do that very thing. Every time he closed his eyes, he conjured an image of Meg surrounded by falling water, the picture of abandoned worship. In a public garden, of all places.

Jack suspected there was symbolism there somewhere. Meg had something vital that he was missing, but his life would get very complicated if he couldn't keep his distance from her.

Suddenly the door to the street opened, admitting a tall figure in dark-green uniform. The man's face was shadowed by a big cream-colored Stetson, but Jack instantly recognized Vernon Rook's hip-shot John Wayne stance, and the arrogant tilt of his head.

Something about the way Rook checked over the room as he entered kept Jack from calling out to him. Melting into the shadow between the video machine and the wall, Jack glanced at Tomás. The boy was so intent on his game that the President of the United States could have walked in and he wouldn't have noticed.

Jack watched Rook approach Manny and Efrin; the border patrol agent towered over the two smaller men, thumbs hooked in the front of his belt. Both Mexicans looked up and froze.

Jack could only see Rook's back, but the fear on Manny's face was palpable. Jack would've given anything for a mike on that three-minute conversation. Rook raised a finger, pointed it straight at Efrin's forehead, and then turned to let his gaze sweep the hot, noisy little room. The cold brown eyes passed Jack's corner without stopping; if he saw Tomás, he didn't acknowledge the boy. The thin mouth pulled into a straight line. Without another word, he hitched his pants up and left.

Jack stayed where he was until he was sure Rook wasn't coming back. Laying a couple of quarters on the arcade table to keep Tomás occupied, he approached Manny.

Manny gave Jack a gallows smile, but said mildly, "You're

making my little brother a video addict. I'd better get him home to bed."

"Hey, you're not leaving me to pay for drying all these clothes," Efrin protested.

Jack tilted his head toward the door. "Trouble with *la migra?*"

Manny shrugged. "Always the questions, just because we're brown-skinned. Lucky you were on the other side of the room."

"Lucky, yeah," Jack agreed. He looked at Efrin, who didn't seem as shaken as Manny, despite Rook's threatening gesture. "That guy seemed to know you. Has he hassled you before?"

Efrin sneered. "He's a big clown, but me, I'm badder."

"No worry," Manny insisted. "We all got good papers."

"Still, you better watch an *hombre* like that." Jack kept his tone friendly, concerned. "He'll find a way to send you back over the border, papers or no papers. And you know Tomás is under age."

Manny's lips tightened. "Tomás helps feed our mother and little sisters. I wouldn't let him stay if he had another choice."

Jack lifted his hands. "Hey, no criticism intended. I'd just watch my back if I were you." Jack pulled over a plastic chair and leaned close to Manny. "I got family in Juarez myself."

Manny's expression remained polite. "You're not *nativo?*"

Jack shrugged. "My parents came over to work the dairy farms out in the country. They went back when I was about Tomás's age." He tried to gauge the other man's expression. "I still go down to visit sometimes."

Efrin jumped in. "Would you like to bring them back over?"

Manny gave his cousin an annoyed look, which Jack ignored. He shook his head. "They're old, and the trip is too hard." Looking at Manny, he injected a note of machismo into his voice. "But I have connections to help others who want to come."

Manny Herrera could have made a fortune at poker. His stoic expression changed not by the twitch of an eyelash.

Efrin, however, vibrated like a tuning fork. "What kind of connections?"

"I have two cousins who are the best coyotes in the business. We own a safe house outside Eagle Pass, and I handle transportation." He paused. "You know anybody who needs a good driver?"

"We're looking—"

"Shut up, Efrin," said Manny with a chopping motion of his hand. He frowned at Jack. "What makes you think I know anything about it?"

"I know a farmer's co-op when I see one." Jack leaned back in his chair. "This is a perfect hub to collect the *pollos* and send them north. You're making a bundle, and I want in on it."

Manny shook his head. "I don't make any decisions on my own."

"I appreciate caution." Jack smiled.

After a tense moment, Manny's thick mustache turned up on one side. "I'll see what I can do."

"Okay. That's all I ask."

Tomás's game ended with an explosion of electronic beeps and flare of lights. "Come on, Torres!" the boy called, dancing around the machine. "Let's play again! I'm on a roll!"

Jack grimaced at Manny. "I think you'd better make the kid go home before he cleans me out of change."

He sauntered back to the arcade, fishing quarters out of his pocket.

Jack yawned as he parked his bike in front of the old-fashioned brick church building. Meg's church, he reminded himself, trying to repress a vague sense of apprehension no doubt brought on by fatigue. Ramón Santos had called yesterday and twisted his arm, promising a game of racquetball after church.

He and Carmichael had spent most of last night firming up plans for the sting on the Herrera outfit. Clearly, Manny was fairly low on the food chain, but working with him was a start toward nailing the leader.

Rolling out of bed at seven o'clock this morning had been a killer.

The sun cut sharply through an empty cloudless sky as Jack surveyed the church grounds. The steeple perched on the roof was painted a neat white, and he could smell freshly mown grass. A virulent aqua sign in the yard announced that the *Iglesia Evangelica Hispana del Sudoeste*—Southern Evangelical Spanish Church—met here.

On the way across the parking lot, he noticed Meg's Mustang. The right rear tire needed some air. Realizing he was feeling entirely too proprietary about a car that didn't belong to him, he hurried up the front sidewalk. It occurred to him that he hadn't been to church since Rico's funeral.

He slipped inside and found himself nearly knocked backward by music echoing off cinderblock walls and wooden floors. Just as he was beginning to feel self-conscious, he spotted Meg waving at him from a pew near the back. Benny leaned around Meg to give him her radiant smile as the two girls shifted to make room for him. Crazy, but Jack felt at home.

A young man with a battered acoustic guitar was leading a worship chorus, an overhead projector splashing the words in Spanish on the wall next to the baptistry. The tune wasn't that complicated, and Jack watched the guitarist's hands, trying to figure out the chords.

The song reminded him of Rico's funeral held in El Paso just over a year ago. There had been music that day too. Hopeful music, because Rico always said he was headed for Heaven on the day he'd die.

Along with five other agents, Jack had been a pallbearer at the memorial service. During the graveside service he'd stood beside his partner's widow, holding Rico's son asleep on his shoulder. He'd promised himself then that he'd find the monster who'd authored this scene of pain.

Caught in the memory, Jack pondered the sunlight pouring through the window behind the guitarist. The guy was about Rico's size and age, which was probably why he looked familiar.

Unexpected grief, hard and deep, sliced through Jack. He wanted to clutch his middle and roll over in a ball, as he had the night his friend died. Fleeing the flashing lights and wailing sirens into a nearby field, Jack had thrown himself on his knees and sobbed until his stomach ached and his throat was raw.

He didn't realize his eyes were stinging until Meg leaned into him with her shoulder against his upper arm. Blinking, he steadied himself.

Ridiculous to get so emotional over a song.

Five minutes after the final "amen," Meg could tell Jack was ready to leave. He'd finally come to church, but not until Ramón had run interference for her.

Doesn't matter why *he came,* she told herself. The important thing was, he was here. Ignoring Benny's raised eyebrows, she hauled Jack across the room to talk to Ramón.

Ramón shook hands with a rapid flood of Spanish welcome.

Jack responded in kind, and Meg watched him relax as his gaze skimmed the pastor's jeans and casual polo shirt. Though she caught only the words "hungry" and "eat," she was glad Jack seemed to be comfortable.

Catching her eye, Jack switched to English. "What about you, St. John? Got lunch plans?"

"Well…"

"Come on, the more the merrier," boomed Ramón. "Connie will need another girl to talk to while I beat Jack on the racquetball court—"

"While you do *what?*" Ramón's wife, Consuela, walked up with a little black-haired girl on each hip.

"Uh, racquetball? Is that okay?" Ramón looked abashed. "Can we make the tamales stretch a little farther, honey?"

Connie's brows rose in momentary alarm, but she smiled, used to her husband dumping unexpected company on her. "Certainly," she said. "You can eat three like a normal person, instead of twelve." She poked her husband's stocky middle. Her older daughter, sporting a new pair of tiny wire-rimmed glasses, giggled.

"I'll stop for soft drinks," Meg volunteered, happy to be included in the party. She tickled little Valentina, who chuckled again. "Want to come with me, sweetie pie?"

Face dripping with sweat, his gym shorts and T-shirt soaked, Jack leaned against the back wall of court number three at the seminary rec facility. To his surprise, he'd found that the preacher boy might be a foot shorter and nearly that much bigger around, but he was a dynamo on the court.

"Hey, *muchacho,* you got the legs left to walk over to the Union for a drink?" Santos, breathing just as hard as Jack, waggled his empty water bottle.

Jack grinned and mopped his face with a towel. "I could carry you piggyback, you sissy."

Trading good-natured insults, the two men stepped out into the afternoon sunshine. Santos walked along, swinging his racquet and jabbering in Spanish flavored with Puerto Rican slang. He apparently didn't care that Jack did more listening and head-nodding than responding.

"Your Spanish is really good for somebody that grew up in the States," Santos commented as they walked up the broad steps of the Student Union.

"The education of the *barrios,*" Jack said dryly. He stopped and looked up into the vast atrium of the rotunda, with its marble floor and ornate brass chandelier dripping with crystal tears. An enormous leather-bound Bible rested in ancient dignity atop an antique table under the grand curving staircase.

"Have the people in your church seen this place?" Jack pictured the tiny, '60s–era two-bedroom apartment the Santos family inhabited and the hearty but cheap food served by efficient *Señora* Santos.

"They're proud that their pastor is about to graduate from such a fine institution."

"And will they continue to be proud when their pastor skips on to greener pastures?"

Santos's smile broadened. "I'm not going anywhere." He pushed open a glass door leading into a snack bar, where he bought two large fountain drinks. They sat at a table under a broad bank of windows looking out onto a grassy field.

Jack drank deeply and sighed with satisfaction. "So explain to me," he said, eyeing Ramón across the table, "why a man would come all the way from Puerto Rico to graduate from a place like this, and then waste it on a little bilingual mission church."

"Same reason the Son of God came from Heaven to a desert to preach to a bunch of fishermen and tax collectors and prostitutes."

Jack eyed Santos with amusement. "You are good, you know that, Preacher?"

Santos grinned. "So my wife tells me. I'm glad you came today, even if it *was* on account of Meg."

Jack made a face. "Obvious, huh?"

"As a tick on a white dog."

"There's something about her all right." Jack shrugged. "I've never been to a Hispanic church just like this one."

"I'll take that as a compliment." Ramón grinned. "I'd like to know what impressed you—" Santos smiled "—besides *Señorita* Meg."

"I don't know exactly. The music's great. Never heard people sing like that." Jack hesitated. "Who was the guy with the guitar? He's really good."

"Yeah, he is. Name's Oscar de Fuentes."

Jack sat up. "I thought he looked familiar! He played shortstop for the Rangers, I think, five years ago!"

Santos's smile quirked one side of his mustache. "Yeah, well, *two* years ago he was in a Dallas detox facility. Now he's in my music missions class at the seminary."

"You're joking."

"Ask him."

Jack shook his head. "What a waste."

"Torres, what would you consider a life well spent? Or an afternoon for that matter?"

Ah, the trap, set with clever conversation, baited by a master. This guy was way more subtle than Meg's roommate. Jack laughed. "You want to talk about the meaning of life, Preacher?"

"Well, I'd just as soon talk baseball, but you gave me a perfect opening." Santos chuckled. "I'd be an idiot not to walk on through."

"Yeah, I guess you would." Maybe he was unconsciously looking for answers. "Okay, an afternoon well spent would be a wide-open ride on my Harley down a long stretch of highway. A well-spent life?" He shrugged. "The pursuit of justice maybe."

Santos raised his brows but remained comfortably slouched in his chair. "Justice, huh? What about mercy?"

"Preacher, the merciful end up dead."

The pastor whistled. "You say that like a man with an agenda."

"An agenda?"

"Yeah. I think you're after something. But what you're gonna find might surprise you."

"You're talking in riddles."

Santos sighed. "Meg told me you made a profession of faith at some point."

"When did she tell you that?"

"We prayed for you last Sunday."

Jack looked away, trying not to feel annoyed at the invasion of privacy.

"I asked her to let me talk to you," Santos continued.

"I knew this was a setup!" Jack sat up straight. Apparently the gloves were off.

"You knew it was all along," Santos said patiently. "Didn't you? And you came anyway."

Jack gave the pastor an amused look. "Yeah," he admitted. "God has seemed a lot more—" he hesitated "—real to me than He's been in a long time. Do you think He's chasing me again or something?"

"Brother, once God gets hold of you, He doesn't let go."

"Well, I don't particularly like the way He operates." Jack

met Santos's sober gaze. "All I know to do is function on a day-to-day basis and get along the best way I can. I believe in taking care of myself."

Santos's dark eyes lit. "You know what? Salvation *is* for life, but you don't stick it in a drawer like a policy manual and forget it until you need it. Let me ask you something, Jack."

Jack. Being called by name in that blunt, friend-to-friend tone got his attention. "Okay, shoot."

"Are you happy?"

Jack snorted. "I don't know anybody who's really happy." Well, except maybe Meg St. John.

"Okay, then, content," persisted Santos. "Are you content?"

"No! No, I'm not content." Jack felt his shoulders tense, though he tried to keep his tone light. "I'm confused and I'm sorry I even brought the subject up."

Santos smiled, but his gaze remained steady. "Listen, everybody gets confused sometimes. We're *all* lost, like dumb sheep. You know what? I think when you were introduced to the Shepherd you didn't stick around long enough to get to know Him."

"I've got to go," Jack muttered. How could this man know so much about his feelings? He gave Santos a cautious look. "What do you mean?"

"The Christian life is a relationship with the Shepherd, man. Jesus isn't some impersonal cloud in the sky, or the crack of doom waiting to get everybody. He knows me and you by name, and He's got an individual call for each one of us. But you gotta listen and follow. You get in trouble when you try to stumble around on your own. *You* don't know what you need, but He does. He loves you, simple as that."

Jack looked away. This was the same thing Dottie Rook had tried to tell him. And Rico.

But Rico had been murdered, and Jack had to somehow make that right before he could look God in the face again.

"I've got to go," he said again.

"All right, we'll finish this conversation later," Ramón said, looking disappointed.

"I'll be ready for you next time, Preacher." Jack stood up. "What time is it?"

Ramón looked at his watch and jumped to his feet. "Aw, man! Nap time's been over for thirty minutes. Consuela's gonna fillet me!"

Chapter Ten

The Fourth of July dawned hot as a firecracker under a cerulean sky nearly empty of clouds. In a busman's holiday, Meg decided to use her day off to organize an installation party for the design she'd drawn for the churchyard. Dressed in overall shorts and T-shirt, with thick socks and work boots protecting her feet and a baseball cap to keep the sun out of her eyes, Meg issued orders to her fellow church members and family.

She sent Benny and Elliot, the first to arrive, to the home improvement store with a plant materials list, and put the Santos family in charge of yanking weeds. After setting her parents and the remaining volunteers to work digging up old shrubs and trash trees, Meg went into the sanctuary to turn on the sound system and open all the doors and windows. As she danced back outside to the beat of a Hispanic Christian rock tune, she spotted a familiar multi-colored pickup truck pulling into the parking lot, and promptly fell over a rake somebody had left on the sidewalk.

"Manny! Jack!" Delighted, Meg brushed off her stinging

knees and hobbled over to greet her regular work crew. "I didn't know y'all were coming!" The two men got out of the cab, while Tomás and Diego piled out of the back.

"We help much and see fireworks," Tomás said with his beaming smile. "You said eat on the dirt, too?"

Meg laughed. "Dinner on the ground, yes." She met Jack's grin behind Tomás's back. "I'm so glad you came! Come on, I'll put you seasoned soldiers in charge of the recruits."

Four hours later, mission accomplished, Meg leaned against Manny's truck, surveying her handiwork. She felt as if she'd just earned a million dollars, rather than skinned knees, sunburnt shoulders and blistered palms.

The cottonwood tree by the church's front door was now the centerpiece of a brick-lined bed filled in with ground cover. Pink, purple and white impatiens spilled on either side of the walkway from the parking lot. Even the grass had been plugged with new sod, and then neatly mown, edged and watered.

Now it was time to celebrate at her parents' place out in the country.

Meg had just dispersed most of her ground troops to assemble mess. Jack, who had somehow taken on the role of second-in-command, had stayed behind to help Meg store the tools and conduct a follow-up inspection.

"If they gave a Nobel Prize for persistence, St. John, you'd win hands down," Jack said, opening the passenger door of the truck with a weary sigh. "I've about had enough dirt and grass for one day. Let's go get some grub."

Meg's stomach grumbled at the mention of food. "Good idea." She got behind the wheel of Manny's old truck and found it tattered but clean. When the engine cranked easily, she pulled out into the street. "How come you changed your

ind about helping out today?" She'd mentioned the project
Jack during Sunday lunch, but he'd claimed he already had
ans for the Fourth.

Jack propped his knees on the dash and laid his head back
gainst the seat. Under the ever-present bandanna, his long
air spilled freely on his shoulders. "I wanted to talk to the
eacher boy," he said without opening his eyes.

Meg blinked. "Did you?"

"Yep."

Silence. They got on the interstate and headed toward south
ort Worth. Finally, Meg blew out a breath. "That is so low."

Jack's mouth curled a little. "What's low?"

"Getting my curiosity up and then making like a Sphinx."

The black eyelashes lifted a fraction. "You're gonna have
help me out, Spanky. What's a—"

"Oh, for crying out loud, quit that. You probably know
ore about the Sphinx than most college professors." Meg
yed his gray T-shirt. "I bet you even graduated from Yale,
idn't you? Benny says—"

"No," he interrupted. "I did not." He looked at her uneas-
y. "What did I say wrong?"

"You—" She stopped, frustrated. "You're evading my
uestion, which happens to be one of *your* prize-winning tac-
ics. What did you and Ramón talk about?"

"Sheep."

"Sheep," she repeated blankly.

He chuckled. "Yeah, and shepherds, and following voices.
went home and studied John 10 last night. It suddenly made
ense to me, like I'd never read it before." He paused. "Which
had."

Meg could feel her face splitting in a big grin. "Are you
elling me—"

"Now don't go getting all excited. I'll probably never be as spiritual as you are. But I had a really good friend who passed away about a year ago." Jack cleared his throat. "The guy was a Christian, and he led me to believe, too, only he died before I got very far in my faith. So I got derailed and mad at God, and I'm just now seeing how He might have some purpose for me after all."

Meg felt almost light-headed, listening to Jack tell her things she'd longed to know all summer. "You know He does, Jack," she said softly, feeling her eyes sting. Pulling off the road might stop the flow of Jack's words, so she kept driving.

"I guess." Jack glanced at her, then out the window. "But my life is extremely complicated right now, and that's about all I can tell you about myself. The rest is not fit for someone like you to hear. Just pray for me, okay?"

"Of course I will. But you can trust me—"

"It's not that." His voice remained tense. "Just—don't push me. I've been keeping an eye on you all week. Have you noticed anything else out of place in your car, or anything suspicious at your house?"

The abrupt change of subject nonplussed Meg so that she almost missed the exit to Mansfield, where her parents had a small working farm. Fortunately, traffic had thinned considerably as the scenery became more and more rural. She slammed on the brakes and turned.

"No, I'd almost forgotten about it." In fact, Meg had felt so safe knowing that Jack was watching her back, she'd quit triple-checking her locks every time she got out of the car.

"Don't get too blasé," Jack warned, folding his arms. "I rode by your house a couple of nights this week."

"So that was *your* motorcycle that woke me up at two a.m.

ast night?" She looked at him, scandalized, and gave him a
Stymie impression. "Boy, you's gettin' to be a noosum!"

Jack shook his head. "Just how many *Little Rascals* vid-
os have you memorized?"

"Enough to keep you busy for a couple of years catching
up." She grinned at him.

He snorted. "I'm sorry if I woke you up, but I have to agree
with your dad. You and the Ben-ster picked a pretty sorry
neighborhood to set up house in. I'd be surprised if there
wasn't some drug traffic going on in the house across the
street."

"You're kidding! What makes you think that?"

"Meg, it was lit up like a Christmas tree until the wee
hours of the morning."

Meg had to push her jaw shut. "Wow."

"Yeah. So don't ever leave the house by yourself after dark."

Refusing to dignify that outrageous and impractical command with an answer, Meg turned in at the gravel drive of her
parents' farm. Passing through the iron gates, which had been
swung open in welcome, she honked the horn, startling a herd
of Black Angus grazing next to the fence.

"Here we are," she said with more confidence than she felt.
Introducing Jack to her parents shouldn't have any particular
significance.

But somehow it did. Oh, yes, it did.

Jack grabbed the door handle and rubbed the other sweaty
palm down the leg of his jeans. "This is where you grew up?"

The house was an enormous stucco-and-brick two-story with
a landscaped driveway circling the front yard. Meg had parked
behind a Lexus SUV whose license plate said "KIDDOC."

Having spent most of his adult life with military and law

enforcement types, Jack had never been comfortable hanging out with doctors and lawyers. Generally he didn't worry about his appearance while undercover; the scruffier the better. But he wished he'd had time to shower and change clothes before coming out here.

"Come on, Torres. I'll protect you." Meg was leaning in the window, grinning at him.

"Boy, this am a residence de-*luxe,*" he drawled as he opened the door. Pleased at Meg's delighted shout of "Buckwheat!" he followed her up the short sidewalk to the door.

Her eagerness and joy were contagious. He wondered how it must feel to be welcomed into a home like this, the child of parents who gave you everything. As Meg opened the door without knocking and called out to her mother, Jack thought of Ramón's sermon yesterday morning.

"The Father loves you more than you know, beloved," the pastor had said, translating in herky-jerky fashion from Spanish to English. "No matter what your circumstances or background, you're precious to Him. Whatever you need, feel free to ask."

Ramón had explained the Hebrew term *abba*—the intimate address of a child to his daddy. Because Jack had never had a real father, the idea went straight to his heart. As he walked into Meg's home, he repeated it to himself, suddenly filled with peace and confidence.

"I'll show you around a little before we go out on the patio," Meg said as they entered a sunny foyer, where a skylight poured sunshine onto the split-brick floor. Bursts of laughter, conversation and music filtered in from outdoors.

As Jack looked around, the mirror above a pine cabinet cast back his dark reflection, reminding him to guard his tongue. He was an interloper here.

At the click of toenails scrabbling on the floor and heavy canine breathing, he turned to find Meg bending to receive the slobbery kisses of the weirdest-looking dog Jack had ever seen. Brown spots splattered an ugly beige coat, and Jack looked twice to make sure he wasn't seeing things: one of the dog's eyes was pale blue, the other a light cinnamon color.

Laughing, Meg ruffled the dog's ears.

"Looks like somebody was foolin' with the DNA on that one," Jack said.

Meg laughed. "This is Julio. Registered Catahoula cur. Isn't he gorgeous?"

"He was bred to look like that on purpose?" Jack snapped his fingers. "Come here, fella." The dog sniffed Jack's fingers and gave them a slurp. Jack scratched him under his leather collar and made a friend for life. "You'd make cat-bait out of that twerpy little dachshund, wouldn't you, big guy?"

"Hey!" exclaimed Meg, setting her fists on her hips, and Jack grinned at her.

"Meg, is that you?" somebody called from another room.

Meg tipped her head. "Come on and meet my mom."

Jack would rather have tangled with a mound of fire ants, but he gave the dog a last pat and stood up, brushing his hands off on his jeans.

Meg led the way through a dining room featuring a mahogany table with a floral centerpiece. She stopped in the doorway of the kitchen, taking Jack's elbow and tugging him closer.

"Mom, this is Jack Torres."

Distracted by the feel of Meg's fingers against his skin, it took Jack a moment to find the tall, middle-aged woman who stood at the sink wrestling with an ice-cream freezer.

"Welcome." Rose St. John took in her daughter's hand

clasped around Jack's arm. Her brows, straight and dark like Meg's, climbed a little. "Have you met Benny?"

Meg's roommate, who had just closed the refrigerator door with her elbow, faced Jack with a loaded vegetable tray. "We've met a couple of times." Her expression was knowing, but kind. "Hey, Jack. The men are all outside, fighting over who's got the best grilling technique."

Jack shifted his weight and glanced at Meg.

Eyes sparkling, she released his arm to pluck a carrot from the tray. "Go on out and show 'em how it's done," she said, gesturing toward the back door. "I'll give you the grand tour some other time."

Gratefully Jack headed for wide-open spaces.

Jack sprawled in a lounge chair by the pool, watching the sun meet the horizon in a blaze of orange, pink and violet. In his lap was a guitar he'd borrowed from Meg's brother's old room. He'd been enjoying the luxury of having nothing more pressing to do than run scale patterns and watch Meg and Connie dunk the little Santos girls in the shallow end of the pool.

Ramón, Elliot and Benny were supervising the fireworks on the far side of the lawn, and Meg's mother walked around plying everybody with iced lemonade. Not an alcoholic beverage in sight.

Which was fine with Jack. Much easier not to have to deal with the complications of pretending to be bad-news scum with a drinking problem.

"Okay, that's it, son, now gently press the shutter."

Meg's father was crouched near the edge of the pool, explaining the operation of a digital camera to an intent Tomás Herrera. They were practicing on the bevy of mermaids in the pool. Meg and Connie, knee-deep in the water and still dressed in shorts and T-shirts, had been drenched by the squealing and splashing little girls. It was quite a sight.

Jack grinned as Meg received a strangling hug from a pair of wet little arms. "Take me under again, Miss Meg!" choked Valentina, who had refused to remove her new glasses. Jack remembered praying in the ice-cream shop for her eye exam.

"Is very cool, *Señor* Doctor!" exclaimed Tomás. "I am good, *sí?*"

"You're a natural, kiddo," said Dr. St. John, chuckling as the teenager viewed the picture through the monitor and preened at his success. "Would you like to take it home with you and practice some more?"

Tomás looked at the tall, silver-haired doctor wide-eyed. "You are kidding me, right?"

George shrugged. "You can learn more just messing around with it, than if I stand here and lecture you."

Tomás's Adam's apple bobbed. "*Caramba.*" He lifted the camera to his eye again and focused the lens on Jack. "Look, Torres, I'm a photographer." He pronounced the word carefully.

Jack shook his head. The generosity of the St. John family had him nearly as flummoxed as Tomás. They were treating this scraggly and underdressed lot like long-lost relatives. On the patio, three long tables groaned under the weight of hamburgers, side dishes and desserts—and no telling how much money they were blowing up in fireworks.

"Guard it with your life, boy," Jack said in Spanish to Tomás. Tomás flashed his quick smile and snapped Jack's picture.

"So, Jack—" Rose St. John set her tray on a table and perched on the end of the chair next to him. "Meg hasn't told us much about you. Did you grow up in Texas?"

Distracted by the sight of Meg climbing out of the pool

with Valentina clinging monkeylike to her waist, he answered without thinking. "Yes, ma'am. Eagle Pass."

The curiosity in Meg's eyes as she dropped cross-legged onto the concrete beside her father warned Jack that he'd better be careful.

"Jack doesn't talk about himself," Meg said, tucking the little girl into her lap. "I don't even know where Eagle Pass is."

Jack glanced at George, who pulled Meg into a hug. It was clear from his watchful expression that the man was waiting for Jack's answer. "It's down on the border."

"Is that where you met your friend who led you to Christ?" Meg smiled up at her father, as if to say *See, he's a good guy.*

"That's right." Out of the corner of his eye Jack saw Rose's expression relax. Her husband, however, frowned.

"Discipleship is critical," George said mildly enough, but Jack heard the warning. Apparently the good doctor was more generous with his material possessions than with his daughter.

Which, as far as Jack was concerned, was not a bad thing. "I've attended Meg's church a time or two," he said.

Meg started to speak, but her father forestalled her. "And where do you see yourself, say, five years down the road?"

Jack smiled at the doctor's "Boy, this better be a good answer" tone. "It's pretty clear God has some kind of plan for my life," he said with a shrug. "I'm just not sure what it is right now."

George looked dissatisfied, but Rose said brightly, "Do you still have family down south, Jack?"

Jack smiled. "Real far south. My mother went back to Mexico."

"Ah." Rose rattled the ice in her glass. "Any brothers or sisters?"

"Not that I know of."

"You can have mine," said little Valentina Santos unexpectedly, and all the adults laughed.

"Your mommy might not like that," Meg said, kissing the top of the child's head.

"I can do a fish-face," Valentina announced, hanging on to the spotlight. "Athena's too little." She arched her brows, sucked in her cheeks and wiggled her puckered lips.

Relieved at the shift in conversation, Jack sat back and enjoyed the sight of the three other adults and Tomás mimicking a four-year-old's facial contortions. Dr. St. John seemed to be the only grown-up who could get it right.

Meg dissolved in laughter as Tomás aimed the camera at her father. "You're caught on film, Dad!"

"Reckon they teach fish-faces in medical school?" Jack stood up and plucked Valentina out of Meg's lap, then extended a hand. "Come on, let's go show the kids what to do with a sparkler."

"Okay." Taking Jack's hand up, Meg smiled at Tomás. "I asked Dad to get some bottle rockets, too. Want to come?"

"Bottle rockets?" Tomás looked puzzled.

Jack translated, demonstrating with his hands. "Trust me, it'll be right up your alley."

Tomás leaped to his feet, handing the camera reverently over to its owner. "I'll be back," he said.

The four of them left the lights by the pool and crossed the lawn through the mounting darkness, Jack carrying Valentina.

Meg looked up as a Roman candle exploded overhead in a shimmer of red and gold. "So you grew up in Eagle Pass."

"Yes." Jack felt his body coil. He should have known she wouldn't be able to leave that alone.

"Come on, a little more information would be nice." She bumped his elbow with hers. "What happened to your parents?"

Jack was used to telling partial truths, but found himself stumbling with Meg. Every lie he built between them was going to matter. He measured his words. "I don't remember much about them. I was really small when they went back to Mexico."

Meg took a sharp breath. "Without you? They left you on the street?"

Jack could feel compassion radiating from Meg in almost physical waves.

"Pretty much. Child Protective Services put me in a home, but I started running with a gang when I was about ten." Jack paused. "Before I had a chance to get in much trouble, though, one of my elementary school teachers snatched me up and made me fly right."

"Must have been a special lady. Was she a Christian?"

"Yes, she was." Jack smiled at her automatic assumption.

"You need to call her," Meg said. "I bet she'd love to know what happened to you."

"Maybe." He sighed. "I still don't know why she cared anything about me."

"Tell me about her."

Jack hesitated. If he kept handing little pieces of his life to Meg, could he trust her not to throw them back at him later in a moment of confrontation?

"She took me home with her after school sometimes and fed me. I stole things from her. Money from her purse, mostly." He glanced at Meg and found her eyes swimming with tears.

"Did she know?"

"I don't think so. Before long, I realized anything I needed, she would make sure I got. She and her husband wanted kids but couldn't have any." Jack shifted Valentina in his arms. "I quit stealing things, but I still lied to her and shucked off into trouble every chance I got." Meg grabbed his hand and squeezed, and he was suddenly grateful for the darkness. "When I've told you more than you want to know, just say 'when.'"

"It's just that I want so bad to *fix* what happened to you, and I can't."

"Well, that's just it. As nice to me as Mrs. Rook was, as hard as she tried, she couldn't make me whole. I used to look at people like you and wonder why I didn't deserve—"

"Jack, half the time I feel *guilty* for being so happy." Jack could hear Meg's voice wobbling. "But I do know Jesus is in control, and He's put me where I am for a reason."

Jack could only breathe, throat working. "Maybe some of us are here to take out the adversary."

"Not by yourself! Nobody's strong enough—"

"If the life I've lived to this point is going to have any meaning at all, Meg, that's got to be it."

He felt no relief in having emptied his soul at her feet, only a clearer understanding of the chasm between them. He was going to have to stop this right now.

Chapter Eleven

Meg had forgotten she had Jack by the hand until he let go. They had stopped walking, while Tomás went on to join the others.

Valentina had fallen asleep; pressing her higher on his shoulder, Jack looked up as a bottle rocket streaked past and exploded against a fence post. His hard profile bore an expression Meg couldn't interpret.

After a moment he sighed and looked at her. Even against the chancy light of sparklers hissing in the background, Meg could see a longing in Jack's eyes that quickened her heartbeat and made her take a step toward him.

"I'm not going to ask you out, Meg," he said, halting her in her tracks.

"Wh-what?" she stammered.

"You're one of the most beautiful women I've ever met, but your father would cut my liver out if I made a move on you." His mouth quirked.

The double-edged effect of the compliment wrapped in such blistering candor took her breath away. She stared at him, speechless, shaking her head.

"Oh, yeah, he would, and I have too much respect for your respect for him to step over that boundary."

"Daddy doesn't know you."

"That's right, and what he *doesn't* know, he'd like even less than what he sees." He paused. "I sort of hinted at this before, but…Meg, I really need you to back off. If I ever kiss you, there won't be any going back, and I just can't afford to go there, okay?"

Feeling her cheeks flame, sucker punched, she could only be grateful for the darkness. "What did I ever do to give you the idea I like you that way?"

"Meg, come on. You're a perfect lady, but there's some major tension going on between us." He seemed to be picking his words with care. "Look, you should know I'm not going to be here much longer. You're all wrapped up in your church and your family, and I'm moving on at the end of the summer."

Through a haze of pain and embarrassment, she said, "Does Sam know?"

Jack nodded, a jerky dip of his head. "He knows. I just thought it was only fair to tell you before…well, you know."

He walked off, leaving Meg to gather herself as best she could. After a moment she followed, the words *If I ever kiss you* sending sparkles of longing through her chest. Until he'd said that, she hadn't realized how much she wanted him to.

Jack handed Valentina, still sound asleep, over to her father, then sat down beside Bernadette on the tailgate of the hay wagon. All the fireworks having been consumed, Ramón swayed gently with his sleeping daughter in his arms as he talked to Manny and Tomás. Something to do with baptism.

Jack hardly listened. His focus was on Meg, who sat down, glassy-eyed, on the other side of her roommate. He knew he had hurt her badly. It was one of those situations where he had to do it now to avoid exponential pain in the future.

He had no idea how long it would take to put the Warner outfit in jail; until then he couldn't tell anybody—especially Meg—who he was. She would eventually find out, of course. But by then, if he did his job well, she would have developed a thorough disgust of him.

Even if Meg were to forgive all the truths he'd kept hidden from her to this point, he could just see George St. John's face if Jack offered to take his daughter off to some lonely border outpost. During long stretches of living undercover, maintaining a relationship was next to impossible. Jack had seen marriage after marriage crash and burn. Meg deserved better.

Depressed, he reminded himself of the immediate goal—working his way inside this smuggling organization. Herrera hadn't yet given him details of the next run on the border, but had promised they would meet soon.

Angry voices exchanging Spanish insults snagged Jack's attention, and he looked up to see Tomás ducking away from his older brother's attempt to grab him by the arm.

"I'm old enough to make this decision on my own." Tomás folded his arms and stepped closer to Ramón.

"You were baptized as a baby," said Manny, lifting his hands. "Why do you need to do it again?"

Tomás's chin came up. "I gave my life to Christ in a new way, Manuelo. I read it in the Bible. It's called being born again."

"The Bible is for priests to read and explain to us." Manny glanced at Ramón. "He doesn't know enough to understand it."

"That's because we never went to church back in Mexico," said Tomás. "But Meg gave me a Bible, and I *did* read it. I'm not stupid, and I'm going to stay here and go to school this fall so I can understand it *all*. I might even be a photographer to put myself through college like Meg's father did." The boy's defiance turned to cajoling. "Please, Manny, I just want to be baptized. It's what Jesus told me to do. Torres says he'll do it if I will."

Every eye focused on Jack.

"You've never been baptized?" asked Benny.

"He's never been baptized?" Meg echoed.

Manny looked an accusation at Jack. "How come you are leading my little brother astray?"

Just shoot me now, Jack thought. Among other complicated questions, Tomás had brought up the issue of baptism this morning on the way to the church, as they rode alone in the back of the truck. Jack had answered what he could and deferred the rest to Pastor Ramón.

Now he was backed into the proverbial corner. He needed Manny's goodwill, yet he was most inconveniently reluctant to discourage Tomás's obedience to Scripture.

Plus, there was Meg's eager gaze fixed on his face.

Jack found himself lifting his hands in an attempt to placate Manny. "All I said was, I got baptized as a baby myself, but there comes a time when a man has to make decisions of his own. Who you gonna follow, know what I'm saying? Doesn't mean you turn your back on the church or put down your parents' dedication ceremony. Just says you're making a new start." He glanced at Ramón, who nodded and gave him a quick thumbs-up. He could hear Benny quietly translating his words into English for Meg.

Manny's face was a study in confusion. "I'll think about it. You and I have much to discuss." Looking at Meg, he switched to English. "Ma'am, we thank you for the meal and fireworks. We must go home and get ready for work tomorrow." He gestured to Tomás and Diego. *"¡Vamanos!"*

Jack slid off the tailgate, avoiding Meg's eyes. "Thanks for the party, St. John. See you in the morning." He shook hands with Ramón. "Find a couple of hours in your schedule this week, Preacher, and I'll stomp you in a game of racquetball."

"In your dreams," Ramón said with a grin. "Appreciate the help with the yard," he called as Jack followed the Herrera men toward the front driveway where they'd parked.

Waving a reply, Jack forced himself not to glance over his shoulder at Meg. He was going to have enough trouble sleeping as it was.

Warner picked up the phone on the first ring, checking the other side of the bed to make sure Jeri was still asleep. She mumbled something about plugging in her curling iron, then rolled over with the pillow covering her head.

Tucking the cordless phone between his shoulder and ear, Warner dragged his pants on and padded barefoot downstairs.

"Don't call this number again," he said as he sank into his recliner in the family room. "You'll wake up my family."

The Wolf laughed. "Like I care."

"You'll care if we get caught," Warner growled. "What do you want?"

"I want money," said the Wolf. "I got guys down at the border sitting on ready, but they'll go elsewhere if we don't start the show soon. What's the holdup?"

"Hiring transportation," said Warner. "We've just found a guy—new man in our company. Bilingual, been in prison for trafficking. He got out when he turned in somebody bigger."

"Really." To Warner's relief, the Wolf sounded a bit less contemptuous than usual, maybe even satisfied.

"Yeah. We've got the run set up for the nineteenth. Tell

our men to hold on for two weeks and we'll make it worth their while."

Silence crackled over the phone for a moment. "They'll hold on," said the Wolf, "but I need cash now. Five hundred dollars by Thursday or I'll turn you in. You can leave it in our safety deposit box."

Warner's patience snapped. "I don't have money to give away. And if you turn me in, your little cash cow dries up."

"Warner, I happen to know you just joined the country club last week. You're rolling in it. So pay up—or you don't pass 'Go' and you don't collect two hundred dollars."

Warner was in too deep now to back out. He had bills that couldn't be put off. His biggest mistake had been working through *El Lobo* without knowing the man's identity. Maybe there was a way to track him down.

Fear coiled in Warner's belly as he clicked off the phone. Prison was not on his list of vacation spots this year.

On Thursday afternoon, Jack stayed after work to help Meg pull plant material for the next day. It was a backbreaking and monotonous job. After clearing the end of the largest greenhouse and cordoning it off with fluorescent tape, they moved the three-gallon plants closer together, then began shifting flats of color. Having everything together would speed up loading in the morning.

Meg would have done it by herself, but she was relieved when Jack offered. Surprised, too. He'd kept his distance since the Fourth of July party, and she hadn't pushed him. What else was there to do when a guy told you in no uncertain terms to back off?

Better to take a leaf out of Benny's book and avoid men altogether.

Still, as she crouched between two rows of impatiens to check for consistent color and leaf density, Meg was very aware of being alone with Jack in the moist, warm interior of the greenhouse.

"I called Miss Dottie last night," he said suddenly, as if continuing a conversation.

Startled, Meg glanced over her shoulder. "Who?"

Jack looked at her through the feathery foliage of a Japanese maple. "My teacher. The one who helped me when I was a kid."

Meg's defenses dropped. "What did she say?"

Jack set the tree in the corner with the others and arched his back. "She asked me how I was doing, why I hadn't been to see her in such a long time."

"I told you she'd be glad to hear from you." Meg crab-walked along the row, examining plants. "These are fine. Let's take the first ten out of both rows." She glanced at Jack again and found him bent over, hands on his knees. "What's the matter?"

Jack spoke downward, voice harsh. "Meg, she's dying."

Meg sat down and stared at him. "Oh, Jack."

"She needs a kidney transplant." Jack turned his head to look at Meg, and her stomach clenched at the sorrow in his eyes. "I wish I could give her one of mine."

"I know you do. I don't know what to say."

"I wasn't going to tell you." Jack squatted beside Meg, close enough that his knee brushed hers. "But I figured you could pray for her."

"Of course I will." She wanted to touch him, but didn't dare.

"What bothers me most," he continued, "is I don't know what her husband's gonna do when she dies. Vernon's kind of a jerk, but he loves Miss Dottie." Jack looked away, absently fingering the petals of a lipstick-colored impatiens. "On top of everything else, he's apparently made some real dumb investments, and they could lose their property. No family to bail them out, and I can't help. I don't have any money, and even if I did, they wouldn't let me give it to them."

Meg gripped his wrist, and felt the powerful muscles of his forearm bunch as he clenched his fist. "Jack, I know I've said it before, but there's nothing in your life——or in Dottie and Vernon's——that God doesn't have under control. I'll pray with you and we'll wait to see what God leads you to do."

Jack turned his hand to clasp hers, and his expression as he looked at her made the breath back up in her chest. After a long moment, she closed her eyes and bowed her head.

"Lord, thank You for being close when we need You. We don't know how to help Jack's friends, but we pray for Your guidance. Please, if it's Your will, let a kidney be found, and I pray You'll help Vernon see You working in his life. Thank You…" She took a sharp breath when Jack squeezed her wrist. She could feel every scratch and callus on his palm and fingers.

"I agree. Amen," he murmured. Meg looked up to find Jack staring at her. "I guess telling you was the right thing to do."

But Meg wasn't so sure. Somehow Jack had her hand in both of his, tracing the lines in her palm with his thumbs. She couldn't remember a prayer ever before reducing her to such a mass of quivering emotion.

Suddenly the greenhouse door opened, and Sam stuck his head in. "Hey, you two, I'm outta here. Meg, don't forget to lock— What's the matter?"

Meg had snatched her hand from Jack's and jumped to her feet. "Nothing." She hopped across two rows of plants, putting a safe distance between herself and Jack. "We're finished.

I mean, everything's ready for in the morning. We were just leaving, right, Torres?"

Jack pushed to his feet and gave Meg a small, sad smile. "Oh yeah. We're done."

Sam watched the door shut behind Jack, then turned a frown on Meg. "What was that all about? And don't tell me it's none of my business."

Meg grimaced. "If I knew, I'd be happy to elaborate."

"I know what it *looked* like."

"It wasn't, Sam. I promise."

Sam just looked at her. "Meg, be careful."

"I am." She avoided his eyes. "Are you and Grace coming to the baptism on Sunday?"

"We'll be there." He opened the greenhouse door. "Go on home. I'll lock up behind you."

"Thanks." Meg mustered a smile for Sam as she headed for the parking lot.

What she needed was a nice long bubble bath and a Max Brand Western. Wait, scratch that. Too many handsome Latino cowboys in Max Brand's stuff.

She unlocked the Mustang with a sigh.

Too many handsome Latino cowboys *everywhere*.

"I'm not much of a water person." Jack kicked a rock into the muddy Trinity River, the site of the church's monthly baptismal service.

Meg, standing beside him, nudged him with her elbow. "You want a life jacket?"

Jack was seriously considering it.

Winding through the Metroplex like a lasso, the Trinity River snaked among cemeteries and residential areas, freeways and railroads, wooded parks and botanical gardens, and even the occasional golf course. On the less appealing side, the Trinity also hosted several industrial complexes and a gigantic sewage treatment plant.

Jack had wondered if he and Tomás were doomed to baptism in pollution, but he needn't have worried. Clearly Ramón Santos had connections.

This section of the river looked like a photograph from *Southern Living*. Lush shrubbery, cottonwoods and water oaks lined the opposite bank, casting their reflections onto the water and veiling residential developments miles in the distance. Cottony clouds scudded along in the blue sky overhead, and birds intermittently interrupted the quiet. Church members and guests who had come to observe the baptism stood at the water's edge, marveling at the beauty of the place.

Besides Meg and Benny, Jack's only personal guests were Sam Thornton and his wife. He'd wanted to invite Dennis Carmichael and Mrs. Rook, but under the circumstances…not a good idea. Tomás had talked Manny, Diego and even Efrin into attending.

Jack came out of his reverie as Ramón, dressed in jeans and a white polo shirt, walked up and whacked him on the shoulder. "Showtime, brother. You ready?"

Though large amounts of water made him queasy, over the past few days Jack had spent a good bit of time thinking about this baptism thing. Undercover or not, he knew it was time to publicly declare his identification with the Lord.

"Yeah." Jack took a breath. "I'm ready."

Following the baptism, everyone moved to Professor Anderson's deck for a celebratory hamburger cookout. After they'd both gone through the buffet line, Jack pulled Manny aside. "If we're gonna talk, now's the time."

Holding plates piled high with burgers, baked beans and potato salad, the men found seats on a wooden bench looking out on the river. The wife of Ramón's seminary professor, who had hosted the after-baptism party, proved to be a world-class cook and a generous hostess. "Eating on the dirt," as Tomás insisted on calling it, seemed to be a favored activity for these people.

Manny leaned close and lowered his voice. "I've got to know if this religion thing is gonna throw a kink in our plans."

Taken aback, Jack took an unhurried look around the grounds before answering. Meg and Tomás had gone inside to use the professor's computer to look at the pictures she'd taken, and the rest of the company had scattered in all directions to enjoy the food, scenery and conversation.

Jack crinkled the soda can in his hand. "This is business. Why?" He had changed to dry clothes, but still felt the peace that accompanied his act of obedience. He had to force himself to think like an outlaw.

Manny stroked his mustache. "I can't trust anybody completely. But you've kept your mouth shut about Tomás."

"I always keep my word."

"Good." Manny's dark, scarred face took on a pinched expression. "Because if we don't do the run by the middle of the month, they're gonna send my wife and kids back."

Jack choked on a mouthful of soda. "Your *what?*"

"You think I'm gonna leave my family in Mexico while I'm living the good life here?"

A mental image of the bug-infested hotel they both lived in flashed across Jack's brain. "Where are they?"

"Nearby. It's not your problem. But can you move that fast?"

"I think so. Herrera, who's your boss?" Jack had never come right out and asked.

Manny shook his head. "He'd kill me." He continued in a matter-of-fact tone, "You'll need a couple of trucks, and places to wait if you have to go under. Guns for protection."

"No problem." Jack would call Carmichael tonight, put in a request for money and arms. It was a relief to have a target date at last.

"One more thing," Manny said. "The meeting place is *el puente negro* in Eagle Pass. They've paid off *la migra* to look the other way."

Jack had suspected as much, but the confirmation made him ill. He nodded. "How does the nineteenth sound?"

Sickened, Meg stared at the computer screen, while conversation in the kitchen behind her buzzed in and out like a bad cell phone connection.

This couldn't be what she thought it was.

After going through the lunch line, she and Tomás had come inside to view his picture disk, a series of playful and remarkably clever amateur shots of his family and friends. At first, Tomás had looked over her shoulder, pointing people out and providing a running commentary. Eventually, though, he'd bounced outside to play Frisbee with the Andersons' black Lab puppy.

Meg had been about to put the computer to sleep when she'd noticed a video file at the end of the still photos. Curious, she'd opened it up.

And now would give anything if she hadn't.

What she had here was a three-minute video clip of a party. As shaky as her Spanish was, Meg recognized vulgar language when she heard it. A couple of brown bottles were being passed around and, judging from gestures, ribald jokes as well.

Before she could react, the clip was over and had looped back to begin again. Stung, Meg closed the window and ejected the disk. Stuffing it into her pocket, she jumped up from the computer.

She'd seen worse things on the six o'clock news, and Jack had been in the room only briefly. But it hurt to see him there, along with Manny, Efrin, Diego and a couple of other men she didn't recognize.

Stumbling outside to the deck, she saw Jack deep in conversation with Manny. They'd evidently just finished eating; empty paper plates and crumpled soft drink cans lay on the bench. Jack's hair was still damp, leaving wet patches on his shoulders, but the peaceful expression he'd worn following his baptism had disappeared.

He looked watchful, dangerous. A lot like the first time she'd met him.

"*Está bien,*" Manny was saying as she walked up to them, "*voy a pagarte cuando me los entregues.*" He looked so grim that Meg would have given anything for her Spanish dictionary right then. Her imagination went wild. There had to be a way to find out what was going on.

"Hey, y'all," she said, summoning up a smile. "I just discovered a pinball machine. Anybody want to take me on?"

Jack stood up with a lazy smile. "Put a bowl of homemade ice cream on the line and I'm your man."

Meg gave him a pitying look. "Loser serves the winner, and I like caramel sauce and whipped cream on mine."

Jack snorted. "Whatever." He jerked a thumb toward the lawn, where Tomás was still roughhousing with the puppy. "Manny, you better go rescue that dog before the kid wears him out."

One of his rare smiles glimmering, Manny picked up his

empty plate. "Okay. And I come rescue *you*, when Miss Meg squashes your ego like a bug."

Mentally stringing together what she was going to say, Meg led the way back into the house. "I don't think I've ever seen Manny relax like this," she began. "You think he'll forgive Tomás for joining our church?"

"Manny's all right," Jack said. "He just wants the best for his little brother."

In the empty game room, Meg turned suddenly, so that Jack bumped into her, steadying her with his hands on her upper arms. She could smell river water on his skin, mixed with the clean-laundry scent of his clothes. "What is he hiding?" she whispered. "I can't help worrying about him."

"I think the old saying 'don't ask, don't tell' applies." His tone was light, layered over a note of command.

Staring up at Jack's firm, humorous mouth, Meg wished desperately that he would tell her what was going on so she didn't have to ask. It was so tempting to just close her eyes and fall in love with him in spite of all the warning bells.

Don't ask, don't tell. Maybe that was her answer for Tomás's video clip as well. Her conscience squirmed, but she wrestled it down. "Let me know if there's anything I can do, okay?"

Jack released her arms, leaving her feeling cold. "You're a good person, St. John, but I'm not feeling sorry for you when you lose." He plucked a token off a stack on the pinball machine. "Hope your dipping arm's in shape." He pulled a lever and released a ball.

Lights, bells and whistles went off.

Meg moved to watch, very much afraid that she was one of those idiots who, refusing to learn from history, would be doomed to repeat it.

Chapter Twelve

There was plenty of activity in the Electric Q tonight, even on a Sunday night. Maybe, Jack thought, *because* it was Sunday. He looked for Carmichael and found him at their usual table.

Jack shook hands and sat down.

"Developments?" Carmichael said without further greeting.

Jack waved away the waitress, who pouted and turned to Carmichael.

Jack leaned in. "We're set to go on the nineteenth."

"Fine." Carmichael surveyed Jack with narrowed eyes. "What's wrong?"

Jack chose his words carefully. "I told you somebody was stalking my boss—the woman." He hoped the depth of his feelings didn't glow like neon in his face. "I've been watching her."

"I would expect you to." Eyes twinkling, Carmichael rubbed his hand over his mouth. The waitress delivered his drink. After he'd paid, he turned back to Jack. "Any other activity?"

Jack cleared his throat. "Apparently they found whatever they needed from her and shifted attention to me."

Carmichael frowned. "How do you know?"

"Somebody searched my room."

"Are you sure? When?"

"Night before last. I leave markers in strategic places. They've been moved."

"I know you well enough to know you didn't leave anything damaging lying around. Any ideas who it was, or why?"

"Maybe just Warner checking me out. Herrera seems to trust me."

Carmichael pulled on his lower lip. "I'd be worried if they *didn't* check your ID."

"Right. But…there's something else bugging me. Do you know a guy named Vernon Rook?"

Carmichael thought for a moment, then nodded. "Slug working out of the Euless office."

The term for officers close to retirement who spent their days pushing paper and little else just about fit Rook to a T. "Yes, sir. How long's he been in this region?"

"I don't know. Less than a year, I guess. Why?"

"I knew him down south. Actually I've known him since I was a kid."

Carmichael sat up straight. "And he's seen you here?"

Jack nodded. "The first time I ran into him he challenged me, and I told him I'd gotten out because of…because of Rico, you know. He seemed to believe me. The second time I didn't let him see me. He was bullying the Mexicans in the laundromat near my hotel, but I wasn't close enough to hear exactly what was going on." Jack had regretted that more with every day that passed.

Carmichael whistled. "Coincidence?"

"I hope so. Can you check him out to make sure?"

"Sure. I'll let you know. What else you worried about?"

"What do you mean?"

"I ain't been in the agency this long without learning to read people. You're on edge. There's something different about you."

Jack uttered a short laugh. Not a good sign if he was that transparent. "Just personal stuff. Nothing that'll interfere with the job."

"You're not falling for that woman, are you?" Carmichael persisted. "You get her involved and you're both in danger."

Jack didn't try denying it. "I've got it under control." He laughed again. "She thinks I'm scum."

Which was probably the most depressing truth of all.

"Why didn't you tell me Torres is a cop?" Warner demanded, clutching his cell phone to his ear. Sitting in a golf cart just short of the eighth green, he checked to make sure his buddy had moved onto the green to putt and couldn't hear. He lowered his voice anyway. "Is this your idea of a joke?"

"You didn't need to know," said The Wolf, "until I decided what to do with him."

"I don't believe it," Warner said stubbornly. "He fits in with those lousy wetbacks like a long-lost brother."

An impatient snort blasted Warner's ear. "It's his *job* to fit in, Warner."

"Well, what are we going to do?" Warner asked. "I've got too much invested in this next run to cancel it."

"We're not going to cancel it. You're going to take Torres out."

"Take him *out?*" Warner yelped. "I didn't get into this to murder a cop! I'm just making a little side money in the transportation industry."

"You don't have to be anywhere in the vicinity," The Wolf said reasonably. "Simplest thing to do is arrange for an accident. He works a construction site, right?"

Warner forced himself to calm down and think that over. He really, really hated being told what to do. On the other hand, he couldn't think of a better plan.

After a moment he gritted his teeth. "All right. But you do know we'll have to find another driver for the run."

El Lobo grunted. "Let me worry about that. This guy's got to go."

Warner clicked off the cell phone and stuffed it into his golf bag. He sat there scowling at his scorecard. Two under par and the game had been ruined.

Meg stood under the carriageway, watching the rain come down in dense sheets and listening to thunder boom overhead like a celestial bowling party. If this kept up much longer, the entire front entrance was going to wash away—including the mountains of gravel and dirt and landscape timbers positioned for filler.

"I vote we head for 7-Eleven and take on a Big Gulp," said Jack, who had just dodged into the downpour to retrieve a couple of shovels. He wrung out his shirttail. "This is a lost cause for today." He popped the tools into their slots against the side of the truck, then sat down in the open cab with a distinct squish.

Manny shook his head. "Already missed three days last week because of rain." He was neatly coiling baling wire around his hand and stuffing it into a burlap bag. Manny never wasted anything. "The men need to work."

"Yeah, but if we get out in that mess, somebody's gonna get electrocuted." As if to prove Jack's point, a jag of lightning split the leaden sky. A second later, thunder crashed.

Meg jumped. "Mrs. G called twice this morning to remind me they're doing the photo shoot here on Friday." With fatalistic humor she added, "I'm thinking we put Rosalee in the hole we dug for the oak tree, and call it 'The Princess Bride Goes Mud Wrestling.'"

Jack laughed, and even Manny gave an appreciative half smile.

"You're the boss, Spanky," said Jack. "I can't get any wetter, that's for sure."

Meg surveyed the idle backhoes and box blades stranded outside the carriageway. "Mr. Warner said he's not paying to rent the heavy equipment after this week, and the budget's getting pretty skimpy." She put her hands on her hips and looked up at the sky as another deafening crack of thunder boomed. "So, what am I supposed to do, Lord? This is serious!"

"What've you got, a direct line up there?" Jack demanded as he walked by Meg on the way to round up the rest of the crew, who had retreated into the carriage house.

Within ten minutes, the rain had stopped as if turned off by a giant faucet, and the sun lit up a rainbow that streaked in glorious Technicolor across the roof of the house.

Meg grinned at Jack's obvious stupefaction. "Sometimes I think God just likes to make me laugh."

He looked up at the sparkling sky. "Maybe so, but this is just…spooky." Shaking his head, he disappeared into the carriage house.

Fortunately, the men were eager to get back to work. Within minutes, they'd pitched in to help plant a twenty-foot live oak, which Manny had driven all the way to Lewisville to obtain.

Manny himself operated the front-end loader with the tree suspended by straps from the bucket. From the top of the incline, he maneuvered the tree ball closer to its intended spot, while Jack directed, holding his hands above his head and bringing them closer together to indicate Manny's distance from his target. The other men waited nearby, ready to guide the tree into the hole.

Meg was leaning against the extended-cab, checking a blueprint, when one of the cables holding the tree suddenly snapped. Hearing Manny shout, she watched in horror as the huge tree wobbled and fell.

Tomás was right in its path.

Meg screamed "Move!" and the men shouted as the tree hurtled downward. Frozen, Tomás looked up, mouth and eyes wide.

With a speed she could only later recall as a blur of time and motion, the men all scattered except Jack. He dove at the boy's knees, knocking him out of the way.

He was almost clear himself, but the tree rotated on one strap, the trunk bouncing against the front-end loader. The second strap snapped with a gunshot-like pop, sending the tree arcing. The heavy root ball of the tree clipped the back of Jack's head, then landed with a thud on top of a pile of dirt. Jack sprawled motionless at the base of the new retaining wall.

As Meg ran for Jack, her peripheral vision caught a white-faced Manny ramming levers to lock the loader in place. He launched himself to the ground, sparing a look to make sure Tomás was safe, then slammed to his knees beside Meg. The other men formed an anxious circle around them.

"Dead?" asked Manny.

"No." Meg could feel Jack's shallow breath when she put her cheek close to his mouth. Her own heartbeat roared in her ears. Manny reached to turn him over, but she stopped him. "Wait—I think you're not supposed to move people when they're unconscious."

She probed Jack's head with gentle fingers. A huge lump

was forming behind his ear, but there was no blood that she could see. Was that a good thing or a bad thing?

Manny frowned. "We better call an ambulance."

"I should've thought of that." Meg scrabbled for her cell phone and punched in 9-1-1.

When the operator promised that an ambulance would arrive shortly, Meg settled cross-legged on the ground, close to Jack's head. His skin was pasty-gray under the olive complexion, but his breathing seemed normal. The bump continued to swell.

"We should put some ice on this," Meg fretted. She gently smoothed her fingers across Jack's forehead and black hair, skirting the outside of the purpling wound. "Come on, Torres, wake up!" she muttered.

Somebody handed her a cold drink cup, and she looked up to find Tomás leaning close, his young face puckered in concern. "Thanks," she told him and carefully touched the cup to Jack's bruise; he flinched but didn't rouse.

Tomás nodded. "I am dead if Torres does not push me."

What if Jack dies? The thought nearly shut down Meg's brain. *Oh, please let him come around.*

Fifteen tense minutes later, Jack still hadn't moved or even groaned. Meg tugged her shirttail out to wipe sweat off his upper lip and forehead, vaguely worried because it wasn't that hot out here after the rain. His skin was clammy to the touch, his cheeks and jaw shadowed by a faint, scratchy beard. She looked at her watch for the hundredth time. Traffic in this part of town could be horrible, and it was getting on toward late-afternoon rush hour.

Where was the ambulance?

On the thought, a siren pierced the general traffic noise. Within moments an ambulance wheeled, lights flashing, into the messy dirt-packed area and backed toward them. The amulance doors burst open, and the crew peeled out of the way, eaving an opening for the EMTs and their equipment.

"What happened?" asked a uniformed woman who knelt eside Jack and began to check his vitals with stethoscope and blood pressure cuff. The driver and other tech hauled out a stretcher, backboard and neck brace.

Meg twisted her hands with anxiety. "A tree strapped to a front-end loader came loose and hit him on the head."

"Where was his hard hat?"

Meg looked blank. "This is a landscaping crew."

The EMT directed an impatient glance at Meg, continuing her gentle but thorough examination of Jack's body. "Has he been conscious at all?"

"No." Meg's voice clogged. "Is he going to be okay?"

"We'll do our best. Have you moved him?"

"No."

The woman nodded approval. "Look, sit with him and let me ask your boss some questions before we move him, okay?"

"Okay." Meg looked up at Manny for support, and he unexpectedly pressed her shoulder. She gave him a wobbly smile. "But *I'm* the boss."

The EMT blinked and gave a small grin. "Cool. Okay, boss-lady, does anybody know this guy well enough to know if he's allergic to anything? Any previous conditions or other medications he might be taking?"

"I don't think any of us knows him that well," Meg said. *And not for lack of trying.* "His name is Jack Torres. I've never seen him take any drugs, and as far as I know he's as healthy as a horse, but—" She looked down at Jack's still face and shrugged. "I think he's afraid of water."

The EMT snorted. "Well, that's real helpful. What's your name, sweetie?"

"Meg."

"Okay, Meg, scoot back out of the way and let my guys in to give Jack some oxygen."

Meg complied, crouching as close as she could without getting in the way so she could watch the medical team work. While the woman placed a C-shaped collar about Jack's neck, one of the men attached a plastic pincherlike object to Jack's finger, then checked his pulse—which seemed to be normal if the medics' expressions were any indication. Lifting Jack's eyelid to note the pupil's response to light, the male medic frowned. "Probable concussion," he muttered. The third partner took notes on a clipboard.

The lady tech continued to address Meg. "Now I need to know about the accident. First of all, *was* it an accident?"

Meg looked up at Manny again. His whole face tightened with fear. "Of course it was an accident," she said quickly. "Manny here was operating the machine, moving a tree over to plant near the retaining wall. It swung out unexpectedly, and one of the guys wound up underneath. Tomás, over there." Meg gulped. "Jack took time to shove him out of the way, but the tree caught him—Jack, I mean—on the head."

"How long has he been out like this?"

"Twenty minutes now, I guess." Was that too long? Was Jack actually in a coma now?

"Hmmm. How high up was the tree when it started to fall?"

"About—I don't know! Manny, what was it, about five feet?" Manny shrugged, and Meg gestured helplessly. "It hit the wall and the strap broke, so it must have been coming down pretty hard."

The medic responded to the panic in Meg's voice with a sympathetic look. "All right," she said, "no I.V. and no drugs for now. He looks good, except for that bump and zero LOC.

Let's package him and get on the way. Hopefully he'll come around soon."

Near tears, Meg stood back and watched the medical crew roll Jack onto his side and slide a backboard beneath him, keeping his body carefully aligned from head to foot. One of the medics removed Jack's wallet from his hip pocket in the process and tossed it to Meg. As they lifted the backboard onto a stretcher, the female EMT said over her shoulder, "Look through there and get Mr. Torres's date of birth, social security number, and anything that might tell us about his previous medical condition."

"Okay, but—"

"Come on, you can ride in front."

Relief flooded Meg. She'd been afraid they'd make her stay behind. She turned to her foreman. "Manny, you're in charge. Take the men and all the equipment back to Sunset and make sure Sam knows what happened and where we are—" She turned to one of the medics, who had just slid the stretcher into the back of the ambulance and locked it to the floor. "Which hospital?"

"Harris Methodist on Pennsylvania."

"You got that, Manny?" Meg backed toward the passenger door of the ambulance, Jack's wallet in her hand.

"*Sí. Vaya con Dios.*" Manny lifted a hand, then turned to give instructions to the other men. The last thing Meg saw before getting into the ambulance was Manny slinging his arm around his little brother's neck and walking off with him toward the company truck. The other men followed, though Efrin hesitated, turning to watch the ambulance.

At least Tomás was all right. *Thank You, Lord, and please be with Jack.*

* * *

Jack came out of black, blanketing darkness to find his arms strapped to his sides, something plastic up his nose and all kinds of noise aggravating a monumental headache. Radio static, a woman's unfamiliar voice chattering to him, and above it all a siren wailing. He couldn't get his eyes open.

"Shut it off," he said, and immediately felt the woman's ear at his mouth.

"His lips are moving," she announced. "Breathing returning to normal. Let's see your fingernails, sweetheart." He felt her mash a couple of them. "Oxygen perfusion is nearly normal now," she said to someone, presumably not Jack, because he didn't have a clue what oxygen perfusion was. "Can you wiggle your fingers for me?"

"You talkin' to *me?*" he said in his best DeNiro voice, which was pretty weak at the moment.

The woman laughed. "Yeah, I'm talkin' to you, cute thing. Come on now, show me your stuff." Jack clenched his fist and received a pat on the hand. "Good boy. What day is it?"

"Monday, July eleventh. Is Tomás okay?"

"Who? Oh, you mean the little guy you tackled? Just fine. Walked off without a scratch. Next time you decide to play hero, though, you might want to wear a hard hat."

"Yeah, I got a bit of a headache." He tried opening his eyes again. The interior of the ambulance was dimly lit, but it still felt like shards of glass entered his skull directly through his eyes. He groaned.

"Don't look," he was advised. "Just lie still and enjoy the ride." Since he was strapped down like a victim in a Vincent Price movie, Jack could hardly argue. "However, if you're in a chatty mood," the EMT continued, "you might help me finish filling in this form. Is all the info on your driver's license correct?"

"Yeah." It was, to a point. Deep undercover, he was given altered ID for just such a situation as this. No need to panic.

"Good," said the medic. "Since you were unconscious, we gave your valuables to your boss. Your beeper and keys…"

Jack missed the rest of her sentence as a buzz of adrenaline nearly blacked him out again.

"Whoa!" he heard through a fog, "we're losing him again, guys. Radio the ER, tell them…"

He didn't hear what she told them because disaster poured through a brain that currently had the retention capacity of a sieve. He was too sick to think, too sick to pray.

Okay, God, what are you up to here?

The Harris Hospital emergency room was nowhere near as chaotic as the inside of Meg's head. No sooner did she grab on to one thought than another one chased it off. She laid her head back against the wall, jingling Jack's keys. What was she supposed to do with them? The Harley was parked at Sunset, along with her Mustang.

When it had occurred to her that she didn't have a ride home, she'd decided it was a good time to use her cell phone to page her father. She found him, fortunately, next door at the Cook Children's Medical Center. He'd promised to pick her up as soon as he wrapped up his evening rounds.

Since she wasn't a relative, the nurses wouldn't let her in to see Jack. Just told her he'd be kept overnight for observation. With a severe concussion, he'd be subject to violent headaches and nausea for a few days, then gradually get back to normal. Whatever normal was.

Meg gripped Jack's keys until the jagged edges bit into her palm. The EMT's questions had brought home how little, beyond basic phone number and address information, she knew about Jack.

Well, she knew that his commitment to Christ had begun to change his behavior. And that he was funny, tender and courageous to the point of idiocy.

But there were so many things that didn't match up. His secrets with Manny and his prison time, which he still refused to talk about.

Lord, she admitted, *my emotions are way out of control. Can't You turn them off, like You did that thunderstorm this afternoon?*

Ha. Like that was going to happen. God might enjoy making Meg laugh, but He seldom rescued her from the consequences of her own choices.

Chapter Thirteen

Early the next morning, Meg parked outside Jack's room at the Starlight Inn. It had occurred to her that he might appreciate a change of clothes; her plan was to pick up a clean pair of jeans and T-shirt and drop them off on her way to work.

And, in the dark recesses of her heart, she had to admit she wanted to look around. Since she had a key, that wouldn't technically be breaking and entering.

Still, she sat in the car a minute or so with the engine running, working up the nerve to get out. Without Elliot's genial bulk, the neighborhood scared her a little. The sky was dark with a brewing dust storm, the sun still cowering behind the buildings up and down the street. Nobody was out and about, but she watched a stray dog snuffle around somebody's garbage a few doors down. Would it attack when she got out of the car?

You're being silly, she told herself.

Standing outside Jack's door, her hands shook a little as she tried to fit the key in the lock. A siren wailed a few streets over, and the smell of the garbage made her nose wrinkle. *Let's get this over with and get out of here.*

Just as the rusty lock finally gave, she felt a hand on her shoulder.

"'*Dias, señorita.* What are you doing here?"

Meg jumped a foot and turned around with her hand on her throat. She fell back against the door. "Efrin! You scared me to death!"

Efrin Herrera grinned. "I scare you?" he repeated. "That's good." He did not, Meg noticed, remove his hand.

She shrugged it off. What did he mean by "that's good"? "I wasn't expecting to see anybody I knew," she said nervously. "I came by to pick up some clothes for Jack Torres." There was no reason to explain herself, and judging by Efrin's quizzical expression, she wasn't sure he'd even understood her. Babbling just seemed to help. "Well, goodbye. See you at work."

She turned the doorknob, all but fell into the dark room, and slammed the door in Efrin's face.

Praying the door had locked behind her, she felt for the light switch. To her relief, it came on. She wandered around the tiny room, touching Jack's pillow, the guitar leaning against a chair, and the leather Bible lying on a lamp table beside the bed.

Marveling that the bed was neatly made—the last time she'd made hers up had been about five years ago when her grandmother came to visit—Meg sat down and opened the Bible. Inscribed inside its cover, in a lovely, old-fashioned script, were the words "To Jack, with love from Dottie and Vernon." Flipping through it, she saw notes inked in the margins, in spiky, masculine print that only increased her curiosity. Here was the private side of Jack: possessions kept not to impress anybody, but to sustain the soul.

What sort of man played the guitar, wrote in his Bible... and lived in a place like this? He had to make a decent salary. Did he save his money, or did he spend it all? Did he have large debts? For all she knew, he had a drug habit or a wife and children somewhere that he had to support.

The thought made Meg's stomach lurch, and she couldn't help looking around for pictures. There were none. Just stark, pathetic bareness. The room of an intrinsically lonely man.

It was then that the guilt of snooping overcame her curiosity; after choosing jeans and a green T-shirt from a stack inside the cheap dresser, Meg drove straight to the hospital, determined to dig information out of Jack. All he could do was tell her to mind her own business.

Standing outside the partially open door of Jack's hospital room, Meg shifted the grocery sack in which she'd packed his clothes, and lifted her hand to knock. She hesitated when she heard someone else in the room. A doctor, judging by the hale and hearty tone of voice.

She was about to walk down to the nurse's station to ask for a cup of coffee, when she heard Jack's raised voice.

"Look, you can't file that report, I don't care what kind of OSHA rules you break." Jack sounded tired, upset, yet somehow in command.

Meg found herself utterly incapable of walking away. Why wouldn't Jack want the doctor to file a simple OSHA report? Was he concerned about getting the company into trouble?

The doctor seemed equally mystified. "Mr. Torres, this is just standard procedure for head injury cases. Nobody's going to prosecute *you*. It's your employer's responsibility—"

"All right, Doc," Jack interrupted. He lowered his voice so that Meg had to lean closer in order to hear. "I'm going to hold you to patient confidentiality here. Can you handle that?"

"Well, I—sure, I suppose so."

"Okay. I'm a border patrol officer, and if you put my name on that document, you'll get me in serious trouble. If you want to check it out you can call this number." Jack rattled off a phone number that Meg was too astonished to memorize.

Jack was an undercover officer? Border patrol?

She sagged against the wall.

Once, when Meg was seven or so, her brother had told her she couldn't ride his new ten-speed bike because she was too little. The minute he went into the house, she'd wheeled the bike out of the garage, mounted it from a patio chair and sailed down the driveway. After successfully navigating the first block, she got cocky and decided to experiment with those fascinating gears.

A trip to the emergency room for eight stitches, another one to the dentist to replace a front tooth, and the forfeiture of six months' allowance to pay for the repair of the bike, were enough to convince Meg that discretion was most definitely the better part of valor.

Standing in this hospital corridor, Meg had something of the same feeling of finding herself in sudden face-hands-and-knees contact with a concrete sidewalk.

All the pieces of information she'd collected about Jack crashed through her overloaded brain until she wanted to lean over and empty it all out again.

The innate fineness that characterized him, in spite of his prison record and apparent contentment with living in a slum. The intent way he'd questioned her about her crew being busted. His insistence that she not report Manny and Tomás.

She would bet there'd been something on Tomás's video clip that would have clued her in had she bothered to translate it.

And reeling through Meg's brain went the few pieces of his past that Jack had let her have. Was every bit of it fiction? Could she believe *anything* he'd told her?

Come to think of it, how did she know that what he'd just told the doctor was true? He could be covering some crime and planning to slip away before he was caught.

Suddenly the door beside her swung open, and the doctor came out, mumbling into a voice dictation recorder. He passed her without a glance.

What should she do? Confront Jack? Pretend she hadn't heard?

She laid her head back against the wall. "Lord, it's me," she whispered. "I feel stupid and betrayed, and I don't know what this means. Please give me wisdom."

Taking a deep breath, Meg knocked on the door. When Jack called "Come in," she peeked inside. Despite her anger and confusion, her heart clenched at the sight of all that vital masculinity confined to a wrinkled hospital gown and an IV drip. Fortunately, he'd thrown an arm across his eyes, giving Meg time to blink away her tears.

She cleared her throat. "Jack."

He lowered his arm, his expression wary. "Hey, St. John. What are you doing here?"

"I brought you some clothes."

Alarm flashed through his eyes. "I wondered who had my keys." When she didn't respond, he gestured toward the bedside chair. "You can sit down if you want to."

Meg shook her head and swallowed. As she continued to hover near the door, silence grew into an awkward blank.

Jack's brows drew together. "Come here, Meg." His voice had that authoritative note she'd heard when he spoke to the doctor.

A law officer's authority. Drawn to him by his compelling eyes, Meg sidled closer.

"How long were you standing outside the door just now?"

Meg set the sack of clothes on the table. "You must think I'm an idiot," she blurted.

The heart monitor whirred softly in the silence. "I wasn't trying to make a fool of you. I was doing my job." Jack gave her a half-caressing, half-aggravated look that made her insides flip. "If it makes you feel any better, you and Dr. Guthrie are the first people to blow my cover in more than five years."

She didn't know how she felt, but it certainly wasn't *better.* "You weren't going to tell me at all, were you? You've been using me to get information about my employer and my friends."

"If that's how you want to look at it. But you only have to worry about your friends if they're breaking the law." He frowned. "Meg, when I'm undercover, I can't tell *anybody* who I am."

"Well, I can't *un-*know what I know!" She lifted her hands. "What am I supposed to do?"

"Simple. Just keep your mouth shut. You breathe so much as one word to anybody, and you're under arrest."

Meg stared at him, tears of humiliation pricking the backs of her eyes. Evidently all the lazy, teasing and borderline admiring things he'd said to her had been part of his James Bond act.

Stung, she lashed out. "Of all the condescending—"

"I didn't mean it like that," he said wearily. "But if my ID is compromised I could wind up in the morgue, not just in the hospital with a concussion."

Meg's eyes widened. "Why? Do you think this wasn't an accident?"

"I don't have any reason to think so at this point. But…" He hesitated. "The more I think about that break-in at your house, the more I'm afraid it was related to this whole deal."

Cold fear twisted a knot in her stomach. "Were you ever going to tell me?"

"No. I told you, I've been watching out for you." He sighed. "You can't believe how this complicates things."

"What exactly are you trying to accomplish? Are you after somebody inside the company, or are you just trying to send home all the illegal aliens we hire?"

"I can't tell you anything else. Just leave me alone and let me do my job."

She flinched. "I thought we were friends."

"Everything's different now—"

Suddenly a brisk knock sounded on the door, and Meg's father walked in.

"Hi, Sweet Pea," he said cheerfully. "How's your guy feeling this morning?"

Jack wished he could pull the sheet up over his head and go back to blessed unconsciousness. He'd said every wrong thing possible to Meg, and the hurt on her face made him want to throw something. No way to dig out with Papa Bear in the room.

He played the sympathy card. "I feel like I got hit on the head with a twenty-foot oak tree," he said, avoiding Meg's eyes.

Her father ambled over to stand at the foot of the bed. "I passed Dr. Guthrie in the hall. He said you're ready to go home."

Jack looked at him blankly. "I guess I'll have to call Sam—"

"Nonsense." Meg's father unclipped the stuffed koala on his tie and stuck it in the pocket of his lab coat. "I've finished my morning rounds, so I'll take you."

This was getting worse and worse. Jack needed to talk to Meg, but not in front of her father. "Thanks, but I'll just—"

"No problem. I'll clear your paperwork and we'll be on our way." Dr. St. John disappeared, leaving Meg and Jack staring warily at one another.

"Dad's a good guy."

Jack could tell by the look on Meg's face where her thoughts were leading.

"He is, but you can't tell him who I am. Let him think the worst. All the better for what I have to do." Headache raging like a wild animal, he rubbed his eyes. "Meg, promise me."

"Of course I promise." Meg's expression was troubled. "You look terrible. Maybe you shouldn't stay by yourself. Mom and Dad would be glad to——"

"No! I mean it, Meg. You're a sweet kid, but you're out of your league on this one."

To Jack's relief, Meg visibly drew herself together. She gave him a wobbly smile. "Well. Okay, then, I'd better get to work. Sam asked about you, so I'll tell him you're on your way home. Just—just call me—us, I mean, if you need anything." She whisked out the door without looking back.

Jack slowly sat up and reached for his clothes. He didn't look forward to caring for himself alone in that motel room, but there was no other choice. If he was right in suspecting Warner had had somebody rig the belt on that truck, the stakes had just been raised exponentially. He couldn't embroil Meg or her family in this mess any further.

Even if she managed to keep her mouth shut, it was going to be tough to resist his growing desire to share everything with her. This new and insidious longing for a life partner had begun to overpower his instinct for self-preservation.

Dangerous in the extreme.

For thirty-six hours Jack lay in his scuzzy little hotel room, picturing Meg sorting through his T-shirts. He wished he could call her. If she'd bring him soup or sing some goofy song, or read to him or even smile at him, he'd feel like a new man.

As it was, the only person he could call was Dennis Carmichael. The OIC advised Jack to lay low and take as little pain medication as possible.

"You're gonna need all your wits about you, boy. I'd come over and see to you, but they're watching."

"Yes, sir, I understand," Jack said, gripping his pillow as a wave of nausea rolled over him. When it passed, he continued, "I've got to get back to work and figure out what caused that strap to break."

"You do that. What about the doctor who treated you at the hospital? Any indication he turned in that report?"

"No, he was cool after he understood what was going on." Jack hadn't mentioned his confrontation with Meg. He had her under control.

Hopefully.

"Good. So there's no kinks in the plans for our little sting operation."

"No, sir. We're good to go."

Carmichael grunted in acknowledgement. "Listen, I followed up on Vernon Rook. The guy's nothing but a paperpusher, but his record's clean. He went to Presidio ten years ago, and stayed five years before transferring here. There's no apparent connection to anybody involved in what happened to you and Valenzuela."

Jack closed his eyes, relief warring with disappointment. Things would have been a lot simpler if he could have nailed Warner's accomplice without making the trek to the border himself. On the other hand, it would be terrible for Miss Dottie if her husband were on the take.

Still… Rook had unexpectedly appeared in Jack's territory

twice. Jack's instinct told him that wasn't a coincidence. If he'd followed his instincts a year ago, Rico would still be alive.

"All right, boss," he said slowly. "But do me a favor and keep your ear to the ground. If Rook steps one toe out of line I want to know about it."

There was a brief pause. "You gonna be okay, son?" Carmichael asked. "I'll send somebody out to check on you if—"

"No, sir. I'm fine. I'll check in with you after the doc clears me to go back to work."

When Carmichael hung up, Jack threw his arm across his eyes. The faulty air conditioner added to his discomfort.

He groaned aloud when somebody banged on the door. Tomás was a good kid, but Jack wasn't up to dealing with his high-energy conversation.

Dragging himself to a sitting position, he let his head quit spinning before he tried to stagger to his feet. When he finally got the door open, he was glad he was leaning against the wall.

Standing before him dressed in impeccable gray slacks and a striped golf shirt, black medical bag in one hand and an enormous picnic basket in the other, was Elliot Fairchild.

"Lurch!" Jack said without thinking. "Dude, you missed the pediatric unit by a few miles."

Fairchild didn't seem bothered by the pejorative nickname. He sighed. "Yeah, house calls in this neighborhood don't pay real well." He hefted the picnic basket. "Meg wanted me to check on you, and Connie Santos sent you some…uh, soup I think."

Jack's nose had just zeroed in on the delicious smells issuing from the basket. Nausea disappearing, he backed away from the door to let the young physician in.

Fairchild looked around and chose the pressboard dresser as a receptacle for his Meals on Wheels offering. He set his medical bag on Jack's rickety table and took out a stethoscope. He gestured toward the chair. "Sit down and let's see if you permanently dislodged anything. Do you feel as bad as you look?"

Jack shook his head, but his knees buckled as he more or less fell into the chair. "I got a pretty hard head." He submitted to the stethoscope, breathing deeply as instructed, and followed the light with only slightly blurry vision. "I don't guess you have a Tylenol or something in that bag?"

"Sure. You're a little bigger than my usual patients," Fairchild commented as he put away his instruments, "but it's safe to say you'll live. Now maybe Meg will leave me alone."

Jack felt himself sagging a bit with the effort of sitting upright. "A bit on the persistent side, isn't she?"

"That's a euphemistic way to put it." Fairchild nodded toward the bed. "Go lie down before I have to scrape you off the floor. Can you handle some soup?" Jack's stomach gave a loud growl, and Fairchild laughed. "I'll fix it before I go."

Jack lay on the bed wondering at God's weird way of answering prayer. He felt cared for in a way he'd rarely experienced. Even though Meg wasn't physically in the room, he sensed her presence in the doctor's efficient movements, in the thick, warm chicken broth and noodles that filled his stomach, and in the get-well card that had been signed by half the membership of the church.

If Jack couldn't have Meg herself—and he couldn't, not until justice for Rico was paid out—then he could tell himself the Holy Spirit worked this way. As Someone you couldn't see, but Who made Himself known in a multitude of practical ways.

Jack was almost asleep when Elliot Fairchild took the bowl out of his hands and told him to lie down again.

"You'll feel a lot better in the morning," Fairchild said,

picking up his bag, "but don't try to go back to work this week
Oh, and one more thing." He turned off the light and opened
the door. "If you hurt Meg, it'll take more than chicken soup
and Tylenol to bring you back after I get through with you."

The door closed gently, and Jack began to laugh.

Warner was in the middle of a cattle roundup when his cell
phone vibrated against his hip.

"I thought you were going to get him out of the way," said
the Wolf. "A simple accident—no problem, right? What
happened?"

A herd of longhorns thundered past, followed by a couple
of whistling, shouting cowboys on horseback, and Warner
choked on a cloud of manure-laden dust.

"Wait a minute, I can't hear you," Warner said, coughing.

Adjusting the earpiece of his cell phone, he took his son
more firmly by the hand and pushed through the crowd of
tourists lining Rodeo Street. Jeri was out of town on a cheer-
leading gig with Brittany, so Warner had agreed to chaperone
Sean's second-grade field trip to the Stockyards. He was already
hot, dusty and irritated with the stench and the noise. Hearing
from his annoying partner put the perfect cap on the day.

"Don't worry, I've got a backup plan," Warner said, pulling a whining Sean into the air-conditioned lobby of the Vis-
itor's Center. "Here's some money, buddy. Go buy a souvenir."
He lowered his voice as his son ran toward a glass case full of
tin badges and cap guns. "But Torres isn't the entire problem.
Herrera's giving us trouble, too. He wants out after this run."

El Lobo grunted. "I hope you told him that ain't gonna
happen."

Warner watched the clerk give Sean a badge that said "U.S.
Marshal." Sean pinned it on his T-shirt. Warner could some-

what understand Herrera's weariness with *El Lobo's* constant demands. He hadn't made nearly enough money to make up for all the headaches this business had caused. Maybe he'd make this his last run, too.

"I'll make *sure* Herrera knows how serious we are," Warner said with more confidence than he felt. He hadn't gone to college for six years to learn how to whack nosy border patrol agents or intimidate recalcitrant wetbacks. He supposed it was a skill one had to learn on the job.

Chapter Fourteen

The Wednesday after Jack returned to work, Meg knelt in the shady herb garden, enjoying a break from the day's manic pace. The crew had worked like slaves for the last three days, leaving only the gazebo and a retaining wall to finish. If nothing else interfered, the Grover-Niles wedding would proceed as scheduled.

Meg broke off a sprig of mint and sniffed it, enjoying the pungent scent. In her opinion, Jack was going at it too hard— sunup to sundown, barely stopping for lunch—and the other men followed his example. He only spoke to her long enough to get instructions for the next project, and then he didn't meet her eyes.

She'd found herself watching him anxiously. His color was back to normal, and he'd lost the gaunt look he'd had when he first came back. He'd thanked her for sending Elliot to see him, commented on Connie's soup…and that was it.

This morning Sam and Mr. Warner had come out to the site for a surprise inspection. When Warner insisted on tramping around the estate, dragging along the supervisory crew, Meg had sensed Jack's presence behind her as potent as a physical touch. But when she glanced back, all she saw was her reflection in his sunglasses.

At least, Meg thought with a shiver, Warner had kept his slimy eyes to himself. He'd spent most of his time firing questions at Sam, who answered with the patience of Job. Then, to Meg's astonishment and rage, Warner had sent her off for an early lunch break while he stood in the open door of his car talking baseball with the men.

The last thing she'd seen as she rounded the corner of the house was Jack giving her one of those under-the-chin Spanky waves behind Warner's back. Cheered, she'd repaired to the herb garden to enjoy her burrito.

Okay, so it wasn't in the same league with "I came across time for you." At least the man had a sense of humor.

By Thursday, Jack was feeling like his normal self. Manny caught him as he was getting in the truck to move a load of field stones for a retaining wall that Meg wanted to build at the top of the steep hill above the creek.

Jack looked around to make sure they were out of earshot of the crew, and found them along the slope passing the water jug as they waited for instructions. Meg sat in the cab of her truck at the bottom of the incline, going over blueprints and gnawing on a pencil.

"Arrangements made," Manny said quietly. "We move tonight."

"*Tonight?* Why so little notice?"

Manny shrugged. "Arrangements are made," he repeated. "We have to be in Eagle Pass by two a.m. or miss the cover. Pick me up at eight."

"*El Lobo* will be there?"

Manny flinched as if the name struck a raw nerve. "I don't know. He stays in the shadow."

Jack had seen the same reaction when Vernon Rook had walked into the laundry three weeks ago. Instincts on end, he said offhandedly, "He's somebody local then?"

Manny stepped back. "They don't tell me much," he said. "I am small potatoes in this pot of soup."

Certain this quiet, capable man knew more than he let on, Jack decided to let it go for the moment. He had a six-hour drive to pick Manny's brains.

"All right. I'll get the truck and meet you at the church." He climbed behind the steering wheel of the truck. "I've got to move this thing, and I don't want to run over the stakes for the concrete. Direct me?"

"*¡Como no!*" Manny tucked his clipboard under his arm and backed down the hill to make room for Jack to navigate the truck.

Jack checked the rearview mirror. Here the lawn took a beautiful, steep incline, sweeping between terraced retaining walls, which would later be landscaped with flowering shrubs and ground cover. He'd give kudos to Meg for the clever design, but it was a tricky place in which to maneuver heavy equipment.

Watching Manny's minimal gestures in the side mirror, Jack released the emergency brake and began easing the truck and its still-loaded trailer backward down the hill. In the rearview mirror he caught a glimpse of Meg's truck. He wondered how she was going to handle the inevitable crash of her career when the company went down the tubes. She was going to have to start all over with a new boss, a different web of interoffice politics, and a major dent in her faith in people.

Good thing he wasn't going to be around to watch it happen. He'd be back where he belonged, doing what God had appointed him to do. Guarding the borders. Making sure people like Meg were—

Jack could feel it when the brake failed. Felt the pedal clank onto the floorboard, felt his stomach turn wrong side out, felt the death grip of his hands on the steering wheel as the truck accelerated down the hill.

The stone-laden trailer swung a wild arc to the left. Sickening paralysis pounced, as it had when the tree was about to smash into Tomás. Manny ran sideways, stumbled and rolled. The truck lurched, and the loaded trailer wrenched the steering wheel out of control.

Events unfolded so fast, Jack couldn't tell what had happened to Manny. The trailer crashed against Meg's pickup, halting the truck with a grinding of gears and motor.

Meg had been in the cab with the door open, seat belt off.

Aftershocks jolted Jack's body. He fumbled to open the door, fell out, spat dirt out of his mouth, then pushed to his knees and looked wildly around. Manny lay a short distance up the hill, clutching a leg bent at a weird angle.

"Meg!" Jack shouted. Not seeing her, he staggered to his feet, a hand on the open door of the truck for balance. "Meg!"

He skidded the last few feet down the hill, past the trailer imbedded in the back of the little Toyota. Clambering over the trailer, he hit the ground on the other side. The door was still open. Relief blindsided him when he saw that Meg wasn't inside.

Head spinning, he leaned against the buckled-in bed of the pickup. He had to get to Manny. He was vaguely aware of the rest of the crew running toward him. Shouts, both English and Spanish, blew past him, as the men ran to help the injured crew leader.

"Meg, where are you?" Jack's stomach heaved, and he put the back of his hand hard against his mouth.

Suddenly there she was, flinging her arms around his waist, burrowing her head against his chest. "Jack, are you all right?"

"Meg!" He enfolded her, held her strongly until she squealed in discomfort. "Sorry." He eased his hold. "I'm okay, but Manny—"

"I've already called an ambulance. Jack, you better sit down."

He stared at her, hands on her shoulders. Reality crashed down. It was his own fault Manny was injured and Meg had nearly died. He'd been thinking about her, not paying enough attention to operating the truck.

Like Rico had been distracted, worried about getting home to Isabel, just before the snipers in Eagle Pass had mown him down.

"I said I'm fine." He sent Meg away and turned to walk up the hill. "I'll sit down later."

Meg watched the ambulance scream away toward the hospital. It had felt weird not to go with Manny, but she'd made the tough decision to send Diego instead. With Jack still looking like a pasty-faced caricature of himself, Meg knew she needed to stick around. She'd go see Manny after dealing with the trauma onsite.

Meg turned to find Jack moving into the open door of the truck, where he collapsed onto the seat. Concerned, she bent to study his face. She wanted to touch him, but was held back by the stiffness of his body. He was a man apart right now.

"Okay," she said on a deep breath, "tell me what happened."

"The brakes went out." Jack lowered his head. "I could have killed you and Manny both."

"And yourself." She shuddered.

"Maybe." He gripped his thighs, and she saw that his hands shook. "Meg, I want you to quit this job."

"Are you crazy? I'm just about to get my promotion."

"Then take a vacation. It's not safe while I'm here." He looked up, eyes fierce.

Her breath left her. "This wasn't an accident, either, was it?"

His mouth was a hard, grim line. "I've made somebody really mad, and until I find out who—" Abruptly, he stood up. "Listen, Meg, it's time we laid our cards on the table. I've spent more time with you than any woman in my adult life. Not because I had to, but because I *wanted* to." He cut himself off, then continued as if the words were ground out of him. "I'm not going to let you stick around where people keep arranging accidents."

"You're not going to *let* me?" she demanded, half angry, half amused. "What do you propose to do about it?"

Before she could blink, he'd hauled her close, taking the back of her head in his hand to tilt her face up. He covered her mouth with his, absorbing her shock, kissing her with frustrated tenderness and deadly purpose until she had no choice but to kiss him back.

A long moment later, Jack pulled away and laid his forehead against hers. She waited in vain for a declaration of love or explanation or…well, *something*.

She cleared her throat. "That—um, that's the way to chase me away."

"Meg." His voice softened. "I told you if this happened, there wouldn't be any going back. But I have to do my job. And I need you out of the way."

Meg gulped. If *what* happened? The accident and that kiss had been just about on a par for cataclysmic events.

"Would one of you two lovebirds like to explain what's going on around here?"

Meg's glance jerked up and over Jack's shoulder. "Sam! Boy, are we glad to see you." She put her fingers to tingling lips. They probably glowed like neon.

"What is all this?" Sam thundered, the sweep of his arm encompassing the two trucks sandwiched together and the crew milling about the site like discombobulated sheep. "I get a call that one of the men has been run over by one of our own vehicles. Then I get here and find you two—"

"It's not what you think," Meg said, wincing at Sam's snort of disbelief. "Jack was moving the field stones, but the truck's brakes gave, and Manny couldn't get clear fast enough. My truck was in the way, too, but I got out." She crossed her arms. "I was—we were just relieved. A lot."

Sam removed his glasses and pinched the bridge of his nose. "It's a mercy nobody was killed," he muttered. He moved to survey the wreckage. "All these vehicles are serviced and checked regularly. How could the brakes have gone out?"

"They were fine this morning when we came on-site," Jack said.

Sam held up his hands. "Meg, get your crew and equipment rounded up, knock off for the day, and both of you meet me in my office in an hour."

"But I wanted to go to the hospital to check on Manny," Meg protested.

Sam sighed. "I know. But we can't leave this without investigating its cause. There'll be a pile of reports to fill out, and since you were a witness I need your input. And Torres—" Sam paused with a grim look "—keep your hands to yourself."

* * *

In Sam's office, Jack watched Kenneth Warner come unglued.

After interrogating both Jack and Meg for nearly an hour, Sam had paged Warner. Most unhappy about being called out of an executive finance meeting, Warner had listened to Sam outline today's accident in brutal detail.

Warner scowled at Meg. "How could you let this happen?"

"Meg had nothing to do with it," Sam intervened in his deep, measured drawl. He glanced at Jack. "I had a conversation with the mechanic a little while ago. He confirmed the brakes on that truck were fine. Now this is serious business. My people start getting injured, I'm thinking we need to call in the police." Sam steepled thick fingers against his chin. His tone sharpened. "What about you, Mr. Warner?"

Warner sat up in alarm. "We don't need the police anywhere near us. We just bid on some city contracts. They'll go out the window if there's any hint of scandal."

"Scandal!" Meg blurted. "What about the poor guy who's in the hospital with his leg in traction?"

Warner gave her a harassed look. "Herrera will be taken care of, naturally. But since trouble seems to be following you around, I suggest you let the big boys take over from here."

Meg's eyes kindled. "Trouble might not find me such an easy target if the big boys would do more than chest-bump one another on the way to the next business deal."

Jack was glad he had situated his chair so that he could observe both Thornton and Warner. Maybe he was about to sort out the buzzards from the cuckoos in this crowded nest.

Thornton hid a smile, but Warner's expression hardened. "Keep in mind, sweetheart, you won't have a job if the company folds. Mr. Crowley seems determined to keep you on, so you might as well swallow the hard facts. Running this business isn't all grubbing in the dirt, or even painting pretty designs on the computer. It's winning new contracts, shuffling paper and looking good for the government agencies that keep tabs on us. And then there's keeping the payroll under control—" Warner wrenched his tirade short.

Jack decided it was time to weigh in. "If you don't mind a comment from a guy who grubs in the dirt—" he looked at Meg and watched her eyes light "—we all appreciate your efforts to keep the company solvent." Warner looked mollified. Jack continued with a slight edge. "Still, I suggest we at least attempt an in-house investigation. You know, to cover our bases."

Warner's eyes narrowed. "That sounds reasonable." He paused and fiddled with his tie. "Do you think you were the intended target?"

"Target?" Jack rubbed his nose. "Don't know if I'd go that far. Anyway, Herrera drives that truck as often as I do."

"Herrera?" Warner snorted. "Why bother with him?"

Wanting to shake this rat by the neck, Jack shrugged. "Herrera's a good man, and I'm not gonna stand around and watch him get run over again. Figuratively or literally."

Veins popped out above Warner's pristine collar. "*I* certainly wouldn't want to be the one to cross you, Torres."

Satisfied that he had made his point, Jack looked at Sam. "Meg and I need to check on Herrera. Are we done here for the day?"

Sam rolled back in his chair, rubbing the back of his neck. "Go ahead. I'll finish up this paperwork and talk to you tomorrow."

As Jack followed Meg out of the office, he intercepted Warner's baleful glare.

Sam, apparently not noticing, was shaking his head and muttering to himself, "Mr. Crowley's gonna have an aneurism."

Warner left Sam Thornton and went straight to his office, pausing only to bark at Sharon Inge, who was e-mailing a picture of a tulip farm in Oregon to her sister. On company time.

"But I was on my break!" Sharon protested as Warner slammed the door on her.

He punched in the emergency number the Wolf had made him memorize. "He's threatening me now," Warner announced. "This thing's out of control."

"What happened to your grand scheme?" mocked *El Lobo*. "Knocking off two birds et cetera?"

"All I can say is, that truck should have killed them both. Herrera's in the hospital with his leg in traction, so I think he's scared enough to keep his mouth shut. But Torres walked away without a scratch."

There was an exaggerated sigh on the other end of the line. "All right, here's what we'll do. Send him on down to the border for the transfer tonight. There'll be plenty of crossfire to take care of him." *El Lobo* paused. "In fact, I'll handle it myself. Should have done it from the get-go."

"I don't like this," Warner said. He could feel a tension headache coming on. "What if he's setting us up?"

"What if he is?" The Wolf sounded not at all concerned. "Forewarned is forearmed, right?"

"Yeah, but there's the girl. What if she goes to the police when Torres doesn't come home?"

The Wolf's tone turned ominous. "Why would she do that?"

"I'm fairly sure she knows who he is." Warner didn't know any such thing, but he could manipulate facts to suit his purposes. "One of my men saw her at his apartment after the first accident. And just now, the way he looked at her..." Warner swallowed the bile of envy. He had many reasons to hate Torres.

"Then I'll just have to take care of her, too. Where did she go after the meeting?"

"She and Torres were going to the hospital."

"All right. Just sit tight, Warner, and let the pros handle the situation."

At this point Warner had no alternative. "Lobo, if you're double-crossing me you'll be sorry," he blustered.

The Wolf chuckled. "You might want to get ready for your own run for the border."

"Meg, I want you out of this mess. This situation could blow up at any minute."

Meg looked up at Jack, who had leaned down to prop his folded arms along the open window frame of her car. They'd just spent an hour with Manny, making sure he was comfortable. At least, Meg assumed that was what they'd been doing; more than half the conversation had been conducted in Spanish.

"Find another job," he continued before she could do more than shake her head. "Your dad would set you up with your own business if you just crooked your little pinkie."

"I've worked too hard to get where I am." She looked at Jack's mouth, barely six inches from hers. "I could put my pinkie to better uses."

He looked away. "Meg—"

"Jack, we have to talk about this. I'm not going to ignore—"

He gave her a slow grin. "Oh, you mean that little song and dance for Sam's benefit."

Meg's emotions took a cold-water bath. "What does Sam have to do with it?"

"I figured he'd yank you into the office ASAP if he saw a little fraternizing going on." He stood up and winked. "You didn't take it seriously, did you?"

"Of course not," Meg said, swallowing. "I was just making sure *you* didn't." Her cell phone rang, and she fished for it in her purse. "I'd better take this. It might be my parents."

With a lazy salute, Jack walked toward his motorcycle.

Meg blinked. The blinding afternoon sun that reflected off her rearview mirror would explain why her eyes were watering.

The phone rang again, and she finally found it under the seat. "Hello?"

"Meg! Where have you been?" exclaimed Benny. "I've been trying to call you for hours. My missions appointment came through this afternoon!"

Jack decided his next move should be a consultation with his OIC. He paged Carmichael and met him at the bus station. Over a cup of coffee in the lounge, he filled Carmichael in on the truck incident and the ensuing meeting with Warner and Thornton.

"I can't decide if Warner was targeting me or Herrera," Jack finished. "I just spent an hour with Herrera at the hospital. Warner knows where Herrera's wife and kids are, and has threatened to hurt them if he talks."

Carmichael, who had listened without comment, rubbed his hand over his face. "Does Herrera know you're border patrol?"

"No," Jack said. "But he knows I didn't run over him on purpose. He asked me to do what I can to protect his family from the goons."

"That's useful." Carmichael frowned. "But there's another complication. Your instincts about Vernon Rook were dead-on. I finally hit the right channel to confirm that he's been under internal investigation. They were keeping it quiet because of all the media coverage focused on the agency lately."

Jack felt like he'd been hit in the stomach. "I can't believe Vernon's gone that far off the deep end. He's been in the service for forty years!"

"It wouldn't be the first time it's happened." Carmichael looked grim. "Word is, his wife's illness has taken its toll. People do crazy things when they're in financial straits."

"So Rook didn't believe me when I told him I'd gotten out?" Jack gripped the table, wishing the thought of his former mentor going rogue hadn't been confirmed. "He's the border patrol connection of this gang?"

Carmichael shrugged. "I think that's pretty clear."

"Cute little triangle they've worked out." Jack released a slow breath. "They've got Rook controlling the crossing points, Herrera providing the coyotes and mules, and Warner taking care of distribution on this end."

Carmichael was silent for a moment. "The only way to take down the whole cartel is to stick to the original plan."

"I don't know, Carmichael. These guys aren't playing games. With Herrera in the hospital, I'll be on my own down there."

"I don't think we've got any other option. It's all set, right?"

Jack nodded. "I drive the truck down to Eagle Pass tonight for the pickup. Soon as Warner pays me, we make the bust."

"I've alerted handpicked agents in Eagle Pass. They'll be watching out for you." Carmichael squinted, watching Jack narrowly. "Something about the setup bother you?"

"It's just…" Jack paused. "I've been working this case all summer. Herrera's just a poor chump who tried to sneak his family across the line the cheap way, and wound up in over his head. If we could offer him immunity, I bet we could get more out of him."

"I'm willing to entertain the idea. Let's see how things go night, then we'll see where we are." Carmichael reached to his pocket and pulled out a cigar. "What are your plans ter we have these clowns behind bars?"

Jack shrugged. "Back to the border, I guess."

A puff of smoke hid Carmichael's irregular features. "What out the young lady? You gonna take her with you?"

Jack didn't pretend not to know what the OIC meant. Meg's a landscaper, Carmichael. Nothing grows down there it carrizo and rattlesnakes." Jack shifted in his chair. "Bedes, I wouldn't put anybody I cared about through what Isel Valenzuela has gone through since Rico died."

The smoke cleared enough for Carmichael's dry smile to ppear. "That's a mighty pessimistic outlook."

"Just realistic." Jack more than cared for Meg. He loved her ith a passion that wanted the best for her. He couldn't ask er to give up family, career and mission to follow him. But hining about it wouldn't change anything. Jack pushed back is chair. "Better go. One more thing to take care of before I ave."

Carmichael looked at his watch. "All right. What's your metable?"

"I'm supposed to hit *el puente negro* no later than two m." Jack stood up. "I'll be at the Spanish church on James r the next hour or so. I'm leaving from there."

Carmichael looked curious. "I wouldn't have taken you for religious man, Torres."

Jack hesitated, rubbing the back of his neck. He had no idea here his OIC stood with God, but Meg and Ramón would all this an open invitation. Time to quit being a coward.

"It's not just religion, Carmichael. I'm learning to take my ith into every part of my life." Jack managed a sheepish grin.

"When you're going into battle, a little spiritual armor can' hurt, right?"

"I guess not," said Carmichael dubiously. He stubbed ou his cigar and dismissed Jack with a cynical flip of the hand "Give my regards to the Man Upstairs, then, would you?"

Inwardly wincing, Jack nodded and left. At least he'd tried

Chapter Fifteen

"Benny, I'm home!" Meg pushed the kitchen door shut with her foot and wearily leaned against it. She wished she could as easily close the door on her anxieties.

In six weeks, Benny was going off to Mexico. Not just a short-term Backyard Bible Club mission, but for keeps. Leaving America behind.

Leaving *me* behind, Meg thought, gaze skimming all the little indications of her roommate's personality. A collection of pictures on the refrigerator, teenagers Benny had been praying for. A pair of orange rubber flip-flops beside the door. A Greek Bible commentary on the table. A Brazilian butterfly pressed between glass disks hanging on the wall. It was going to be awfully lonely around here without Benny's calm, steady presence.

Jack's going to leave me behind, too. No matter what he said, that kiss hadn't been anybody's song and dance. Possessive came close to describing it. And he was off playing hero now. She could tell by the way he'd walked away from her without looking back.

"Why'd I have to fall in love with a guy with a hero com plex?" she muttered, pushing away from the door. She raise her voice. "Ben, where are you?"

"I'm at the computer," she heard from the living room "Come here, Meg, and tell me what this is."

Meg shoved open the swinging door between the two rooms and found Benny sitting on the sofa with her compute in her lap. Her curly hair was twisted on top of her head and secured with a yellow pencil, and a pair of gold-rimmed read ing glasses perched on her nose.

"What's what?" Meg said lightly. No sense making every body depressed by airing her discontent.

"This picture disk. Who are these people?"

Meg leaned over Benny's shoulder to see what she was looking at. "Oh, those are some photos Tomás took with Dad's camera after the Fourth of July party. Didn't he do a good job?"

"Yeah, but have you seen this video clip at the end?" Benny double-clicked an icon, and it began to play.

Meg abruptly straightened. She didn't want to see Jack act ing drunk again. "I meant to erase that."

"It looks like Tomás was hiding when he filmed it. See the weird angle? And it's partially obscured by a curtain or something."

Meg came around the sofa to sit down beside Benny "What are they saying? It went by so fast I couldn't trans late it."

"They're talking about transporting something across the border."

"Oh, that." Meg laughed. "Apparently they were all chicken farmers back in Mexico. I heard Manny and Efrin talking one day—"

"Meg, *'pollos'* doesn't just mean 'chickens.' That's also what they call people who come across the border illegally."

Meg stared at her roommate. "How do you know?"

"Never mind, I just know. Did you hear them talking about coyotes, too?"

Meg nodded, wide-eyed. "What does that mean?"

"A *coyote* is a guide, the person who arranges tubes to cross the river and safe houses and transportation north."

Meg's eyes widened as she remembered the conversation she'd overheard at Jack's baptism. "Benny, what does *'pa-arte'*...um, something like... *'cuando entregues'* mean?"

Benny slammed the computer shut. "'I'll pay, you deliver.' Meg, we'd better take this to the police."

"No, wait a minute!" Meg put her hands to her face, thinking. Jack had been living among these men all summer, probably setting up some kind of sting. He'd made her promise not to tell anybody who he was. How was she going to keep Benny out of it? "Let me have the disk, and I'll take it straight to border patrol."

Benny frowned. "What do you know about border patrol?"

"Nothing," Meg said hastily. "But I'm going to find out." A thought occurred to her. "Benny, what did they say after Jack left the room?"

"Something about taking out *la migra.* That's border patrol." Benny's face flamed with uncharacteristic fury. "Meg, I cannot *believe* we fell for this con man. You take care of this and call me back within an hour, or I'm going to the police myself."

Speechless with shock, Meg nodded.

"Taking out *la migra*" meant Jack.

They knew who he was. They were going to kill him.

Jack didn't know why the church had been left unlocked. He could only reflect that God knew his need. Face down, arms pulled into his chest, he half knelt, half lay at the bottom of the carpeted altar steps. All his life he had responded to threat with action. Now he could only lie still under God's hand.

Jack rolled onto his back, feeling the edge of the altar steps dig into his shoulder blades. The only light switch he'd been able to find had lit the foyer and the choir loft, where a rustic wooden cross hung. The sanctuary was shadowy and stuffy and smelled like dust. He tipped his head back so that he looked at the cross upside down.

Something had compelled him to come here, no doubt not knowing what might happen tonight. He thought about Meg's refuge at the Water Gardens.

Water, water, everywhere…

"Wouldn't be my first choice of places to go," he muttered aloud. Feeling God smile at him, he relaxed. "Yeah, so I'm afraid of water and I'm afraid to die."

Well, that wasn't exactly it. He wasn't afraid of death anymore. But he sure wasn't *eager* to die. He'd really like to see where this thing with Meg might lead.

Then the truth slammed him between the eyes. He'd been right to mislead her earlier, downplaying his feelings for her. His job, who he *was,* affected the people he was close to. He couldn't claim to love Meg and endanger her life on a daily basis.

It would be cowardly to start anything with her.

Well, judging by that intense kiss, things were a little more than *started.*

"Okay, God, why'd You send along a woman like her in the middle of this mess? You've yanked the rug out from under me so many times—"

He covered his eyes with his forearm, obliterating the cross, but other images kept flashing. The ambulance pulling away with his mother. Screaming sirens and lights flashing across Rico's broken body. Dottie Rook's tired voice on the phone.

"What if I die? What if I live and I have to leave Meg?" *What if, what if.* "I can't do this again."

Above the unanswerable questions, Scripture drifted into his mind. *I lay down My life for the sheep, and they will listen to My voice.* Tired of struggling, he let tears run down his temples and into his hair.

Okay, take me, Lord. Take my weakness and fear. Take my selfishness, rebellion and resentment. Do what I can't do. Go where I can't go. Break me apart and put me back together.

In thirty-two years he'd never felt so alone and vulnerable. And, paradoxically, so sheltered. Maybe Vernon Rook was a traitor, but Jesus had dealt with worse.

He'd just read in the Bible this morning that God would work good out of the worst circumstances.

Help me hold on to that, Lord.

He was just about to drag himself to his feet when his beeper buzzed against his hip. Sitting up, he looked at the number in the display window.

He didn't recognize it and almost deleted it.

Something made him press the save button.

In the parking lot behind the Euless border patrol office, which shared an unassuming brick building with Immigration, Detention and Deportation, Meg stopped next to an SUV with a border patrol insignia on the door. It was late, almost seven o'clock, but maybe somebody would still be here. She locked up the Mustang, then headed for a glass door with modest block lettering.

A secretary looked up as Meg entered the main office area. "May I help you?"

"I'd like to speak to Agent Jack Torres." Meg had no idea if Jack would actually be here. But surely someone would know him.

The woman lifted a pair of reading glasses hung on a chain around her neck. After surveying Meg thoroughly, she pushed a button on the phone. "Sir, there's a young lady here to see Agent Torres."

After a brief silence, someone barked over the intercom. "What?"

"I said—"

"Never mind, send her in."

The secretary jerked her head toward the door behind her.

Meg knocked timidly, opening supervisory agent Dennis Carmichael's door when she heard him growl, "Come in."

A craggy-faced, middle-aged man with thinning gray hair, agent Carmichael stood as Meg entered the room. He wore a border patrol uniform, one empty sleeve of which was pinned to his shoulder. With his good hand he gestured toward a folding chair. "Sit down. I'm Torres's supervisor. What can I do for you?"

Meg sat. "I'm Meg St. John," she began, nervously looking around the windowless office. The metal desk was piled with towering stacks of overstuffed manila files, two half-empty mugs of black coffee, and a stinking Skoal can that apparently served as an ashtray for the cigar clamped between Carmichael's teeth. She gave him a cautious smile. "First of all, Jack would be really mad if he knew I'd come here."

The officer plucked the cigar from his mouth, and Meg noticed his lips looked funny on one side. "I'm guessing you have a good reason," he said.

"Yes, sir. I tried to get hold of Jack, but his phone's been busy, and I'm not sure he's even—" She stopped, feeling utterly stupid now that she was here. "I thought somebody needed to see this." She laid the picture disk on Carmichael's desk.

"What is it?"

"Somebody in the company I work for is running a smuggling operation. There's a video on that disk that proves it." Meg pressed her fingers between her knees. "I called once before, but the only thing that happened was, I got reprimanded for disloyalty."

Carmichael jammed the cigar into the Skoal can. Without further comment, he sat down and put the disk into his computer. After a moment the video clip appeared on the screen. When it blinked off, he turned to Meg. "Where'd you get this?"

"A young man on my crew took it with my dad's camera, and I wound up with it. I've had it for a few weeks, but—" Something told Meg not to bring Benny into this. "It took some time to translate the Spanish."

Carmichael rubbed his hand across his mouth. "I see. Miss St. John, would you be able to identify the men in the video?"

"Yes, sir. I work with them every day."

Carmichael nodded. "Good. I need you to come with me."

Meg caught her breath. "Come with you? Why?"

"Obviously Torres is walking into a trap. He's already left for the border. We've got to stop this."

"But—" Meg stood up so fast the chair rocked on two legs. "You want me to go all the way to the *border* with you? I can't do that!"

Carmichael looked stern. "I'm afraid you have to. Jack's life is in danger."

Meg stared at Jack's supervisor with her mouth open.

She'd known instinctively that she'd seen something critical, but it hadn't occurred to her that she was directly involved. Fear kicked her in the stomach.

Lord! I'm no super-chick. What am I supposed to do?

Meg tried to think. "Okay. Okay, can't you just call Jack and tell him—"

"He's deep undercover. If I call him, he's dead."

Meg sat down again, abruptly. Her love for Jack canceled her fear for herself.

"Okay. I'll come." Her voice shook, and she cleared her throat. "Let me just call my roommate and tell her where I am."

"You can't tell anybody." Carmichael turned to shut down the computer. "He's already got a good head start, so we have to leave now."

"Now?" Meg suddenly felt like an overcooked spaghetti noodle. "*Now?*"

Without answering, Carmichael opened a drawer and pulled out a handgun, which he slid into a holster at his waist.

"I guess now's as good a time as any," Meg said meekly.

Jack pulled the eighteen-wheeler up to a pay phone in a nearby gas station. He got out, pushed his money into the slot and dialed the number on his pager display window.

The phone rang once before it was answered by a familiar gravelly voice. "Rook here."

"Vernon, how did you get this number?"

Rook ignored Jack's question. "Where are you?"

"Where are *you?*" Jack retorted. "I already told you—"

"Listen, son, I got information related to your case. We need to talk *now.*"

Jack's mind raced. Carmichael had said Rook was under investigation. Besides that, new information should have been forwarded directly to Jack, not passed through an agent un-related to the case. What was going on here?

"Okay," he said. "I'm at a quick-stop at the corner of James and Felix."

"Don't move. I'll be there in ten minutes." The phone went dead.

Jack looked at his watch. He had an hour to kill, so he could afford to hear what Rook had to say.

Back in the cab of the truck, Jack sat with the windows down, listening to the desultory sound of traffic lurching by on James Avenue, punctuated by the occasional boom of hip-hop music blaring from an open window. The sunlight had faded to warm, murky dimness. He was due at the border by 2:00 a.m., where he'd shuffle the aliens to a safe house under cover of darkness. They'd hide out during the daylight hours, then complete the trip north tomorrow night.

The minutes inched by. Jack pulled out a stick of gum and, to pass the time, opened his Bible to Isaiah.

Those who wait on the Lord will find new strength. They will fly high on wings like eagles. They will run and not grow weary. They will walk and not faint.

Pretty good bunch of words for a guy headed to a show-down in Eagle Pass. Jack prayed for Meg, the Herreras and Miss Dottie, then for Carmichael's salvation and for a safe trip tonight.

Fifteen minutes went by, and he considered calling Rook again. Or calling Meg. His stomach churned.

Don't get distracted, Torres.

He was looking at his watch again when Rook's border pa-trol cruiser suddenly pulled into the gas station.

Jack got out and slid into the front seat of the sedan. He forced himself to relax. "What's up, Vernon?"

"Hey, kid." Rook reached to turn down the radio static. "I hear you got a big party on for the next couple of days."

"What are you talking about?"

"I got reason to believe Carmichael may be on the take."

So the gloves were off. Unexpected rage flared in Jack. Where did this slug get off accusing *Carmichael* of treachery? He took a breath to keep his tone cool. "What am I supposed to do about it?"

Rook leaned forward to prop his arms on the steering wheel and glanced at Jack. "Don't go through with this run tonight."

Was that a warning or a threat? Baffled, Jack studied Rook's puffy face. He'd lost some of the red-brown sunburn that characterized officers who spent much of every day patrolling the border in the baking south Texas sun. As a young cop, Jack had trusted Vernon Rook with his life. Rico Valenzuela's death, however, had shaken Jack's faith in almost everyone.

"Okay, Vernon. Warning taken."

"So you're not going?" Rook's stare was steely, as if he were back to giving instructions to a rookie.

Jack shrugged. "Let's just say I'm not changing any plans until I know where you got your information."

Rook glared. "I don't think you're takin' me seriously."

Jack rubbed the back of his neck. Sitting here in the presence of his enemy, he didn't know what to believe. But a shadow of frustrated near-panic in his former mentor's faded brown eyes kept him in the car. "Look, I know what I'm doing. But I gotta tell you, Vernon, you worry me. How long before you retire?"

Rook gave a short guffaw. "Retire? Boy I ain't *retirin'*. I got a bunch more good years in me." Rook's once-handsome face tightened. "I've been up for sector chief for some time, and I'd like to see it happen before they put me out to pasture."

Alarms went off in Jack's brain. Here was motivation that confirmed the crime. Still, a grain of sympathy, maybe even respect, remained for this limping, toothless, aging wolf.

Jack put his hand on the door. "I hope you make it, Vernon. But don't worry about me, all right? Give Dottie my love."

As Jack moved to get out of the car, Rook grabbed his shoulder hard. "I'm telling you one more time, boy, don't believe anything Carmichael tells you." The deep voice turned harsh. "You'll get yourself killed if you do."

Jack just looked at him. This was crazy.

An insane man was an extremely dangerous man.

"All right." Jack shrugged off the older man's hand. "I've got an idea. I can't change what's set up for tonight, but you can come with me."

Hoping *he* hadn't just gone over the edge, he watched relief lighten Rook's expression.

"You're serious?" Rook demanded.

"Yeah." Jack checked the time. It was after eight. "But we gotta leave now. It's a long way to the border."

Keeping Rook under surveillance was either the stupidest or the most brilliant idea Jack had ever had.

He hoped it was the latter.

Meg stared out the window at empty prairie cut only by the ribbon of black highway. The sun was steadily melting into a puddle of magenta and orange that blended into the evening sky.

She was shivering, and not just because Agent Carmichael was apparently at home in meat locker temperatures. Chauvinistic bosses, undocumented crews, even wrestling with the Sunflowers That Ate Fort Worth paled in comparison to the pickle she was in.

She glanced at Carmichael, wishing he'd tell her more about

what was going on. She was getting a very queasy feeling about this expedition. Carmichael might be Jack's boss, an officer of the law, but when it came down to it she didn't know him from Adam's housecat. It was after dark, and she didn't know when she'd be getting back home. Her dad was going to kill her.

She folded her arms. "Mr. Carmichael, you have to let me call my parents. They'll be worried about me. I promise I won't tell them anything about Jack's…uh, operation. Whatever you call it." After thinking about it for two hours, the whole thing was sounding too melodramatic.

Carmichael glanced at Meg in surprise, as if he'd forgotten all about her. "No phone calls."

Meg stared at him bewildered. "But why?"

Carmichael's focus returned to the highway. "Miss St. John, you're just going to have to trust me. Why don't you fill me in on what you know about your employer?"

Meg shook her head. "Mr. Crowley's a fine man."

"Maybe. Maybe not. You called border patrol back in April, and again in June. You must suspect somebody in the company."

"I did make a call in June, but that was the only time—" She stopped. "That means somebody else has noticed something funny going on." She didn't like the look on Carmichael's face. "But I don't know anything for sure."

"Who else have you talked to about your suspicions?"

"Just—nobody but Jack."

"Are you sure? It's very important that you not lie to me."

"Mr. Carmichael," she said, "the only reason I called INS that day was because I was tired of losing my crew every other week. I generally keep a low profile to keep from being Mr. Warner's punching bag."

"How did you find out Torres is border patrol?"

Meg looked at him uneasily. Would Jack be in trouble because of her? "It was an accident. I brought him some clothes when he was in the hospital. I heard Jack telling the doctor not to file some OSHA report."

"Are you and Torres lovers?"

"Of course not!" Meg exclaimed, horrified.

"You were seen going into his room."

"But he wasn't even there!"

"He kissed you today."

"How would you know that?" Meg's voice rose. "Did Jack tell you—"

Carmichael chuckled. "You're a beautiful girl, and I'd be surprised if Torres *hadn't* decided to mark his territory. How well do you know him?"

"Jack hasn't told me much that's personal," Meg managed to get out in spite of her embarrassment. "And I'm sure most of what he *has* said is a lie."

Carmichael shot her an amused glance. "You sound resentful. You in love with him?"

Unable to deny it, Meg looked away.

"Unfortunately, it's part of his job to keep things from people." Carmichael's voice was sympathetic. "If you decide to stay with him, you'll have to learn to live with that."

"He's made it clear I won't have to worry about it."

Carmichael shook his head. "Give him time. He lost a partner in a shoot-out about this time last year."

"So at least *that* was the truth," Meg blurted.

Carmichael looked at her sharply. "He *has* talked to you."

"He just said a close friend had died. I didn't know it was his partner." Sadness for Jack swamped Meg, for the moment displacing her anxiety. No wonder he had a hard time allowing anybody close to him.

"The boy's seen a lot of violence," Carmichael said. "He's a former Marine."

Meg swallowed. "Really?"

"Border patrol has a new program of bringing in veterans of the wars in the Middle East." Meg tried to pin down something odd that had seeped into Carmichael's tone. "Supposedly they've got the training in covert ops that we're looking for. These young guys will eventually replace all of us old guard."

"That must make you feel sort of…strange."

"I've learned to deal with it."

For some reason, a shiver went down the back of Meg's neck. After an uncomfortable moment she said, "How much farther?"

"We'll be in Eagle Pass in about four hours. But we'll stop for gas in San Antonio."

Meg's pulse jumped. Maybe she could get to a phone then. "That sounds good," she said agreeably. "I didn't have any supper and I'm hungry."

Truth be told, her stomach was the least of her concerns right now. She was trying hard to appear calm and cool, but what she was, was scared and confused.

God seemed as far away as the stars winking overhead. But experience had taught Meg that He often went silent during the times He was working major change.

Lord, she thought, *please be close to Jack right now. I don't know where he is, but maybe he needs You as much as I do.*

Chapter Sixteen

Jack's prayers continued to zoom through his mind as he and Rook left San Antonio behind.

He knew God was listening, even in the silence.

And Rook was silent. He'd been sitting on the other side of the truck for four hours, with his hat on one knee.

Finally Jack had had enough. He reached over to turn the radio off. "Vernon, what were you doing outside the ice-cream shop that night?"

Rook looked at Jack. "Saw you and Carmichael at the Q one night," he said. "So I followed you to see what you were up to."

"What did you think, when I told you I'd left border patrol?"

"I didn't believe you." Rook flapped the hat against his leg. "I knew you must be cut up about Valenzuela. Dottie had been pestering me for months to call you, but I kept putting her off." He shrugged. "You know I ain't much for the touchy-feely stuff."

Jack snorted. Couldn't argue with that.

"Figured you must be after Valenzuela's killers." Rook cleared his throat. "I decided if you were too stupid to see through Carmichael, I'd better watch your back."

"Is that right?" Jack had to laugh.

"You're the one with the college education," said Rook with a sour smile. "But sometimes plain old common sense beats a pile of book-learning."

"Point taken. But I can't help wondering what you've been up to during the last six years. You always told me you'd never leave the border."

"Dottie's doctor is here," Rook said. "She's in line for a new kidney, and we have to be close if a donor comes available."

Jack drove in silence for several miles, reviewing what he knew about the case and everything Rook had said tonight. Undeniably, Dottie was a very sick woman. If Jack had a chance to save the life of the woman he loved, there was no question where he'd be.

He glanced at Rook and found him gazing out the window. The older man's face was gray with fatigue and sadness.

Jack found himself saying, "All right, Vernon, I'm going to give you one shot at convincing me Carmichael's the crook and not you. It better be good."

Meg adored cashews, but she looked with revulsion at the bag of nuts in her hand. Fear had a way of making one queasy.

The stop in San Antonio for gas had provided her with no opportunity to find a phone or talk to anyone. Carmichael had accompanied her inside the convenience store and politely waited for her while she went into the restroom. Then he'd bought her a soft drink and a snack before escorting her back to the SUV.

Over an hour ago, they'd passed through the little town of Uvalde. Now they were back in the middle of nowhere, but they ought to be getting close to the border.

I'm not putting up with this anymore. "Mr. Carmichael, did you say Jack's meeting us in Eagle Pass?"

"He'll be there," Carmichael said. Without a signal of any sort, he suddenly turned the SUV into a gravel side road, set off by culverts on either side and guarded by an iron gate. With a neat three-point turn, he backed into place with the rear bumper against the gate. The headlights went off.

Meg's stomach knotted. "What are we doing?"

"Waiting."

"Waiting for what?"

Carmichael just looked at her, then returned his attention to the darkness in front of the car.

Meg remembered an article she'd read about young women tricked into driving off with fake highway patrolmen, never to be seen alive again. But Carmichael was the real deal. She'd actually seen him in his office. Besides, the man's apparent total disinterest in her mitigated her anxiety.

She tried to remember if Jack had said anything to indicate he was planning to leave town tonight.

"I don't think Jack's going to be very happy to see me," she said. "He told me more than once to stay out of this, so I wouldn't get hurt."

"Is that right?" At last she had Carmichael's attention.

She wished she'd kept her mouth shut. "Yes, sir." Maybe she should change the subject. "This must be a really dangerous job," she babbled. "I've been wondering how you lost your arm."

Carmichael seemed to be thinking over whether or not he was going to answer her. "A long time ago," he said slowly, "I made the mistake of getting involved with a Mexican hooker. She stuck a rusty knife in my arm."

Meg's blood turned to ice. Jack's mother had been, in his own words, a Mexican prostitute. "G-got involved? You mean you arrested her?"

Carmichael just looked at her in the darkness. "I sure

did," he said after a moment. "They just sent her back to Juarez."

It couldn't be, the crazy thing she was thinking.

Meg scrabbled for a safe topic. "So, have you lived in the DFW area all your life?"

Carmichael snorted. "Spent my good years down in Del Rio. Dallas sector is where they bring the old *lobos*. Not enough action to get into trouble with."

Meg could hardly catch her breath. But before she could ask more questions, Carmichael gripped the steering wheel. His gaze followed the approach of headlights from the north; a few seconds later an eighteen-wheeler passed.

"Is this where Jack is meeting us?" she asked, appalled at the breathlessness of her own voice.

"Didn't you recognize him?" Carmichael sounded amused, but Meg did not feel like laughing. He had unclipped a set of handcuffs from his belt. "Give me your hands, Miss St. John."

Jack hadn't seen Eagle Pass in over a year, but he figured it hadn't changed much.

A scruffy little border city of approximately 25,000 souls, it was separated from its Mexican neighbor only by the smooth gray-green flow of the Rio Grande. Dope smugglers operating out of Piedras Negras had taken border patrol's efforts to control illegal crossings as a personal affront. Local agents now found themselves facing, with increasing frequency and violence, hidden enemies armed with all the technological benefits of the twenty-first century.

Jack knew how jumpy those agents would be—exponentially increasing the possibility he'd be blown away by the good guys. *El Lobo,* the kingpin, was supposed to have prepared the way. Experience had taught him, however, not to count on anything.

"There's somebody following us," Rook said after a moment. Jack had made the older man take the wheel, so that he could keep his own hands free.

Jack glanced back. The crawling of his skin increased with every mile they got closer to the border. Rico had died on just such a night. Black velvet sky spangled with stars, damp river breeze carrying the unique scents of the river into the open cab.

He could see the international bridge ahead. The searchlights of the border patrol checkpoint flashed on the American side; beyond the river waited the silent darkness of Mexico. Jack had told Rook to avoid that crossing point and head for the old bridge.

Rook kept an eye on the side and rearview mirrors as he drove onto the bridge, unchallenged by green uniforms. The pavement was in bad shape, the old-fashioned railings shallow, the river deep and dark on either side.

Jack swallowed. Fear of water was going to kill him someday. He imagined going under, sucking the river into his lungs.

Mentally he recited the twenty-third Psalm, as Ramón had suggested.

He leadeth me beside still waters. Yea, though I walk through the valley of the shadow of death, I will fear no evil, for Thou art with me.

No fear, he repeated to himself. *No fear.*

Jack released the gun under his arm, which he'd been unconsciously clutching.

At the apex of the bridge, but still on the American side, Jack made out a dark oncoming vehicle. "There's the van." Unlit by headlights, it approached shadowlike. Jack sat up. "Okay, it's showtime—"

His words were cut off by an explosion of glass as gunfire erupted. Rook gasped and slumped over, blood pouring into his eyes. As the truck veered, Jack grabbed the wheel trying to figure out the source of the attack. More shots popped the cab of the truck, and the windshield shattered on the driver's side. Shots from *overhead?*

As the oncoming van accelerated, Jack jerked the wheel and slammed into the side of the bridge. He jammed the gears into reverse, shoving the accelerator to the floor. Deafened by more bullets pinging off the steel beams of the bridge, Jack backed the truck off the bridge.

Out of range of the sniper, he knew he had to get help for Rook. Blood made the steering wheel slick, but Jack somehow managed to turn the truck around. The van screeched across the bridge, avoiding shots from the unseen enemy.

Jack suddenly saw the border patrol SUV that had been following them. It headed right at them, full-speed. Jack managed to swerve out of the way, letting it pass. It bore down on the van, which lurched from side to side as if the driver were drunk. Confused, Jack slowed and pulled to the side of the road.

For a sickening moment it looked as if the two vehicles would crash head-on. But at the last possible second, the van swerved off the road on two wheels. It continued that way for several yards before rolling onto its side in a thick stand of cane alongside the river. The SUV screamed south onto the bridge.

The report of a gunshot was followed by a splash. Something or someone had fallen into the river.

Adrenaline pumping along his nerve endings, Jack put two fingers on the pulse point on Rook's neck. It was there, faint but strong. He took off his bandanna and tied it tightly around the older man's head. All his assumptions had been turned upside down.

Jack looked around, listening for more shots. All was still.

The van lay on its side in the crushed cane, half in, half out of the water, wheels still spinning. Jack fumbled for the door and got out on shaking legs. The grass was tall and coarse, blending into the carrizo. Hunched over, he struggled through it, fell, pushed on and at last reached the van. The bridge lights were off, but by this time Jack's eyes had adjusted to the darkness. He saw that the van was a boxy old green Chevy with ratty plaid curtains on the back windows.

Jack struggled to open the back doors. They were locked. Confused cries from inside increased his haste. He climbed onto the side of the van, which was now the top. He felt it sway sickeningly toward the marshy water. The occupants of the van beat against the door, rocking the vehicle. It was going to roll into the river.

God, I'll go when You say it's time, but please, these people don't deserve to die this way.

He couldn't remember how many times he'd helped rescue illegal aliens abandoned by a coyote. Sick, dehydrated, starving, near-drowned, lost. Hopeless. He'd never gotten used to it.

Anger fueled his struggle to free these few. He wouldn't let them drown.

"Be still!" he shouted in Spanish. "Don't move or you'll roll into the river!" There was another moment or two of confused motion, then gradual stillness. Jack kept the note of command in his voice. "You're locked in from the inside. Somebody reach up—careful now—find the latch."

After a moment he heard, *"Hecho, Señor."*

"Okay, I'm opening the door, but come out one at a time."

The latch was old and cranky, but Jack managed to wrench the door open and slide it backward. Arms and legs and bodies were crammed inside the van like fish in a trawler. In spite of his warning, three men scrabbled for the outside, sending the van deeper into the water.

"Careful!" Jack slid backward to the ground and held out his hand. "Slow now, I said *one* at a time."

Small, wiry people in an amalgam of outdated clothes and plastic tennis shoes crawled out of the van. He worked patiently, steadying the half-floating vehicle as best he could, handing the Mexicans to safety one by one. Imagining a muscle-bound archangel keeping the van from sliding through the supporting vegetation into the water, Jack whispered a thank-you to heaven and kept working.

The last to exit was the driver, a long-haired individual sporting a Fu Manchu beard and enough cheap gold chains to sink the *Titanic*. Jack collared him; the man gave a surprised yelp and submitted without a struggle as Jack yanked both his arms behind his back. Expecting the rest to have scattered to the winds, Jack turned to find the group, about twenty-five in all, huddled in the broken cane along the riverbank.

"Come with me," he ordered, then marched the whole crew toward the Sunset truck, whose windshield was smashed into a lurid spiderweb of cracks. Jack helped everybody into the back of the truck except the driver. He hesitated before closing the door, but decided they'd be safer out of sight. The arrest wouldn't be complete until he returned to Fort Worth and confronted Warner.

He handcuffed Fu Manchu to the side mirror outside the cab.

"You got a cell phone?" Jack asked in Spanish. He wanted to call an ambulance for Rook.

The driver shook his head.

Jack would bet it was in the bottom of the river right now. Pressing the heels of both hands to his temples, he walked down the dark road. Something felt unfinished.

Where was the border patrol vehicle that had run the van off the road?

If the splash a moment ago had been the gunman on the bridge, was he dead? Or was he waiting for Jack to approach in order to finish the job?

He stood there waiting, knowing he must look crazy to the sullen driver. Jack was beyond caring. He'd come this far, and either God was God—or He was not.

Jack chose to believe He was.

Lights approached from the bridge. Headlights and an interior light, a rotating blue strobe. Border patrol.

The cruiser approached and braked with a jerk within a couple of feet. Jack waited, balanced feet apart, both hands shielding his eyes against the lights.

Dennis Carmichael got out of the car, gun drawn.

Right behind him, Meg stepped out, handcuffed.

"Look here, Torres," said Carmichael. "I brought you some company." He put the gun to Meg's head.

The sight of Jack, covered in blood, hands awkwardly raised in the glare of the headlights, undid Meg completely. She lunged toward him.

"Stop right there," growled Carmichael.

"Don't move, sweetheart," Jack said hoarsely. "Carmichael, what are you doing? Have you lost your mind?"

Meg jerked to a halt and glanced at Carmichael.

"Keep your hands where I can see 'em, Torres, or I'll drop her."

Meg started to cry. "Jack, are you okay?"

"I'm okay." Jack swallowed. "Carmichael, let Meg get back in the car. Whatever your problem is, we can work it out without her."

"After I went to all the trouble of getting her down here?" Carmichael shook his head, pushing the gun harder into the base of Meg's skull. "She knows too much." He clicked his tongue. "Thought you were smarter than that, Torres. She had a video clip of one of your planning meetings."

Meg made a distressed noise. Only Jack's cautioning look held her still.

His gaze narrowed on Carmichael. "Rook told me you're *El Lobo,* but I didn't believe him."

Carmichael grunted. "Torres, you really should be more considerate of the people you hang around with. First Valenzuela, then Rook, and now your little lady. You're a walking death trap."

Meg watched Jack's face change in that instant. Cold, controlled, and implacable rage infused every line of his body.

"Jack, I'm so sorry," she whispered. "I tried to tell him you never told me anything."

Carmichael chuckled. "Did you know she's in love with you, Torres? Too bad you won't live long enough to take advantage of it."

Meg could see Jack's hands, curled above his shoulders, tremble. But his eyes, fierce and steady, begged Meg to be still. "Carmichael, why are you doing this?"

"Tell him, honeybunch." Carmichael slid the gun around to Meg's cheek. "You figured it out, didn't you?"

Meg couldn't see her captor, but she could smell rancid hatred pouring off the bulky body crowding hers. Feel the gun, cold and blunt, pressed against her cheekbone. Numb with fear, she locked her gaze on Jack's. She could see his courage warring with anxiety for her safety. It bolstered her own faith.

"I guess you'll have to explain it to him yourself, Mr. Car-

..ichael," Meg managed to get out. Very much to her own sur-
..rise, she stepped away from the gun and turned to face her
..aptor.

Carmichael looked poleaxed. "That's far enough."

Meg looked over her shoulder and gasped. A small, deadly
..istol had materialized in Jack's hands, pointed over Meg's
..houlder at Carmichael's head. A smile curled his lips.

"Drop the gun," Jack said calmly. "You could shoot me,
..ut I'd get you, too, and that's not what you want."

"What you got in that little popgun, boy?" Carmichael jeered,
..ecovering from his shock. "One shot? What if you miss?"

"I assure you, I've been practicing just for this." Jack stood
..eet apart, with the gun braced in both hands. "You know I've
..een looking for Rico's murderer."

Carmichael swallowed, but steadied his gun. He seemed
..o have forgotten all about Meg. "You're a messed-up kid, Tor-
..es. I saw you rescue those wetbacks I ran off the road. There
..ou stand, one of those pro-life, born-again believers, ready
..o kill a man in cold blood."

Meg's hands went to her mouth as she backed away from
..he coldness in Carmichael's eyes. This man had been respon-
..ible for the death of Jack's partner. She'd never known a killer
..efore. She'd actually ridden in a car with this awful man for
..ix hours.

"If I explained it to you, I don't think you'd understand,"
..ack said in a strangled voice. "Why do you hate me so much?"

"Let's just say we got a little payback going on." Car-
..ichael's voice hardened. "You brown-skinned hotshots got
..o business taking over the agency. We're already overrun
..with Mexicans, half the population of Texas don't even speak
..English anymore."

"This won't get you a promotion." Jack jerked his chin up.

"Come on, Carmichael, put the gun down and let me take you in. You need help."

"You want to help *me?*" Carmichael uttered a short laugh. "The ultimate irony is, you aren't really *nativo* yourself."

Jack's eyes narrowed to slits. "How would you know that?"

"Your mother was the wetback prostitute who cost me my arm." Carmichael was practically spitting with venom.

"That's ridiculous," Jack growled. But he looked uncertain. "What makes you think—"

"It happened the night I fished the two of you out of the river," Carmichael said. "It was near-about flood level that night, and the rest of your little flock didn't make it across."

In the wash of light from the SUV, Jack looked stricken, his eyes like black holes in his face.

Relentless, Carmichael continued. "Your mama's name was Adlin. Right? She was young and pretty, and you were just a little fellow. I found both of you a place to stay with some other Mexican women. In return for not sending you back, I came back for some entertainment."

"Shut up, Carmichael," Jack said abruptly. Meg saw the tremor of his gun, and her lips began to move in prayer.

Carmichael's words continued to boil out like poison. "You were playing with a couple other brats in the hallway. Playing with a knife. I guess you thought I was hurting your mother when you ran in. When I tried to put you back out, she grabbed the knife and stuck it in my shoulder."

Meg could see Jack's chest heaving. *Holy Spirit,* she prayed, *keep him, oh keep him.* Her legs wouldn't hold her up any longer. She fell to her knees.

The motion drew Jack's attention for half a second.

Carmichael took advantage and fired.

Meg screamed as Jack lurched, his right shoulder a mass

of blood and torn flesh. Carmichael met Meg's eyes, smiling a little as he turned the gun on her.

Oddly she wasn't afraid, but consumed with fierce sorrow for Carmichael. Still on her knees, she closed her eyes as another blast of noise and the stinging odor of sulfur exploded around her

Her ears rang and rang, seemingly for minutes. But probably only a moment later she realized she wasn't shot after all. She gingerly opened her eyes. The ululating noise cutting through the night came from sirens in the distance, along with the approach of lights.

Meg staggered to her feet and turned to Jack. Facedown across the hood of the car, he gripped his shoulder in an attempt to stem the blood seeping through his fingers.

"Carmichael!" Jack gasped, sliding to the ground at Meg's feet. "Dead?"

She glanced at Carmichael and nearly vomited. "Yes—"

"Make sure."

"Jack, there's no doubt."

"All right, get me something. Gotta stop the bleeding," he said through gritted teeth. "Find something to—" He groaned, his head falling back.

She fumbled in her pocket. "Here's my bandanna."

"Tú eres una joven muy brillante." Jack's white smile glimmered. He'd once again told her she was smart.

Inexpertly Meg tied it around Jack's upper arm where pieces of charred, torn black T-shirt surrounded the wound. Feeling his gaze, she glanced at him, and found him lax, eyes half closed.

"Carmichael forgot I'm left-handed," he murmured in a deep slurred voice.

Tightening the knot, she nodded and pulled him gently

against her. "I hear sirens," she said anxiously. "How'd they know to come?"

"Don't know. Did he hurt you?"

"No."

"Meg, I'm so sorry. This won't happen again."

"You're acting like you just stepped on my foot. Of course it won't happen again. Carmichael's dead."

Jack closed his eyes without answering.

"Jack? What's the matter?" But he had withdrawn into some private ocean of pain that she couldn't penetrate.

As the scene around her came alive with the arrival of local police—flashing lights, wailing sirens, crackling radios, shouts of command—Meg did the only thing she knew to do. She held on to Jack and prayed.

Chapter Seventeen

Meg spent what was left of the night in a blur of the surreal. A uniformed Eagle Pass police officer helped her to her feet and pulled her aside for questioning, while another attended to Rook and Jack. A couple of border patrol cars came to take charge of the illegal aliens clustered near their rolled-over van, and the coroner arrived to deal with Carmichael's body.

When the ambulance arrived, Rook was quickly stabilized and loaded for transport. Somebody finally convinced Jack he'd be little good to anyone if he died from loss of blood; after reluctantly submitting to being strapped to a gurney, he was rolled away to be stuffed into the ambulance.

Forlorn, Meg stood watching its lights strobing through the darkness.

The young policeman who'd questioned her earlier cleared his throat. "Ma'am, where'd you want me to take you? It'll be daylight soon." He paused, scratching his blond buzz cut. "There's a halfway decent motel or two in Eagle Pass."

She suddenly felt a hundred years old. She needed to call her parents. Call Bernadette. None of that sounded appealing.

"I'm not tired," she told the policeman. "Can you just take me to the hospital?"

He looked at her doubtfully. "Are you okay, ma'am?"

She straightened. "Hunky-dory. Let's go."

While the young policeman drove Meg to the hospital, she used the time to call all the people who would be concerned about her. She assured them that she was a bit travel weary, but none the worse for wear. She knew she'd have to provide a better explanation sooner or later, but for the moment she avoided gruesome details.

Her parents were naturally horrified, Bernadette all but apoplectic, as she had been trying unsuccessfully to reach Meg's cell phone since dark. Sam—after making sure Jack was going to be all right—told Meg to get herself home so he could chew her out in person.

"I'll call you soon as I find out anything," she told Sam and handed the nice officer back his phone.

They pulled into the Fort Duncan Medical Center parking lot, which was all but deserted at that time of night—morning, Meg corrected herself as she got out of the squad car at the emergency entrance. She hardly knew what day it was anymore.

She approached a yawning nurse stationed behind a computer just inside the ER's automatic doors. All was perfectly quiet, almost churchlike.

"Excuse me, what happened to the two men who were brought in here about an hour ago?"

"Gunshot wounds? The border patrol agent and the…whatever he was? Druggie?" The nurse frowned, taking note of Meg's bloodstained jeans and shirt. Jack's blood. "Are you related?"

"Jack Torres is an agent, too," Meg said. "And no, we're not related." She rubbed her aching head.

The nurse's face relaxed. "He's still in surgery."

"Is he going to be okay?" Meg's voice wobbled.

Compassion warmed the nurse's eyes. "I'm sorry, darlin', but I can't tell you any more than that. But there's a waiting room with a coffee machine up on the second floor outside the operating room. You can wait there."

"Thank you." In an agony of anxiety, Meg wandered toward the elevator at the end of the hall. It occurred to her to wonder if anybody had called Vernon Rook's wife, Dottie, but she didn't know how to get ahold of the woman.

In the waiting room, Meg stood looking at the coffee machine. She didn't have any cash in her purse.

For some reason, that pushed the tears in rivers down her cheeks. Wiping her face with her sleeve, she collapsed onto a chair. Her bloodstained clothes were beginning to smell, and she was tired and hungry and thirsty. Her head ached, too, so she loosened her braid and finger-combed her hair.

She wanted Jack to be well.

She wanted Jack, period.

She remembered talking with him in the middle of the Water Gardens, both of them getting wet with spray. She remembered the way he'd come up out of the Trinity River at his baptism, his face lit with joy.

She fell asleep remembering the way he'd said, "This won't happen again."

Sometime later Meg awoke at a light touch on her shoulder. "Miss St. John?"

She sat up, startled, disoriented. She didn't recognize the nurse, couldn't even remember where she was.

Oh. Eagle Pass.

"How is Jack?" Meg blurted, rubbing her eyes.

"He came through fine. He's in recovery, awake and asking for you."

Meg's heart bounced. "He is? Where—"

"This way."

Meg followed the nurse through a couple of doors, warmed that Jack assumed she'd be waiting to see him.

"How's Vernon?" Jack demanded before she could get out a word.

Meg blinked. "I have no idea." She walked over to the bed and studied his face. He didn't look too bad, for somebody who'd been shot. His right upper arm was bandaged, and an IV tube snaked into the crook of his left elbow. "How are *you?*" She reached out to touch the thick hair at his temple. He flinched, and she withdrew her hand, uncertain.

"I'm fine," Jack said. "Has anybody called Miss Dottie?"

"Not yet, but I will if you'll give me her number."

"No, I'll do it." The expression in Jack's dark eyes was so remote that Meg hardly recognized him.

Had she ever really known him? After everything they'd gone through, was it possible to know him at all? Everything she'd planned to say to him flew out of her head.

"Jack, what are we going to do?"

He looked away, a muscle in his cheek working. "I don't know."

Meg watched Jack close his eyes. Guilt crushed her. He was in pain, grieving, and here she was worrying about her love life. "Jack, I'm so sorry—"

"No, listen." His gaze skimmed the hair spilling over her shoulders, then met her eyes. "I know this has been a pretty stark reminder of the way I live, but I warned you, didn't I?"

She gave a jerky nod, aware that her world was about to fall apart. "It was awful, but you're alive and I'm alive—"

"All things work together for good, right?" He smiled a little, a terrible, sad smile.

"That's true. You know it's true." Jack was behaving as if he were dying. Or going away, never to return.

"Yeah, it's good you found out, before...well, I'm so sorry for getting you involved in all this."

"You're *sorry?*" She stared at him. "What am I, some brainless idiot who doesn't have any choice in the matter?"

Jack's face reddened. "To be exact, you get *half* the choice in the matter. I don't want the responsibility for another person's life hanging over my head twenty-four hours a day."

Hurt slammed into Meg, injuring pride she hadn't even known she possessed. "For your information, I am not your *responsibility.*" She heaved in a breath. She was not going to cry in front of him. "You know, since you seem to be out of the woods, I think I'd better go make a couple of phone calls. Sam will want to know how you are."

Jack's gaze flickered. "Tell him to call me here, okay? You'd probably better go by the border patrol office first thing tomorrow morning."

"But I'm not going back until—"

"Yes. You are." Jack's tone was implacable. "You're a valuable witness, so you have to go back to Fort Worth today. Right now."

"Who's going to take care of you?"

"There are plenty of nurses around here who'll be happy to wait on me hand and foot."

"But *I* wanted to—"

"Meg." Jack glanced away, looking gray. "Please."

Meg shut her eyes. Clearly Jack wanted her to leave him alone. "Okay, then. I'll be praying for you."

"Thanks."

She backed toward the door, felt it hit her shoulder blades, and searched Jack's unsmiling face once more before sliding into the hall.

Jack knew he should never have asked for Meg, but he'd done it while his common sense was drowned in anesthesia.

Seeing Meg stand there with that thick, red-brown mane flaming around her shoulders had created an image in Jack's brain that nothing short of a lobotomy would remove. Right now he could close his eyes and imagine holding that sweet-smelling mass to his face, drawing her near so that he could kiss her—

Idiot. Thank the Lord he had retained at least that much self-control. Because once he kissed her again he'd be bound beyond redemption.

That he couldn't afford.

He didn't even know who he was. Carmichael's hateful words rang in Jack's mind over and over. *"I fished the two of you out of the river."*

He'd known about his mother, of course, but hearing it flung in his face that way had exploded an essential part of his self-image. Who *was* his father?

Meg wouldn't marry a man like me.

He didn't know where his career was going, either. This part of his job had ended in a mess. Maybe a conviction for Sunset, maybe not. The reputation of the agency in question.

Carmichael dead.

I let everybody down. Meg shouldn't *marry a man like me.*

She'd never be satisfied, staying alone while her husband worked weeks on end away from home. *And, dear Lord, some of the grim places I have to work. What if some other creep decided to take Meg hostage, like Carmichael did?*

I could always quit.

But he couldn't quit. He didn't know how to do anything else. He didn't *want* to do anything else. And the Lord knew Jack didn't fit into Meg's family.

Besides, she'd never said she loved him in so many words, and she'd had plenty of opportunity. A woman with as much fondness for speaking her mind as Meg could surely have uttered those three words if she wanted to. He'd showed her how he felt.

Thinking about it made his head ache, so he turned on the television. A *Little Rascals* short was playing on a classic movie station. "Come on, Algebra, this ain't no place for you!" said Stymie, dragging a braying, lop-eared mule out the front door of somebody's mansion.

Well, that was confirmation. Jack didn't feel like laughing.

Meg drove up to find Bernadette sitting on the front step. When Meg crawled out of the car in her wrinkled, smelly and bloodstained clothes, hair in a tangled ponytail, the usually undemonstrative Bernadette let out a shriek and came running.

"Meg! Are you all right?"

"I'm fine." Meg returned Bernadette's hug. "I just need a bath."

Benny had homemade tortilla soup in the crockpot; she served it while Meg showered and dressed in her Woodstock sleep-shirt. With Gilligan snoozing contentedly on her lap in the Papasan chair, she ate her soup and filled her roommate in on the details of her adventure.

"You could have been killed." Benny's dark eyes were wide. "And Jack—will he be okay?"

Meg set her bowl and spoon on the floor and scratched the dog under his collar. "Physically, yes. But with his boss turning out to be the bad guy..." She swallowed. "That's going to take some time to heal. I don't know if he'll ever be the same."

"In the Lord's plan, maybe that's a good thing," Benny suggested. "Trauma can make you more dependent on God."

But Meg was too tired and sad to be optimistic. She met her friend's compassionate eyes. "Or it can drive you away from Him."

The next morning, the fat hit the fire.

Still in her pajamas, Meg was finishing a bowl of Captain Crunch when Benny came in the kitchen door.

"Take a look at this." Bernadette tossed the morning paper on the table.

A two-inch front-page headline screamed "Business Manager of Fort Worth Company Indicted For Smuggling and Accessory to Homicide."

"Oh, my word." Meg's spoon clattered onto the table. "Boy, that was fast."

The article went on to detail how Kenneth Warner, in collusion with deceased Border Patrol Agent Dennis Carmichael, had conspired to smuggle illegal aliens across the border. Further, they were charged in connection with the murder of Agent Rico Valenzuela, as well as aggravated assault on Agents Jack Torres and Vernon Rook. Manuel and Tomás Herrera, currently being questioned, would be given immunity from prosecution in exchange for information regarding the case. Named as witnesses were Sam Thornton and Meg St. John of Sunset Landscaping.

"Well," said Meg through dry lips, "there goes my promotion."

The phone rang, and Bernadette reached for it.

Meg scrambled to her feet. "If it's my mother I'm in the shower." She was not up to exhaustive explanations.

Benny handed the receiver to Meg with a smile. "It's Sam."

"Seen the paper, little girl?" Sam drawled.

"Sam!" Meg plopped back into the chair, drawing her feet up under her nightshirt. "Did you know about this smuggling stuff?"

"I guess you could say that. Come on into the office. Mr. Crowley wants to talk to you."

"Uh-oh, I knew it." Meg's stomach suddenly hurt. "I'll be there in an hour, Sam." She hit the cancel button and poked Captain Crunch in his silly pink cardboard nose. "Benny, pray for me today."

"I will." Bernadette frowned. "But I think you deserve the day off."

"Me, too, but they want me there." Meg hesitated. "If Jack happens to call, give him my cell number, okay?"

Benny's eyes filled with sympathy. "I will. Call me when you know what's going on."

Meg had only been in Ted Crowley's office half a dozen times. A stocky, well-preserved man with a bad comb-over and a penchant for double-breasted suits, he stood as Meg entered. Indicating that she should take the chair next to Sam, Crowley perched on the edge of his desk and swung one alligator-booted foot.

Sam glowered at Meg as if *she'd* been the one besmirching the company name.

"What'd I do?" Meg muttered.

Mr. Crowley cleared his throat, drawing her attention. "Meg, I want to express my regret for the disturbing things you've had to go through this summer. I'm just—" He spread his hands. "I'm just horrified that your life was endangered. Sam tells me you've handled yourself with courage and grace." He paused. "We're both very proud of you."

Meg looked at Sam with surprise. His scowl had lightened to a mild frown. That might even be a twinkle in his eyes.

She swallowed. "Thank you. Sir."

Mr. Crowley smiled. "Warner's arrest will naturally give us some bad publicity, which makes your project with the Historical Commission that much more critical. Mary Frances has given me nothing but rave reviews on your work at Silver Hill. Media coverage of the wedding will go a long way toward reestablishing us as the premier landscape firm in the area."

Meg blinked. "That's great, Mr. Crowley."

"It is indeed. Which is why you'll be moving into the office as a design consultant effective Monday."

Meg bolted out of her chair. "Really?" She grinned like an idiot at Sam, whose broad smile now lit his dark face. "Sam!" she shouted. "Did you hear that?"

Sam winced. "Yeah, me and half the population of Tarrant County."

Mr. Crowley chuckled. "It's just too bad your boy Torres wasn't a real construction foreman. I'd like to have kept him on."

Guilt burst Meg's excitement like a pin in a balloon. How could she have forgotten about Jack? "I'll miss him, too, but…he's a really great undercover agent."

"Which reminds me," Sam said, "Border patrol called this morning after you left your house, and they want you over at their office for questioning. You're to ask for—" He consulted a paper he pulled from his shirt pocket. "Agent Gil Watson. Somebody in from the Dallas regional office."

Meg looked uncertainly at Mr. Crowley. "Would it be okay if I take the rest of the day off?"

"Certainly," Crowley replied, "take all the time you need to get things straightened out. We want our future dealings with INS to be on the up-and-up."

"Thank you." She turned to Sam. "Can I have next week to finish up the details out at Silver Hill? I hate to leave it—"

"All right, all right," Sam sighed, shaking his large head. "It's your baby, you might as well see it to the end."

On her way out of the office, Meg dredged up a smile for Sharon Inge, who sat at her desk flipping through a fashion magazine as if her boss were arrested every day. "I hear you're moving into Mr. Warner's office next week," Sharon chirped. "If you don't want that plant stand by the window, I'd like to have it."

Meg paused, taken aback. "Um, I'll let you know." She continued on her way, wondering why the knowledge that she'd attained her dream job left her feeling so sad.

Chapter Eighteen

Jack gritted his teeth and somehow got through the nightmare of wrapping up Dennis Carmichael's involvement in the smuggling cartel. Quietly buried without the usual ceremony attending the funeral of an agent killed in the line of duty, Carmichael left behind a stunned wife and two sons—both of whom were border patrol agents stationed in Del Rio.

Then there was Warner's indictment. Conducted in an Eagle Pass courtroom by a Mexican-American judge who showed every sign of throwing the book at the sneering, buttoned-down Anglo executive, the tension could have been cut and spread on toast.

Jack was left with a crushing two-day headache and a throbbing shoulder and arm.

A week later, he was back in Dallas at INS Headquarters, meeting with his temporary OIC. Vernon Rook had been awarded a promotion, but was still on leave recovering from his head wound. Supervisory Agent Gil Watson had been charged with debriefing and reassigning Jack.

Jack checked his watch, impatient for Watson to get off the phone and release him to go back to El Paso sector.

Is that what you really want, Torres? To go back to the same-old-same-old?

"No, Linda, I'm not smoking. Goodbye. I love you, too." Watson's phone clattered into its cradle as he looked with longing at a cigar box on his desk. "All right, Torres. Let's have us a little powwow." He picked up a cup of coffee and slurped it, eyeing Jack across the top of the mug. "You're not lookin' so hot, kid. General consensus is you need to take a few weeks off and reevaluate your career."

"Reevaluate—" Jack sat up. "Am I being fired?"

Watson choked on his coffee. "Fired? Are you crazy, boy? You just brought down one of the most influential smuggling rings in Texas border patrol history. Besides the illegals, these guys have been runnin' guns and coke and more stuff than you can imagine across the border. That's why they were so upset when you crashed their little party. The big dogs want you in Washington to spearhead a task force for smokin' out con glomerate smugglers and eliminating 'em at the root."

Speechless, Jack stared at Watson. "Huh. Washington," he finally muttered. His long-term career goal was being handed to him about twenty years earlier than expected. Dressing in a suit every day, regular hours, probably a nice apartment and educated co-workers.

A place to settle down with the love of your life.

Who just happened to be a Texas bluebonnet with a family so tight she couldn't go a week without having dinner with them.

Watson set down his coffee and picked up a cigar. "Now keep in mind, Torres, you're due for some serious trauma counseling and evaluation. And your testimony is gonna be critical in wrapping up this thing here in Dallas. Plan on sticking around awhile, get your head together and be available to testify." Watson looked at the cigar and stuck it in his mouth without lighting it. "You got a wife, Torres? No? Well, look for one who won't try to run your life for you."

With little fanfare, a bus marked "Immigration Detention and Deportation" pulled out of the Euless border patrol station on the first Friday in August.

"They'll be home by tomorrow morning." Jack touched Benny's shoulder. The two of them stood in the middle of the parking lot after putting the Herrera family on the bus. After testifying, Manny had decided to quietly accompany his wife and children back to Mexico. Tomás and Diego were gone as well.

Benny blinked a couple of times before looking at Jack. "You should have let me tell Meg they were leaving," she said. "She'll be really upset that she didn't get to say goodbye to Tomás."

Jack looked away. "She'll get over it."

Benny gave him a pensive look. "You are such a *pollo*," she said conversationally.

Jack laughed. "How do you figure?"

"You're going to ride off in the sunset and let her think she wasn't good enough for you."

"It's the other way around, and you know it." He shrugged, easing the ache in his shoulder by supporting the weight of his cast with his good hand. "If she asks, you can tell her I said so."

Benny gave Jack an annoyed look. "I'm not telling her any such thing, you big baby." She sighed. "I admit, at first I thought you were the last thing Meg needed. But I've watched you grow this summer, and come through some terrible things like a champion. When you showed up here today, I knew the Lord had gotten a serious hold on your life." She paused, then demanded, "Hasn't He?"

Jack grinned at Meg's drill sergeant/beauty queen roommate. "Yes, ma'am. He has."

"Well, then, if you can trust Him with Your life, don't you think you can trust Him with Meg's? What exactly are you afraid of?"

Jack's grin faded. "I'm not afraid of anything."

"Oh, yeah, right." Benny snorted.

Jack looked away, squirming. "Okay, well, I'm having a hard time picturing her choosing me over her family. And she just got that promotion she's been working for all summer."

He stood there with the sun beating down on his head, feet sticking to the melting asphalt, and Meg's genius roommate parsing him like a badly constructed sentence. Man, it was time to get out of this city.

"Jack, look at me."

He did and found warm compassion in Benny's dark eyes. "If anybody understands feeling unworthy, it's me. I grew up in foster care just like you did, and I was a prostitute by the time I was fourteen."

Jack could only stare at her with his mouth ajar. "No way."

"Uh-huh. It took me a long time to be able to believe it when somebody said they loved me."

"Meg never said she loves me," he muttered.

"Oh, she's said it all right, in everything she's done since she met you. I'm telling you, if you want to be a man, you better give her a chance to say it in words."

On the morning of the "Wedding of the Century," as the *Fort Worth Star-Telegram* termed the impending nuptials of Miss Rosalee Ashton Grover-Niles, Meg was on the way home from picking up her formal from the dry cleaners when she decided to take a detour. Still dressed in cut-offs and T-shirt, she drove out to Silver Hill and parked in the center of the carriageway, then got out and climbed into the bed of the pickup for a survey of her handiwork.

Silver Hill was exquisite in its late summer finery. Her new crew wasn't as efficient as the old one, but they'd still managed to finish most of the details to her satisfaction.

If she couldn't have her own wedding, she was determined to make Rosalee's as close to perfect as possible.

The sprinklers were still going, one on either side of the drive, sending a soothing, undulating *shooshing* sound into the quiet morning. Meg frowned. The one on the left looked like it was hitting the side of the carriage house instead of the lacy blossoms of the oak leaf hydrangea on the corner.

She was about to jump to the ground and move the sprinkler when the raucous sound of a motorcycle from a nearby side street cut into the peaceful scene. She paused with one foot on the side of the truck bed.

Motorcycles were an oddity in this part of town. Heart thumping, she moved to the tailgate of the truck, watching the curve around which the motorcycle would appear. She hadn't heard a word from Jack in nearly three weeks. It seemed inconceivable that he would have left town without saying goodbye, but she wasn't going to throw herself at him. He'd hurt her enough already.

The motorcycle roared around the street corner. It was a Harley the same color as Jack's, and it turned into the carriageway.

But its rider wore light-gray dress slacks, a short-sleeved silky black shirt and a *tie*. And there was no thick black ponytail at the back of his neck. Disappointed, Meg put her hands in her pockets and waited.

The helmet came off, and a bunch of startled butterflies took flight in Meg's stomach. This guy looked like Jack, but an alternate universe sort of way. His dark hair was cut short round the ears, textured and slightly wavy at the top. Not one earring or whisker in sight.

He slung his neatly pressed pants leg across the bike and smiled at her.

Ah, there he was. *My Jack.*

Panic set in. "Did you say hi to the aliens for me?"

"What aliens?" Jack's smile disappeared.

"The ones who abducted you and held you hostage," she said patiently. "I assume that's why you disappeared without even saying 'I'll be back.'" Her Schwarzenegger accent was getting better all the time. She was going to have to take it on the road.

Jack had the grace to wince. "Aren't you glad to see me?"

"Sure, I *like* having people tell me to go away."

Meg was enjoying the feeling of superiority that came from talking to the top of Jack's head, but that sprinkler was driving her crazy. She jumped to the ground, waited until it flung its spray away from her, then dodged in to adjust it.

Jack got off the motorcycle and approached, keeping a wary eye on the water hose. She turned around and watched him standing there looking sexy and classy and endearingly familiar. She glanced at her beautiful black formal hanging in the truck, then looked down at her grubby knees and the grass clippings that stuck to her socks. Ugh.

She supposed she could at least be civil. "How's your shoulder?"

"Healing." He lifted his sleeve, showing the edge of the bandage. "They took the cast off. Want to see?"

"Sure." She sauntered toward him as if her stomach weren't doing handsprings. She got close enough to smell the subtle spice of him and stopped. "Well, maybe not. Why'd you cut your hair?"

"So your father wouldn't throw me out of the house when I asked him for the favor of his daughter's hand in marriage."

"So my—*what?*"

He suddenly looked insecure. "Well, he struck me as the kind of guy who'd appreciate the old-fashioned effort. He took it pretty well, all things considered."

"Wait just a minute." Meg took an ill-considered step backward and felt a wave of water swipe her across the back of her legs. "Yow!" She leapt to the side. "Jack, are you telling me you've talked to my dad about—" She stopped. Maybe she'd misunderstood.

He nodded. "I wanted to make sure your parents know I'm a straight-up guy with a good job. By the way, I just got a promotion."

Meg had the unstable feeling of having a rug yanked out from under her feet. "Okay. And just when did this interview take place?"

"Last night."

"And my *mother* was there?"

"Well, yeah. That was sort of the whole point."

"And she didn't say *one word* to me when she called this morning—" Meg put her hands to her hair. "She let me dress like an extra from *The Dukes of Hazzard,* knowing you were coming over here looking like a movie star—"

"A movie star? Really?" Jack's face lit, and she almost forgot about the last few miserable weeks.

Then she remembered just how unfair this whole setup was. She slowly began to walk backward until she was right in front of the sprinkler, letting the water splash the backs of her legs, zoom over her head, and whirl away again.

"If you want me, come and get me," she said.

Jack watched the sprinkler *shoosh* its way back around to

fling water over Meg's shoulder. "You are so low." But he took off his shoes and socks, leaving them on the sidewalk.

Meg smiled. "I figure you're better off knowing exactly what you're getting into."

"Oh, believe me, I counted the cost," Jack said. "Do you know how much this shirt set me back?"

"About a week's salary, I would say." Meg grinned as water began to drip down her face. He was stalking toward her, with that intense, bad-to-the-bone look on his face, and her heart whirled around like the sprinkler. His shirt and pants were dark with wet splotches, but he kept coming. She danced out of his reach, arms flung wide, skipping in a circle that kept him in the middle of the spray.

He followed. "When I catch you, you're going to be sorry."

"I don't think so."

He suddenly jumped across the sprinkler head, snatching her to him, water pelting them both up the middle. "You're it," he said, and kissed her.

A few minutes later, they came up for air. "You can do that again if you want to," Meg said breathlessly.

He started to, then put his hand across her mouth as though removing temptation. "Wait a minute. There's something you have to do first."

"What's that?" she mumbled.

"You haven't said it yet."

"Said what?"

"You know what."

"Oh." Yes, she knew what. She moved his hand. "Why don't you say it first?"

"I love you, Meg."

"Jack, how many languages do you speak?"

"Four. Why?"

"I want one in each language, then I'll say it. One down, three to go."

"No fair."

"If you want fair, go pester some other girl."

"I think what we have here is a Mexican standoff."

"Oh, you are so funny."

Suddenly Jack pulled her close again and put his mouth next to her ear. "Okay, you want French?" he whispered. "*Je t'adore.* Spanish? *Te quiero tanto.* Italian? *Ti amo, il mio inamorata.*"

Meg's knees were weak by this time. She went limp in Jack's arms. "Oh. My. Goodness."

"You want to translate that?" he said, a pleased smile curling his lips.

"You know I love you."

"I thought so." Jack sighed and kissed her again.

* * * * *

Look for the next book in
THE TEXAS GATEKEEPERS series,
SOUNDS OF SILENCE,
in December,
only from Elizabeth White
and Love Inspired Suspense!

Dear Reader,

The idea for a story about an undercover border patrol officer came about while my husband and I were in seminary in Texas more than ten years ago. This was when I first became aware of the tension between the protection that the border patrol provides for American citizens, and the thousands of immigrants whose desperate longing for a better life in our great country often leads them to ignore our immigration laws. Add to this the growing threat of international terrorism, and you've got a hot-button topic! Years of research and interviews would not be enough to fully cover all the ramifications.

My intent in this story, however, is fairly simple. What happens when compassion meets justice? I wanted to explore the emotions of a man and a woman operating on opposites sides of truth, who genuinely want to behave as Christ would have them behave—despite forced secrets and old wounds. Yes, even when they're reluctantly falling in love.

I fully believe that no situation is too complex or too dark to withstand the illumination of Scripture. If circumstances in your own life seem beyond your ability to resolve, I encourage you to go to God's Word, the Bible, for help and hope. As the Gospel of John says, Jesus Himself came to be the Light of the World.

I love to hear from readers via my website, www.elizabethwhite.net. Or you may write to me at Steeple Hill Books, 233 Broadway, Suite 1001, New York, NY 10279. In the meantime, I hope you enjoy the story! Stay tuned in December for *Sounds of Silence,* the second book in the Texas Gatekeepers series.

Blessings,

Elizabeth White

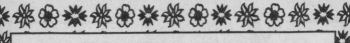

Take 2 inspirational love stories FREE!

PLUS get a FREE surprise gift!

Mail to Steeple Hill Reader Service™

In U.S.
3010 Walden Ave.
P.O. Box 1867
Buffalo, NY 14240-1867

In Canada
P.O. Box 609
Fort Erie, Ontario
L2A 5X3

YES! Please send me 2 free Love Inspired® novels and my free surprise gift. After receiving them, if I don't wish to receive anymore, I can return the shipping statement marked cancel. If I don't cancel, I will receive 4 brand-new novels every month, before they're available in stores! Bill me at the low price of $4.24 each in the U.S. and $4.74 each in Canada, plus 25¢ shipping and handling and applicable sales tax, if any*. That's the complete price and a savings of over 10% off the cover prices—quite a bargain! I understand that accepting the books and gift places me under no obligation ever to buy any books. I can always return a shipment and cancel at any time. Even if I never buy another book from Steeple Hill, the 2 free books and the surprise gift are mine to keep forever.

113 IDN DZ9M
313 IDN DZ9N

Name _____ (PLEASE PRINT)

Address _____ Apt. No. _____

City _____ State/Prov. _____ Zip/Postal Code _____

Not valid to current Love Inspired® subscribers.

Want to try two free books from another series?
Call 1-800-873-8635 or visit www.morefreebooks.com.

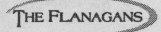